THE LAST BET

THE LAST BET

WALDO CASANOVA

To order additional copies of this book, contact:
Xlibris Corporation
1-888-795-4274
www.Xlibris.com
Orders@Xlibris.com
32450

ONE

H E STEPPED OUT of the elevator, and walked with a brisk pace down the East section of the fourth floor corridor. With a stethoscope hung around his neck and an immaculate white frock that reached down almost to his knees, over an expensive designer shirt and tie, he was sure he looked like a real doctor.

Gray slacks and black, patent leather Italian shoes, completed his outfit.

His short-cropped brown hair was beginning to show some traces of white, and his gray eyes pierced people from behind round, steel-rimmed glasses. At six-foot-two, he commanded the attention of the people he encountered, he was aware of that personality trait, and now was trying to get the most out of it.

"Good evening doctor," the nurse coming from the opposite direction said smiling, out of courtesy, because actually she had never seen him before.

"Evening nurse," he responded keeping his pace and not even looking at her.

Suddenly, out of a side corridor came a big plastic cart full of half empty dinner plates. The eager hospital orderly pushing it had to really dig the soles of his tennis shoes into the polished linoleum to prevent the collision.

"Watch where you're going," he snapped at the man. "Slow down. Where the hell do you think you are? The Expressway?"

"I'm sorry doctor," the man said, averting his eyes.

He stared the man down for a second, and then continued his hurried pace down the corridor. When he reached the nurses' station, he walked into the cubicle without acknowledging any of the three nurses that were sitting there.

"Good evening girls," he said after a few moments in front of the shelf containing the charts of the patients on that floor.

"Good evening Doctor," all three of them said at the same time.

He used his right index finger like a pointer to follow the row of thick binders stacked on the shelf. His finger trembled a little and stopped in front of one that had 'Dr. Arnold, Broderick K.' stenciled on the back, for no particular reason, because he didn't know who that doctor was. He pulled it out of the shelf and opened it.

"When was the last time Dr. Arnold was here?" He asked nobody in particular, without turning around.

"Ahh, . . . I would say about noon, Doctor," the heavyset nurse said, looking up from her paper work and half turning around on her chair.

He wondered if Dr. Arnold was still in the hospital and might appear at any moment. A bead of sweat ran from his scalp into his right eye.

"Did he say if he was coming back tonight," he asked.

"Not that I recall Doctor," the nurse said, "but you know how he is, sometimes he drops by at any time."

He could feel the woman's eyes fixed on the back of his head. With his right hand he smothered another a bead of sweat trickling down behind his right ear. Maybe it had been a poor choice picking Dr. Arnold with his unpredictable visits, but there was no turning back now. If the good doctor suddenly appeared he wouldn't know better, because he had never met him, and then the material would hit the fan at supersonic speed. His heart skipped another beat at the thought.

"Can I be of any help Doctor . . . ?"

"No thank you, I'll take care of it anyway," he said snapping the chart binder close, and walking out of the nurses' station.

The heavyset woman shrugged and looked at the other nurse sitting next to her. "I hope his wife doesn't screw dinner tonight," she said in a low voice, "it seems like he's not in his best mood." They both giggled when they made sure he was out of earshot.

He walked down the hall, and when he was out of sight of the nurses, he looked at the three-inch wide spine of the binder he was carrying on his left hand. Next to "Dr. Arnold", was a computer-printed tag. It read BROWN, MARTIN R. #425 D, and some other information he couldn't decipher. He didn't slow down his stride, trying not to look too obvious while he followed the signs and arrows that would lead him to room 425.

He finally found it and slowly pushed the door open. There were two beds in the room. One was empty. The other one, he assumed D meant door, had to be Mr. Brown.

The room was almost in total darkness. A couple of recessed lights, dimmed, gave enough light to distinguish the patient lying on the bed. The rest of the illumination came from the screens of a couple of electronic monitors, which were spitting information with an eerie green light.

He looked down at the man called Martin R. Brown. It looked like if he was on his late sixties, but he couldn't be sure. The age of people lying on a hospital bed was hard to guess, he thought. The man looked up at him.

He opened the chart binder he had on his hand and started flipping pages again. From what he could understand, out of the huge amount of information, the man has had a colostomy performed the day before. The man was awake and kept looking at him.

"How do I look doctor?" He asked in a low voice.

"You're looking fine Mr. Brown. Just fine," he said.

"Are you sure?" The man insisted. His voice was so low, that it could hardly be heard. "The other doctor gave me the same bullshit answer but he didn't look too confident."

With some reluctance, he picked up the old man's left wrist, and felt for a pulse. The skin felt brittle and cold to the touch. He dropped the skinny wrist after a few seconds.

"We'll see Mr. Brown," he said, avoiding the old man's eyes and looking at the monitors that didn't mean anything to him anyhow. "Right now you're looking just fine. Try to get some sleep."

He didn't have other choice but to make eye contact with the man again. He didn't like what he saw. The man raised the fingers of his left hand, as some kind of farewell.

"Thank you doctor," he whispered and closed his eyes.

He stood there for a minute, paralyzed by panic, looking down at the exhausted body. Had the man passed away? He looked at the monitors. The steady beep was the same and the graphics hadn't changed. He got his breath back and then stepped out of the room. He walked back to the nurse's station, full of apprehension. He had to get out of this place or he would have a heart attack himself. The heavyset nurse, the one that looked like the shift supervisor, was not there. Only one young Filipino nurse was sitting at one of the chairs, completely immersed in the process of filling out some forms. He put the chart binder back on its place.

"Good night nurse," he said walking out of the station.

"Good night Doctor," she answered without lifting her eyes from the papers she was working on.

He walked down the hall, the way he had come, to the elevator bank. Two women volunteers, wearing their white and pink-stripped outfits, were standing in front of the elevators, chatting animatedly in low voices. They stopped talking when he approached. "Good evening, doctor," they both said in unison.

"Good evening ladies," he said. "Working hard I take it. It's kind of late."

"Yes, but we still have a lot to do," one of them said.

"We really appreciate the help you're giving us, I want you to know that," he said.

"Oh, thank you doctor," they both said at the same time.

One set of elevator doors swished open, and a man clad in greens stepped out, surgical mask hanging under his chin. He just nodded and hurried away.

He stepped inside the car. "Going down?" he asked.

"No doctor, thank you, we're going up," they both said at the same time.

He punched a button and let the car go down to the first floor. He decided to go out to the parking lot through the emergency ward instead of through the main hospital lobby, with its full complement of telephone operators, special aides and security guards. He didn't need anybody asking the wrong question.

He followed the signs, and after innumerable turns came abreast a double door with "EMERGENCY", stenciled in red letters. He pushed the one that said IN, and stepped into a different world. The pace for sure was different. The place was really moving, nurses and interns almost running about, stretchers being pushed from one place to the other, a sense of urgency could be felt. The look on everybody's face was one of concern and doom. Men and women in green surgical garments actually had blood smears on their clothing.

Pushed against one wall of the corridor were three stretchers, sitting head to foot. In one of them a young woman moaned continuously, on the other two, a couple of faces that stuck out of the thin blankets that covered them to their necks, just looked vacantly at the ceiling, and were very quiet.

On the other side of the room, across from the middle island intense with the activity of nurses and doctors and interns, were beds separated by curtains. All the curtains were open at the front, and all the beds were occupied, the people on them attached to wires and tubes. In one of them a woman was surrounded by four people clad in green and purple garments, working frantically all over her. He realized he was hardly moving and actually gawking at the surroundings, not what any doctor worth his salt would do. He started walking faster toward the end of the corridor, and the sliding doors that led to the ambulances parking space.

From the last bed on the row, somebody yelled in agony but he didn't dare look, and kept walking toward the double glass sliding doors. Suddenly, somebody grabbed his elbow from behind. He stopped on his tracks, his heart racing one more time, controlling the urge to run out of the place, and slowly turned around.

"Dr. Billings?" the nurse asked. "Are you Dr. Billings, the neurosurgeon?" He looked down at the petite woman with the frantic look on her face.

"No nurse, I'm not," he said. "Can I be of any help?"

"No, thank you Doctor. We're waiting for the neurosurgeon," she said and ran in the opposite direction.

When he got back control of his legs, he kept walking toward the sliding doors. There was an ambulance parked on the other side, its back doors open, roof lights still flashing.

He squeezed between the back of the ambulance and the glass door, and walked outside. The doors slid close behind him.

The night air was warm. He took a deep breath and walked toward the front of the hospital, following the winding path.

When he reached the main entrance, he stood under the brightly illuminated canopy, both hands on his pant pockets. From the other side of the wide rotunda that encircled the big water fountain, a black Lexus came to life. It moved swiftly, and came to a halt in front of him. He opened the passenger door, and dropped into the leather seat.

"My God Jack, you did it," the man behind the wheel said, accelerating out of the parking lot. "Listen to this," he said. He punched a button on some gadget siting on the center console, between the two front seats. A little red light blinked, and then turned to green. The man punched another button.

The previous forty minutes or so came back to life, amid some static and with a kind of metallic twist to it. The footsteps, the background noises, the conversations, even the sound of pages being flipped around. The fidelity of the electronic equipment was amazing. Jack opened his shirt, and peeled the small transmitter off his chest. He laid it on the console, next to the receiver.

"I told you it could be done," he said without too much conviction.

"Well, that's one down. You have two more to go," the man behind the wheel said. He drove out of the hospital parking lot and crossed two traffic lanes at high speed, disregarding the angry horn blasts, so he could make a left turn at the next traffic signal and get into the Expressway ramp.

"Anyway," he said, "the drinks tonight are on me. That was quite a performance Jack, I have to grant you that."

"I'm not sure I want to do it again though," Jack said.

The car slowed down, coming abreast the tollbooth. The man behind the wheel looked at him.

"We made a bet, Jack," he said seriously. "We agreed that you would do it three times. If you chicken out now it's going to cost you. You know that, don't you?" He handed one dollar to the woman inside the booth.

Jack stretched out on the seat, wrapping his hands behind his neck. "I was hopping that maybe we could forget about this one. What do you think?"

"No way, buddy. A bet is a bet."

"Fuck you, Dave."

The light turned to green, and Dave pulled out of the tollbooth, flooring the gas pedal.

"Remember that there's some money involved here," he said laughing. "It was your idea to start with, anyway."

TWO

J ACK PULLED THE lever and let the back of the seat drop down a couple of notches, so he wouldn't have to stare trough the windshield while Dave zigzagged from lane to lane at eighty miles per hour. He thought about the events of the last hour, and wondered if he was loosing his marbles. What was a fifty years old man trying to prove pulling a stunt like that? God Almighty, just thinking of the repercussions, had he been caught, made him cringe. It was really insane.

On the other hand Dave was right up to a point. He had not been pressured to prove anything, and actually had been the one that had insisted that the scheme could be pulled. He shouldn't have challenged Dave to bet on it. Trying to get out of a bet with Dave was no easy matter.

He remembered very well indeed how the crazy idea had developed.

They were having a couple of drinks before dinner at one of their favorite places, a restaurant located on the top floor of a high-rise building on Brickell Avenue, just across from the City of Miami Marina. It had been their regular meeting place for the last four or five years; they loved the subdued atmosphere, the fine food, and especially the fantastic view of Biscayne Bay. The foursome – Dave and his wife Camille, and himself and Alison – met regularly there at least once a week, either for a late lunch, or a few drinks and dinner.

Since his divorce eleven months before, they were not a foursome anymore, but he and Dave had kept meeting there, not as regularly, but at least a couple of time a month. They could keep abreast of things and shoot the shit for a while, without the need of wives, past or present tagging along.

That particular day they had been discussing an article in the newspaper they had both read, about a man who had impersonated an FBI agent so he could get into the safe room of a local police department, and remove some documents that were crucial evidence to a first-degree murder charge against his brother. He had been caught at the last minute by pure chance.

"I don't know where the dumb bastard got the idea that he could pull something like that," Dave said.

"Oh, I don't know about that," Jack replied, "he might have not plan it right," he said draining the last of his drink, "if he had he might have pulled it off. This guy, Ruby, did something like that after the Kennedy assassination. You remember that."

A bartender brought them fresh drinks, a plate with anchovies, small crackers and black olives, and disappeared without a word. Dave lighted a cigarette.

"Forget it Jack, whoever tries some shit like that will be caught in a minute," he said, "that Ruby and Oswald episode its different, that was a political thing. It's very difficult to impersonate somebody you're not, and get away with it."

"Not necessarily," Jack said sipping his fresh drink. "I'm not talking about a high security environment like the CIA, or the Federal Reserve, Dave. I'm talking about a normal, everyday situation. If you look confident enough, and act a little bit aggressively, you can fool people into believing that you are what you are telling them you are." He stabbed an anchovy with a plastic toothpick, put it on top of one of the small crackers, and shoved the combo into his mouth. "People are more gullible than what you think Dave," he said swallowing, "you're a lawyer, you should know that."

"And you are an engineer. I didn't know that you techies were experts in human behavior. Are you sure you could impersonate somebody you are not, and get away with it," Dave asked. He picked up a couple of black olives with his fingers and popped them in his mouth.

Jack thought about that for a moment. He wasn't sure of course. He had never tried it before.

"If I put my mind to it, I'm sure I could do it," he said anyway.

"You're nuts. You could never do something like that."

He sipped his fresh drink one more time, and looked at Dave.

"You want to bet?" he said, and was sorry as soon as the words left his mouth, because there was nothing Dave liked better than to bet on something, no matter how ridiculous or insignificant it could be.

"Yes, I sure would like to," Dave said.

So a bet had been set set. The amount was set at two thousand dollars, way over their regular one hundred or five hundred dollar bets over normal issues as baseball and football games, and some other not so normal issues, as who held the world record for snakebites and was still alive. The stakes were kind of high, but this was an especial kind of bet. Never before it had been as serious as this.

They had agreed that he would impersonate a doctor; he wasn't sure why he had picked to be a doctor in particular, instead of something easier. He would have to make three rounds in a hospital. The days and at what time he would do it, were for him to decide. He would also pick up which hospital he would do it in.

Dave was responsible to find a way to monitor him, so he wouldn't cheat. He had to make all three rounds successfully without being caught, to win the bet.

The whole idea was crazy, and both of them knew it. Grown up men, with half a century of living behind them, law abiding and each one happily ensconced on their professional careers didn't play this kind of games. Still, they went along with it.

"Where are we going?" Jack asked after a while.

"Lets go to the club, it's still early," Dave said. They always called it the club, never "The Skillet", which was the name of the place. When the place had first opened it had been like a semi-private club, catering exclusively to prominent male executives. It didn't advertise, and new clients were introduced to it by word of mouth of the original sponsors. It wasn't legally a private club that required membership, but had a particular way of letting people know when they were not welcome. After some years, and under all kind of different pressures, it had opened its doors a little wider. Now days it accepted women and young male executives that were still a long way from being prominent. Just the extravagant prices for food and drinks was what kept it semi private now days.

Thirty-five minutes after they had left the hospital, they went down the ramp to the underground garage, and parked in front of the elevator. Jack changed into his suit coat, an attendant drove off with the car, and they rode the elevator to the top floor.

The place was still half full. Even if the kitchen closed at ten and the bar at midnight, the younger breed of patrons kept it almost full until the last minute, especially on a Friday night.

Jack and Dave walked to their favorite table, on the south side of the vast room, away from the long bar, where most of the action was taking place. The floor to ceiling glass plate panel gave an unrestricted view of the Bay, eighteen floors below. The marina, with all its lights blazing, was like an explosion against the dark waters of Biscayne Bay. By the time they sat down, Ernesto, who had seen them come in, was setting their drinks on the table. After the usual pleasantry, he disappeared as swiftly as he had appeared.

They sipped their drinks, and Dave lighted a cigarette. Both of them were silent for a while, looking at the incredible view, although they had watched it hundreds of times before. "Quite a sight, isn't it?" Jack said.

"It sure is," Dave said. "I can never remember exactly where my boat is, though. Way over there, isn't it?" He tapped the glass with his finger.

"No Dave, it's down there, toward the southeast." Jack said, and pointed the direction.

"Oh, that's right. I remember now. I guess I get disoriented at night."

"Well, you'd better not get disoriented when you're sailing," Jack said, "you might find yourself in a lot of trouble."

"Oh, it doesn't happen when I'm sailing, it's just the height. Besides, in the boat I have the compass, the navigation system, and as a last resort, the autopilot. It's just from way up here that I kind of loose my bearings." He made a signal with his hand, and they waited until Ernesto delivered fresh drinks.

"It's the height," he said again, "I guess I never could be a pilot," he continued, "I might mistake the runway lights with the expressway lights, and land on the wrong place." They both laughed at their little private joke.

The crowd they had encountered when they arrived had started to thin out almost in unison, like if a silent order to evacuate the place had been given. Just a couple of hard hitters still clung to the bar. Ernesto materialized again.

"The kitchen is about to close gentlemen, would you care to dine?" He asked.

"Yes, we might as well," Dave said. "Do you have any other plans, Jack?"

"No, no, it's completely all right with me. Especially since you're buying."

"I recommend the filet of sole in tartar sauce and the garden salad," Ernesto said. "The wine it's up to you gentlemen, but if I may, I could recommend something really special."

"That's it then Ernesto," Dave said, "surprise us with the wine, but bring us another drink first. We're kind of celebrating."

The waiter departed, and Dave lighted still another cigarette. He tapped it on the ashtray a couple of times.

"About tonight Jack," he said taking a deep drag, "I was so sure you wouldn't be able to pull it off. I was sure somebody, a nurse, a doctor, anybody, would question you. Ask you for some identification, or something. I thought that it really couldn't be done, but from what I heard it looked kind of easy."

Jack sipped his Johnnie Walker Black on the rocks, and smiled at his friend.

"How much did that transmitter and receiver gadget cost you, Dave?"

"Quite a gizmo, isn't it? I bought it in the Spy Shop. Just like the ones the Secret Service uses. It's kind of expensive, though. Two thousand dollars."

"Why did you make me wear it? You thought I was going to cheat, right?"

"C'mon Jack, let's be practical. You could have sat on a waiting room for an hour and then tell me you were doing rounds like if you were a doctor. There's no other way I could make sure. We're talking about a heavy bet here."

"Well, if you loose, you're going to be four thousand dollars in the hole," he remarked.

"That's if I loose, buddy. That is a big if. You have to perform two more times. I'm pretty sure you'll get caught. You were just plain lucky tonight."

Dinner arrived, they waited until Ernesto finished serving, and they started eating. The fish was really delicious.

"By the way Jack, why did you choose to impersonate a doctor? I would think that a construction worker, or a hotel bell Captain would be a much easier target," Dave asked, his mouth full of salad. "I didn't argue the point because the more difficult you make it on yourself, the easiest it's for me to win the bet. But I'm just curious."

Jack thought about the question for a minute, because he wasn't so sure himself he had made the right choice. He finished the fish, picked up the bottle of wine and looked at the label for the first time, before filling his glass again. He smiled to himself. Adding the bottle of wine to the sophisticated transmitter he had bought, if Dave won the bet, he would be way on the red side of the curve anyway.

"An experience I had a long time ago gave me the idea," he said, "I'll tell you about it some other time."

"Okay with me, that's your prerogative," he said still struggling with his mouthful of lettuce, and refilling his wine glass. "At what time are you going in tomorrow," he asked.

"At about nine-thirty. I want to make the morning rounds."

"You want to make the morning rounds," Dave repeated laughing. "I'll be damned. You really sound like a doctor already. What is your plan?"

"You'll find out. You'll be tuned to the transmitter, won't you?"

"You better believe it," he said masticating. He finally managed to swallow the lettuce. "What are you going to wear? Same outfit? Or are you going to try to be a surgeon?" he asked smiling.

"No way," Jack said sipping some more of the wine, "this is risky enough, but actually I'm not doing any harm. They catch me inside an operating room, and God knows what they would think. I won't do it for five thousand. Do you want to raise the ante?"

Ernesto materialized, this time with a helper, and proceeded to clean up the table.

"An after dinner, gentlemen?" He asked.

"Of course," Dave said. "Curvosier please." He lighted a cigarette. "No, I don't want to raise the ante Jack, I was just kidding. You're in enough deep shit right as it is now."

Jack laughed. The after dinner drinks arrived. They sipped their cognac.

"What do you figure would be the worst scenario, in case I get caught?" He asked.

"I really don't know Jack," Dave said. "On the bright side, there could be a real nice hospital director, looking at two successful, middle-aged men involved in a silly bet. No harm done. A slap on the wrist, and a raised eyebrow." He sipped the cognac and lighted another cigarette. "On the darker side, there could be a real mean son of a bitch of a director, attached to a real ambitious lawyer, and you could be facing the biggest law suit you ever imagined."

"Very comforting Dave," Jack said finishing his cognac. "But then, if there's no risk, there's no fun, right?"

"You know it pal," Dave said. "I won't even charge you for the defense."

They got off their chairs and walked toward the main entrance. Ernesto was nowhere to be seen.

"At what time do I see you tomorrow?" Dave asked, holding the door open for them.

"Nine o'clock in the parking lot of the hospital."

THREE

D AVE SQUINTED HIS eyes against the glare of the bright sun as he drove into the parking lot of the hospital on Saturday morning, just a few minutes after nine o'clock. He immediately spotted Jack leaning against the passenger side of his big Ford Explorer. The small parking lot on the ground floor across from the rotunda and the fancy water fountain in front of the hospital, was three-quarter parts reserved for doctors, on the other quarter the very lucky could park, the rest had to find a place somewhere on the six stories high parking garage. Jack was parked on the one-quarter side, and even had a vacant space by its side. Dave slid into it.

"Morning Jack," he said. "Keeping this space for me?"

"Actually yes," he said.

"How did you manage?"

"Oh, I just told the woman that tried to park in here that I was holding the place for another doctor that would arrive any minute. She excused herself and pulled back out. The poor soul is probably still going around and around up there, trying to find a place to park."

He was clad in blue jeans and a white shirt open at the collar, no tie, and the long white coat. This time he wore the stethoscope around his neck.

"I can see you're beginning to like this doctor bit. Enjoy throwing your weight around, eh?" Dave said handing over the little transmitter. Jack checked it to make sure it was on, and put it on his shirt pocket, pulling at the same time the steel rimmed glasses he had bought in a drugstore and putting them on.

"Are you coming in and sit on the lobby, or are you going to stay here on your car, under this hot sun," he asked.

"I had rather stay out here Jack," he said lighting a cigarette, "I don't want to be too close to you in case something goes wrong."

"You're a real confidence builder Dave. There's not a fucking shade in here. Your radiator might explode if you keep your air conditioner on," he said adjusting his glasses.

"I'll take that chance, Jack."

"Well counselor, I have to go. Got to see my patients," he said pushing himself off the side of the car.

"What are your plans?" Dave asked.

"I really don't know yet. Improvisation is the name of the game. You will find out, I'm sure," he said tapping the transmitter on his pocket.

He started walking toward the main entrance of the hospital, a hundred yards away, making his way between the parked cars. The sun felt hot on his head and on his shoulders and it wasn't nine-thirty yet. Another scorcher, he thought.

He wouldn't tell Dave, but actually he had some kind of plan laid out. He needed a different approach. For sure he wasn't going to storm any nurse station, like he had done the night before. Not in the morning, at the beginning of a fresh shift. Everybody would be alert and clear minded, not tired and ready to go home.

When he reached the canopied entrance, he didn't go inside the lobby, but stood to one side of the sliding doors, looking toward the doctors parking lot and at his watch every several seconds, trying to appear like if he was somebody waiting for somebody else to show up, just in case anybody was paying any attention to him. He seriously doubted that he was being scrutinized that close. People coming in or going out through the main entrance of a hospital had other thoughts on their minds and hardly paid any attention to other people around them. In a low crime area like this was, even the security personnel stance was more one of assistance and guidance, than one of law enforcement.

The problem was the subconscious, he realized. The feeling of wrongdoing and guilt, overcame unconsciously the normal behavior of a person. He had to control that feeling and look completely in control and at ease.

Luckily he didn't have to wait long for what he had in mind. After a few minutes a green van pulled up to the curve. A young man jumped out and opened the back door. From the inside he pulled a big flower arrangement, slammed the door shut, and walked toward the glass doors of the main entrance. He immediately followed him in, just a few steps behind, straight to a round reception desk located to one side of the huge foyer. The counter was almost chest high made of polished wood. Behind the desk, two women wearing very smart blue jackets worked the phones and computers. It looked more like the reception desk of a five star hotel than that of a hospital, Jack thought.

The young guy sat the flower arrangement on top of the counter, and one of the receptionists handed him a clipboard with a pen attached to it by a rubber band, while she kept punching keys and talking into the small mike attached to the head set she was wearing. Jack looked at the small envelope attached to the basket with a plastic clip, while the man filled out the form on the clipboard. 'Elizabeth Duran-Room 305', was scrawled on the front.

The man finished filling the log, picked up his basket, and walked to the elevators bank. Jack rested his elbow on the counter and tapped his fingers noisily against the wood counter while he waited for the receptionist to finish giving some kind of instructions over the phone.

"Can I help you, Doctor?" She asked.

"Yes. I'm Doctor Benson. Doctor Arnold told me he had left a message here for me," he said and looked at his watch again.

"Well, lets see . . ." the woman said, searching through a bunch of notes and pieces of paper she had by the side of the telephone keyboard. "Sorry Doctor, I don't have any message for you," she said flashing a charming smile.

"Has he come in yet or not?" He asked in a low tone looking straight at the woman, the piercing gray eyes behind the fake glasses destroying her composure.

"I ah, . . . I really don't know Doctor. I don't have a . . ." She furiously looked at all the notes she had on her desk, while he tapped his fingers noisily again.

"Could you have misplaced or lost the message somehow," he said with the tone of voice you use to address a child that has committed a misdemeanor.

"No Doctor, I'm very careful, I swear. I just can't find a note here," she said, avoiding his stare, her fingers shuffling rapidly through all the papers she had by her side.

"All right," he said looking at his watch again, "when he comes in tell him I'm on the fourth floor. Do you think you can remember that? The fourth floor?"

"Yes, of course Doctor," the woman said cowering back on her seat and avoiding his stare. She felt her heavily sprayed hairdo starting to come loose under the sweat trickling down her scalp.

He slapped the counter top with his right hand, like a final salute and walked toward the elevators. 'Doctor Arnold, please call station 101', he heard over the public address system before he entered the cab. Once inside, he punched the button for the third floor.

The third floor didn't have the same layout as the fourth, he noticed as soon as he stepped into the corridor. The nurse station was toward the end of the corridor, instead of in the center. He approached it with caution. There was another corridor to the right. If there were too many people in the station, he would just keep on walking and turn right on the other corridor.

It turned out that there was only one young nurse on the station and she was talking on the phone. He pulled the black notebook from his coat pocket and flipped some pages, not looking at her.

"Good morning, Doctor," she said after she hung up.

"Good morning, nurse," he said closing the notebook and putting it back on his pocket. "Could you hand me Elizabeth Duran's chart, please."

"Certainly Doctor," she said getting off her chair. She walked over to the shelf, pulled one thick binder out, and handed it over to him. "Here you are. Do you need anything else Doctor?" she asked looking at her watch, "I have to make a couple of rounds myself."

"No, no. You just go ahead. I'll let you know if I need you." He gave her his best smile. She left the station through the other end, and he opened the binder, resting his elbow on the counter, and read the first page.

Elizabeth Duran was a white, twenty-eight years old female, and a Dr. Helen Chang, an orthopedic surgeon, was the physician taking care of her. The young woman had a fractured tibia and a dislocated ankle, product of a car accident. Contusions and bruises to the left part of her body were normal but not really serious he found out, reading between the lines of all the medical mumbo-jumbo of information. She was a little uncomfortable, but not in any danger. All things considered, it didn't look like she was going to die soon. He closed the binder and looked around for the arrows that would lead him to room 305. Nobody he came across in the corridor on his way to the room paid any particular attention to him. Just the occasional nod and forced smile.

He carefully pushed in the door to room 305 and thanked his good luck. His new patient was on the far bed, by the window, and the other bed was empty.

The woman was reading a paper back book, the big flower arrangement he had seen on the lobby sitting on a small table close to the window. He walked over to the bed.

"Good morning Elizabeth," he said.

She put the book down and looked up at him. She was strikingly beautiful, he noticed. Her left leg was on a cast, sticking out from under the covers that reached up to a little under her waist. She was wearing a regular hospital gown, and he noticed a big black bruise on her left shoulder.

"How are you feeling today Elizabeth?" He asked.

"Miserable, Doctor. I hurt all over. Specially here on this side," she touched lightly her left side with her right hand. "It even hurts when I breathe."

He noticed that the gown was not tied at the back, but just lying on top of her. He picked the edge of the gown with two fingers and raised it a little bit. He looked at a purple bruise that ran from under her armpit almost to her hip. He realized that if he wanted to, he could raise the gown some more and take a peek at the gorgeous breasts that were pointing straight up at the ceiling of the room, and nobody would know any better. The thought of a sexual harassment suit combined with one of impersonating a doctor flashed through his mind, and he dropped the flimsy garment.

"That's normal Elizabeth," he said, "you were shaken pretty bad. It will go away in a few days. Is your leg bothering you too much?" He asked.

"Actually no, Doctor. It's really just my side that really hurts," she said. She had a soft, kind of throaty voice, and light green eyes with a kind of mischievous tint to them. She had a beautiful smile and he found himself smiling back at her. He was tempted to take another look at the bruise on her side.

"Do you know when I'll be able to go home?" She asked, and brought him back to earth.

"That will be for Dr. Chang to decide, Elizabeth."

He opened the chart, trying not to look at her eyes. "Listen, I don't want to give you more pain killers unless you're really uncomfortable. The discomfort will be gone in a couple of days anyway."

"It's okay Doctor. I can handle it so far, if I can't I'll scream," she said smiling. He smiled back again and almost forgot what was the real reason why he was in that room.

"Good. Try to rest now," he said swallowing hard.

"If I scream will you come to help me?"

"I . . . I sure will try," he said walking toward the door.

"Doctor?"

"Yes Elizabeth?"

"Will you be back to check on me again?" she asked.

He turned around, his hand on the door handle.

"Ahh . . . yes, I'll probably will," he said pulling the door open. He stepped out into the corridor and leaned his back against the wall.

Jesus Christ, I can't believe myself, he thought. He was playing a dangerous game, and he had let himself be enraptured by a pair of sparkling green eyes and an enigmatic smile. It was actually the first time, in the eleven months of separation from his wife, that he had felt such a wave of physical attraction that aroused him in such a way. Had he felt some kind of energy flow between him and the young woman, or was his middle-aged brain playing tricks on him? Guilt assaulted him because of the thoughts that had crossed his mind, but his ego tried to reassure him that maybe, just maybe, he still made an impression, and was not a discarded old rag. Half a century sounded pretty impressive, but if you said that you had just turned fifty it didn't sound so bad.

"Are you okay Doctor?" the nurse asked him. He realized he had been leaning against the wall and dreaming for too long. He mentally kicked himself. The last thing he needed was call attention to himself.

"Yes of course nurse," he replied, "just making some mental notes." He smiled at her, and she kept going down the corridor.

He approached the nurse station and noticed more people than ever milling around, mostly for what he could tell, interns, nurses and orderlies, but nobody that looked like a real doctor. Nobody paid any particular attention to him when he left the chart on top of the counter and walked toward the elevators. If his luck held a little bit more he would be able to make all his rounds. He crossed his fingers as he pushed the button for the next floor.

On the fourth floor he knew his way around, so he walked to room 425 directly. He gently pushed the door open. The bed by the window was empty, but Mr. Brown was still on the room. He smiled when he saw Jack. "Good morning, Doctor," he said.

"Good morning Mr. Brown. How are you feeling today."

"A little bit better than yesterday, thank you, although I don't know if I'm going to make it out of here." His voice was low and raspy, but he looked alert and very conscious.

"Why do you say that?" Jack asked him.

"Oh, things are happening. Things beyond . . ." The telephone on his bedside table started ringing. He tried to pick it up, but it was out of his reach. Jack lifted it and handed it to him.

"Hello?" He said in a tired voice. He listened and kept nodding his head. "Yes . . . yes, I understand." Some more nodding with his eyes closed. "No. No, I have not . . . I will . . . Good bye." He let the handset slip from his hand. Jack picked it up and sat it on its cradle.

"Doctor, can I have a piece of paper and a pen please," he asked.

Jack pulled his notebook out of his pocket, ripped a page off and handed it to the old man. He then handed him one of his pens. The man tried to write something, but the pen made a hole on the paper. Jack pulled his notebook again, opened it to a blank page, and handed it to the man. The old man started writing on it. When he finished, he handed the notebook back to Jack. He looked at what the man had written. It looked like gibberish. There were just letters and numbers. Some capital letters, some lower case, but actually no real words.

"What do you want me to do with this?" he asked.

"Just hold on to it. If the time comes, I'm sure you'll know what to do. If it doesn't, it's better that you don't know what to do with it. Time will tell."

He closed his eyes and let out a sigh. Jack thought the worst, and almost sprinted out of the room. He held himself and looked at the monitors. The little green peaks and valleys kept running from one end of the screen to the other, followed by dots and dashes trying to catch up with each other.

"I'm tired, Doctor," the man said. "I think I'm going to sleep for a while."

"You do that Mr. Brown," he said. "Just relax. You'll be fine." The man nodded, his eyes closed.

He turned ready to leave, when the door opened and he found himself face to face with the heavy-set nurse of the night before. She was carrying something on her hand. Her eyes filled with surprise when they faced each other.

"Sorry Doctor," she said, "I didn't know you were here. Time for Mr. Brown's pills."

"It's okay, nurse. I was just leaving." He tried to squeeze past her.

"I'm sorry. You're Doctor . . . ?"

"Benson. Doctor Benson. I'm an associate of Doctor Arnold," he said.

"I'm sorry Doctor. I didn't recognize you. Anything new I should know?" she asked. He was at the door and refrained the urge to start running. "No, no. Everything remains the same. Have a good day nurse."

He pulled the door close behind him, and started walking down the corridor, waiting for somebody to yell at him at any time. His back muscles were contracted, like somebody that's waiting for a blow to hit him from behind. He reached the elevators, punched the down button, and tried to look as an unworried doctor should look to all the people that were swarming around him, waiting at the same time for all hell to break loose. The damn thing was taking forever to reach the fourth floor.

When the doors finally opened, he almost jumped inside the car. The elevator stopped on the third and on the second floor. When it finally opened on the first floor and he rushed out, he collided with a man that was also in a rush to get in.

"Hey, watch where you're going man," he said, shoving him. Jack looked at the man. Middle to late twenties he guessed, slick black hair combed back into a ponytail, dark wrap around glasses, a Latino accent and definitely a big chip on his shoulder. He decided to let it go. He just wanted to get out of the place. Maybe the big nurse on the fourth floor had a curious mind and was making phone calls.

He turned around and started walking toward the front doors. The main lobby of the hospital was a beauty from an architect point of view. The roof, made out of glass, was about four stories high covering the gap between the two towers, which were about one hundred feet apart, and let the light shine on the main floor. To one side sat the reception desk, and scattered around, sofas and easy chairs were arranged around center tables, with a profusion of artificial plants. It really looked like the lobby of a five star hotel.

For somebody trying to get the hell out of the place in a hurry, the three hundred feet between the elevators and the main entrance glass sliding doors, looked like a trip to the moon. He started walking rapidly, like all doctors rushing from one hospital to the other are supposed to do.

"Hey doctor, wait." A male voice said behind him. He missed a step when he heard the command but kept on walking. "Doctor wait!" The voice said again. He looked around. No other doctors were leaving the building. The voice was unmistakably addressing him. Damn it! He was so close to make it.

He didn't have any other choice but to stop and turn around. A security guard was walking fast toward him. He almost bolted toward the doors. It took more than he thought he had to stay put.

"You dropped this, Doctor," the security guard said, handing him his stethoscope. All of a sudden, he felt like if millions of ants started running down his body toward his feet. He put out his hand to receive the instrument and it was not as steady as he would have liked it to be, but he couldn't help it.

"Oh. Thank you officer," he said stuffing the gadget on the right pocket of his coat. "Thank you very much."

"No problem, Doctor. Have a nice one," the man said and walked away. He looked around. Apparently nobody else was coming after him. He started walking toward the front entrance again. It was so close, some fifty feet or so, but fifty feet had never seem so far.

Finally the double doors parted open in front of him, splitting his image in two, and the frigid environment of the hospital spitted him out into the blasting sun of the parking lot. Never before a heat blast had felt so good, he thought.

FOUR

WHEN THE ELEVATOR doors opened on the fourth floor the man with the ponytail didn't hesitate, because he had done his homework the day before. He knew exactly where room 425 was. He entered the room and closed the door quietly behind him. The man apparently was sleeping. He walked to the side of the bed, and from the custom-made shoulder holster he pulled the automatic fitted with the long silencer. He tapped the chin of the old man gently with the tip of the silencer. Martin Brown opened his eyes. Jarol Ferrara smiled, moved the pistol a few inches, pushed the end of the silencer against the chest, and pulled the trigger two times. The body jumped and the monitors started screaming. He holstered the automatic and walked out of the room. A nurse was racing down the corridor toward the room. He walked on the opposite direction for a few feet, pushed down the lever on a Fire Alarm station, and made a right turn on a small corridor that led to a door with a sign that said 'Fire Exit Only'. He pushed the bar, the door opened, and he stepped into a steel landing. He went down the fire escape stairs three steps at a time and once on the ground, he walked to the parking lot. Nobody paid any attention to a young, good-looking man, with a ponytail and dark wrap-around sunglasses.

FIVE

H E SHRUGGED OUT of the white coat as soon as he was out of the hospital. He folded it in two and put it under his left arm. He took off the phony glasses and exchanged them for his aviator sunglasses. It was only early June, but the sun felt like a hot blanket on his head and shoulders, and he could feel the hot asphalt of the parking lot through the soles of his shoes. July and August were still a long way off, and by far the hottest months. It was going to be another scorcher of a summer he thought, but then, what else was new in South Florida, he thought.

He walked between his car and Dave's, which had the engine running. He unlocked the passenger door of his car, and Dave rolled down his window. He dropped the white coat on the passenger seat of his Explorer and closed the door.

"Well, my boy, you did it again," Dave said.

He was going to answer, when the short, intermittent blasts of a fire alarm surprised them both. They looked toward the hospital. A couple of security guards were running to the main entrance but besides that, they couldn't spot anything out of the ordinary.

"I hope you didn't set a fire in there, Jack." Dave said.

"If that fire alarm had gone off five minutes before I probably would have jumped out of a window," Jack said laughing nervously.

They couldn't see any smoke, or any major exodus of people spilling out of the building. The loud blasts stopped after three or four minutes. "Maybe it was one of those drills," Dave commented looking at the building.

"Probably was," Jack said. "Anyway, here you are," he said pulling the little transmitter out of his shirt pocket and almost dropping the phony glasses on the pavement.

"Well, you have pulled it two times out of three. Things are looking good for you. You going to try again tomorrow?" Dave asked.

"Definitely not," Jack said. "Tomorrow I rest." He thought about Elizabeth Duran. Forget it, he thought again, don't push your luck. Maybe she would have to stay in the hospital for several days.

"Do you feel like a couple of drinks and lunch some place, Jack," Dave asked. "Maybe that seafood place on the River?"

"No Dave, thanks. I better go home. I have some paper work I have to catch up to."

"Okay then. We'll keep in touch. I'll give you a buzz Monday afternoon." He rolled up his window and backed out of the parking space. Jack watched him get on the broad thoroughfare, and head East.

Five minutes later he was also heading East toward Brickell Avenue and his bachelor apartment. He still couldn't get used to the idea. A bachelor pad in a fancy, expensive high-rise, overlooking Biscayne Bay. Of course, right now he was a little too old for that crap. He would much more rather still be in the nice, spacious house they used to have on Old Cutler Road. But destiny, or whatever you want to call it, and specially his wife, had decided otherwise.

When and where the idea for the divorce had come from, he still didn't know. The suddenness of the decision Alison had taken, out of the blue, without previous bitter arguments about this or that, still baffled him.

One night while having a drink before dinner, she had let him have it. Just like that, no previous notice. She wanted a divorce. Why? What was the problem? He had asked. No particular problem, she had said. They just had been together for too long, that was all. She wanted to be by herself.

"Don't give me a stupid answer like that, Alison. After twenty-two years? Marriages are supposed to last, not be past due after a certain amount of years. Just tell me you have got somebody else, that's more likely. Don't worry, I can handle it," he had shouted at her.

"I don't have somebody else, Jack. I have made up my mind. I want out. We can make the whole thing real easy and smooth, or we can make a real mess. It's actually up to you," she had said. The goddamn lawyer talking, he had thought.

"What about Jackie?"

"I already talked to her. She says that whatever is best for us, it's okay with her."

Typical Jackie, he had dismissed immediately. Not too much help from that quarter about family unity or long lasting marriages. As long as she could stay at Georgetown University, frolicking and bullshitting with her friends of the far left, and the money kept flowing in, she didn't give a flying fuck one-way or the other.

He couldn't find any arguments, not even one specifically, to fight her decision, because her decision was so out of the ordinary. Economically, they didn't have any big problems. He was senior sales engineer for Davidson Avionics, the big electronic-components manufacturer. She was an attorney. They both made pretty good money. They had some investments and money put away. The house was almost paid for.

Socially, they were also normal people, as far as he could tell. They had their friends, they entertained at home, they went out on vacations, and they did what other million of couples did. Their sexual life was not as wild or as usual as it had been in the beginning, but it was still there. So, what the hell was the problem with her?

Jackie, their twenty-three years old daughter, had been just about the only source of a big argument between them. He thought that some of Jackie's ideas were way too liberal, but Alison would back her up nevertheless. They would have an argument, he would express his disapproval, Alison would find some kind of excuse, Jackie would do whatever the hell she had intended to do in the first place, and that would be the end of it, but that was hardly a reason for a divorce. So it had to be somebody else.

The divorce proceedings had gone smoothly, the outcome financially acceptable to both of them, not that he was going to argue any point, but as Alison had said, she wasn't after his balls anyway. They had split everything down the middle; each one had picked up their personal belongings and walked away in different directions.

Apparently, as far as he had been able to investigate, there wasn't a particular somebody else in her life. She kept performing successfully at the law firm, went out to lunch or dinner with different people, mostly business related, attended parties of common friends, and some other friends he didn't know, but emotionally she was keeping to herself. He still couldn't figure it out.

The car phone rang and brought him back to the present. He pushed a button, so he could talk through the speaker without lifting the handset.

"Hello."

"Jack, Milton here." Milton was the owner of the FBO where he kept his airplane. He also rented all type of aircraft. "Listen, are you still planning on taking the Eagle out tomorrow?" He asked. The Eagle was a Christen Eagle, a two-seat, aerobatic biplane he rented sometimes to indulge himself in what he considered one of his little vices. He loved to cavort high over the Everglades on the little open cockpit airplane, rolling and looping and diving at over two hundred miles per hour on muck dogfights against invisible enemies.

"No Milt, can't do. Something has come up. Sorry I didn't call you to cancel."

"No problem. Got a customer want's to rent it tomorrow. Don't know what time yet. I wanted to check with you first. Disregard the message I left on your answering machine. Talk to you later." The line went dead. He punched the speaker button off.

He pushed Alison out of his mind and thought about the morning happenings. He realized that there were hundreds of little things that could have gone wrong, and gotten him into a really embarrassing and maybe quite illegal situation.

It had been stupid to bet with Dave to do it three times. One time, he knew he could do it. Not because he had done it before, but just because it looked kind of easy to him and he figured the odds were on his side. Three times he wasn't so sure now. It was bringing up problems he hadn't foreseen, and chickening out and try to convince Dave that the third trip wasn't necessary was out of the question. Dave wouldn't budge; on the contrary, he would gloat on his failure and insist that their agreement must be fulfilled.

He thought about Dr. Chang walking into the room and catching him lifting the garment of Ms. Duran. A cold chill ran down his spine. Try to explain that to the Police or a Judge and see where it will get you, he told himself. No matter how well he could come out of such a situation, after the press finished with him, the stigma would cling to him for the rest of his life. He definitely had been out of his mind when he did what he had done, and needed more time to plan his next move. What he thought as his failure as a husband and father wasn't reason enough for him to take on endeavors as crazy as this. The idea on the back of his mind, that he didn't have a family anymore to take care of, or protect, and that by himself he could take up any crazy idea that crossed his path, was wrong. Thousands of people got divorced everyday, families got disrupted, children went this and that way, but eventually the dust settled and life kept going on. The chances of middle-aged men pulling stupid stunts and coming out unscathed were very slim, he thought. He would talk to Dave on Monday and try to dismiss the whole thing off, or at least stall it until he came up with a better idea. He mentally started deducting two thousand dollars off his account.

He finally reached his apartment building and dove down into the cavernous underground parking garage. He eased the Explorer into the No.721 slot, and walked to the elevators.

The apartment wasn't large by any standards, but was enough for his needs. After living for so many years in a spacious house, with lot of gardens and yard, and the neighbor's fence two blocks away, it had taken a little time to get used to the cramped space. The wide sliding glass doors facing Biscayne Bay, were really the only assets. The view was magnificent and ever changing. The Bay looked different at different times of the day; from the bright color explosion of early morning, to the soothing tranquility of night, when the stars seemed to fall into the calm dark waters.

It was much more impressive from the top floors, but at ten thousand dollars for every jump upstairs, the seventh level was all he could afford. He had made a study out of the second bedroom, where he kept all the stuff he really cared for. The rest of the furnishings were the product of one visit to a big furniture warehouse, where in one stop you could find everything you needed to furnish a hotel.

He slid the glass door open, to let in the warm breeze from the Bay with its salty smell. He would close it in about a half an hour or so, when the air conditioning unit loosed his battle to keep the apartment cool. He did that everyday when he got home, to get a whiff of the sea, although he knew that the practice was playing havoc with his electric bill.

He fixed himself two inches of Scotch over ice, and went into his study. The answering machine red eye was blinking. He pushed the button and listened to Milton's message. There were no other messages. He sat behind his desk and let his eyes roam over the room, something he couldn't help doing every time he entered it. Two seven-foot high bookshelves held his favorite books, and the walls were haphazardly crammed with framed photographs, some favorite paintings and all kind of mementos of happier times. He knew he had created some kind of cocoon in which he could crawl and return to the past, something that was not healthy, but it was difficult to live in the present. Maybe if the future found a particular heading he would change the decoration.

He actually didn't feel like working, but he had to finish the maintenance contract for Aero Caribe Cargo. He didn't want to loose the customer, but the cheap bastards were screaming for every penny and making his life difficult. He swiveled his chair and switched on the computer.

A couple of hours and two drinks later, he flopped down on the sofa in front of the TV, to watch the late evening news.

" . . . where a man was shot while lying on his hospital bed. Betty Franks has the story."

There was a momentary blur, and then the screen showed a young woman standing on a parking lot, a distressed look on her face and a microphone on her right hand. Behind her, red, yellow and blue lights flashed from the roof of various cars.

"Betty, what have you find out so far?" The anchorman asked.

"Charlie, like I said before, the authorities are not releasing a great deal of information yet. They have confirmed that the victim was shot twice on the chest at very close range. They agree that it looks like a professional hit operation but claim that they don't have any suspects yet."

"Any idea who the victim could be, Betty?" The anchorman asked.

"Not really Charlie, just that probably he was a key witness in some kind of investigation. There are a lot of rumors around here. When I asked about the victim, a spokesperson from Metro Dade told me that he had been booked into the hospital under an assumed name. That could mean that he probably was under some kind of police protection program."

"Did they release a name, Betty?"

"Oh no, they won't until they notify the next of kin Charlie," she said and looked at her pad, "one outspoken official told me, off the record, that it was either John Doe or Martin Brown. Charlie Brown, I guess he meant," she said looking back at her pad. "Like, it could be anybody. It's irrelevant anyway; we know that that it's not the victim's real name. Back to you Charlie."

"Thank you Betty," the screen returned to the studio. "That was Betty Frank, live from West Kendall General Hospital. In another . . ."

Jack bolted upright on the sofa. The anchorman went ahead with some more local news. Jack flicked channels, but there was nothing regarding the shooting in other stations. He picked up the phone and dialed Dave's number. His answering machine told him they would get back to him as soon as possible.

SIX

O N THE WAY to Denny's for breakfast, he picked up the morning edition of the Miami Herald. He found the place half full and walked to a far table against the rear window. A waitress filled his coffee cup and took his order. He sipped his coffee and pulled the Local News section out of the incredible amount of paper. The first page was dedicated to the vitriolic political war between the aspiring Mayor of Miami and the incumbent, leaving hardly space for anything else. He flipped pages and found it on the third page. The newspaper article was more explicit than the evening news. He read on.

The man that had been shot to death on his sick bed, the article said, 'had previously approached the District Attorney's office with a promise to turn over irrefutable evidence of the involvement of some high officials in the local government, along with some very respected executives in the banking industry, with a hardly known, yet very powerful, drug cartel. In exchange for complete immunity and a government protection program, he had promised to turn over the evidence to the appropriate authorities. Tentative conversations had started, when a sudden stomach ulcer problem had come up that required immediate surgery. He had been placed into a local hospital, under an assumed name. Surgery had been successful, but he couldn't survive the bullets of a paid assassin that somehow had found his whereabouts, to the surprise of the agencies in charge of protecting him.' He took a sip of coffee and smiled. What kind of covert operation were the local officials running when a reporter could dig up so much information and publish it? He kept on reading.

'Local officials, from the DA's office, the DEA and the Miami Police Department, were frustrated that a promising key witness against local corruption had been snuffed from under their noses before he could deliver any real evidence.' That was about the gist of the article. Could you smell a rat in here? 'Top local officials were frustrated that a key witness to local corruption had been eliminated right from under their noses.' Frustrated or relieved was a more proper word. Give me a fucking break, he thought. Somebody called Toni Suarez-Smith was the reporter that had written the article and he made a mental note of the name.

He pushed the bundle of paper in disgust to one end of the table to make room for his breakfast. The waitress deposited scrambled eggs with sausage, three pancakes on the side and a double order of toasts. She refilled his coffee cup and he assaulted the food.

After finishing his breakfast and a third cup of coffee, he picked up the Local News section, dropped the rest of the paper on the bench and walked out of the place.

He looked up at the sky while walking over to his car. Clear blue as far as the eye could see. Just a couple of white whiffs way up, maybe at over thirty thousand feet. It wasn't even as hot as the day before. He should have told Milton to reserve the Eagle for him, regardless. It really was a nice day to do some flying.

When he reached his car and opened the door the car phone was ringing. He started the engine still standing out on the parking lot, switched the air conditioning lever to high and picked up the handset.

"Have you read the morning paper yet?" Dave asked without preambles.

"Yes, I have," he said getting into the car and slamming the door shut. "I even watched the news last night."

"Isn't that a coincidence Jack?" Dave said. "The whole thing was happening while we were talking in the parking lot. I'll bet you ten dollars that the guy that did the shooting tripped the fire alarm to create some confusion."

"No way Dave, I agree with that," he said. "But I'll bet you twenty about the victim's name."

They had mentioned the name on the TV newscast, but not on the paper article. That probably had been a slip-off on the part of the spokesperson from the Police Department. The reporter had made a pretty good job of making the name unnoticeable to the public throwing the name of the funnies character along. It was irrelevant anyway because the name was fictitious, to the general public reading the article it wouldn't ring a bell, but it had immediately caught his attention. It would be a chance in a million if there were more than one patient named Martin Brown in the hospital. Apparently Dave hadn't watched the news the night before, not that it would have made a big difference to him because he had never mentioned the name anyway.

There was suddenly silence on the line. He could almost hear the little gearwheels inside Dave's brain grind into high speed, as he tried to figure out what he had meant.

"Shit!" he said after a couple of seconds. "The victim was one of your patients. I know it! Listen Jack, we have to talk. Come on over, and we'll have breakfast."

He laughed at Dave's conclusion, and immediately felt sorry for it. It was not a joke anymore. The old man he had deceived, was dead. The man had sought a professional opinion and he had given him one without knowing what the hell he was talking about. Not that it made any difference now. His only consolation was that he hadn't given him false hopes. Surgery had actually been successful. Or so the paper article said.

"I just had breakfast at Denny's."

"Well, lunch then," Dave said. "We have to discuss this. I'll be waiting for you." There was a click and the line went dead.

Jack dropped the handset on the drivers seat and eased the car into US 1. He needed to talk to somebody anyway, try to sort things out. Try to dump the guilty feeling somewhere else if he could. At the moment Dave was the only person he could confide in, and as a lawyer the most propitious one.

He tried to recall the few words he had crossed with the old man on his second visit. At the time, it had been just a matter of making conversation. A conversation he hadn't paid too much attention to. Something about maybe not making it. Today, the apparently incoherent words of an old sick man, started acquiring different meanings. Whatever he had wrote on his black notebook, unintelligible and unimportant at the time, might hold secrets he wasn't sure he wanted to find. The book, still on the pocket of his phony doctor's white coat, was lying on the passenger seat under the Local News section of the paper.

He made a left turn on LeJeune road, and headed south toward Old Cutler Road and his old neighborhood.

Driving under the canopy formed by the hundred years old oak trees that grew on both sides of the street and joined hands forty feet above the pavement, brought memories of the times when this was his daily route. He unconsciously slowed down a bit when he came abreast the intersection that led to his former home. It had been automatic, something that took over his thinking pattern. He reacted, pressed the gas pedal and kept on going down the road toward the entrance to a plusher neighborhood, where Dave lived.

After a stupid interrogation, the guard at the gate felt confident enough that he wasn't going to blow up a house or rape a seventy-five years old lady, and pushed the lever that raised the plastic arm.

He drove onto the circular, Mexican tiled driveway, and parked in front of the steps leading up to the massive double doors. Two tall columns, on either side of the wide steps, held a small angled roof that sprouted out from the height of the second story. A chandelier hung a foot above the doors, at the end of twenty feet of bronze chain. He pressed the buzzer, and after a few seconds, Camille herself opened the door. Apparently, being Sunday, the hired help had the day off.

"Jack, I'm so glad to see you," she said, turning her cheek so he could give her a peck while she blew a kiss into space. At five feet-eleven, three inches taller than Dave, he just had to turn his face to give her the rigorous social peck.

"Camille, glad to see you again. You are looking as fabulous as ever," he said. And it was the truth. The cream colored silk pants hugged her slim hips and perky ass, just enough. The dark green, long sleeved blouse matched her eyes. The blond, shoulder long hair that usually framed the high cheekbones and stylish long nose, today was held back into a ponytail. It was hardly eleven o'clock in the morning, on a Sunday, and she looked like she was going out for a night on the town.

"Come on in, Dave is out on the terrace," she said closing the door and leading the way to the back of the house through a corridor that bypassed a huge formal dining room, twisted to the left, and ended on a kitchen that would make a couple of restaurants think twice at what a kitchen should be like. Dave loved to cook and had designed the kitchen himself, so it would be an entertaining area as well as a kitchen. The room to its left, facing the back yard and the pool, could easily hold fifty or sixty people. All the decoration was by Camille, who had her own interior decorating company; which his ex-wife had told him wasn't very affordable. She probably was making more money than Dave, and Dave was making a bundle.

At that moment Dave was fiddling around with his barbecue grill and cussing like a trucker not a lawyer, when he and Camille stepped out into the terrace. "Jack is here Dave," she said to his back. He turned around and smiled. "And just in time," he said. "I really need an engineer, this piece of shit won't start."

"David!"

"I'm sorry dear."

"I hate it when he talks like that Jack," she said. "Scotch on the rocks? Or is it too early for that? Dave is drinking beer."

"A beer will be just fine Camille."

"Look at this Jack," Dave said turning back to his sophisticated barbecue grill. "I'm following instructions, like always. Turn this lever to the right. Wait thirty seconds. Turn . . . , these two switches. That's all I need today. Wait another thirty seconds . . . and push this button. You see? Nothing."

Jack got closer and took a look at the front panel. "You see that little gauge, Dave? It says that you're out of gas."

Dave looked at the gauge and then at Jack. "Son of a bitch!" He yelled smiling. "I didn't see that gauge in the instructions manual. Out of fucking gas. I'll be damned."

"David!" Camille said, stepping out into the terrace. She was holding a bottle of beer on each hand, which she handled over to each of them. "Sorry dear," Dave said, "just a slip of the tongue." Camille looked at Jack and shook her head.

"One of these days I'm going to go to one of his trials. Just to see what kind of language he uses in court."

"Very convincing Camille, very convincing," he said, patting her on the ass. She smiled. "Okay guys, drink your beer, I'll take care of the shrimps." She turned and went back into the house.

"Sit down Jack, sit down. Tell me all about it," Dave said. They sat down on easy chairs side by side, in front of a glass-topped table, and Jack replayed his two visits with the man that had been gunned down for Dave's benefit. He didn't mention the notebook though. Not because he didn't want Dave to know about it, but because he wanted to go over it by himself before he asked for any extra help to make any sense of it. Camille had brought them two more beers and they were working on them. Dave lighted a cigarette and automatically offered Jack one, probably forgetting that he had quitted two years before. He hesitated for a moment, and then took the cigarette. He had quitted not because he had really wanted to, but to please Alison and Jackie, who had really gone into the wagon of a smoke free world. Since then he had come to realize that the pleasing game was a two way street, not a one way narrow alley. He choked on the first puff, but enjoyed the second one. The old habit wasn't that hard to acquire back.

Dave had been thinking about what he had said, his eyes fixed on some point on the fence at the end of the property. "Maybe you should go to the police, Jack. That last conversation you had with the man; it might give them some clues," he said.

"Hardly Dave. How do I explain why I was there to start with? I don't think they'll buy the story about the bet. I would look like I was involved somehow."

Dave turned around and sipped his beer. "You're right there. That excuse would look kind of dumb, wouldn't it? I wouldn't believe it myself." He smashed his cigarette on the ashtray and looked at Jack's hand. "You're back to smoking?" He asked.

"You gave it to me two minutes ago, Dave."

"I did? Why did you take it, asshole?"

"Oh, fuck you Dave."

"Jack!" Camille said, coming toward them with a tray on her hands. "Here's your shrimp boys," and deposited the tray on the table. "Jack, you too," she said shaking her head.

"Sorry about that Camille," he said with his best stupid smile. She went back into the house and they attacked the shrimp.

"I'm glad your barbecue ran out of gas," Jack said.

"Why's that?" Dave asked.

"You would probably have burned the critters if it had worked, you asshole."

SEVEN

H E UNLOCKED THE door to his apartment and went straight into his study, the doctor's coat and The Herald 'Local News' section under his arm. He sat on the swivel chair and dropped coat and paper on top of his desk. He was feeling drowsy, they had drunk far too many beers and beer made him feel sluggish. Maybe a Scotch over ice would pep him up, he thought. It was too early to go to bed and too late to start doing anything else. He looked sidewise at the blinking red eye of the answering machine. Finally he decided to punch the button.

"Hi Daddy," Jackie's voice surprised him. "I'm sorry I missed you. Just to let you know that I have a few days off and I'm planning to fly down, probably before the next weekend. Looking forward to get together with you and Mom. Love you. Bye, bye."

The machine hummed for a couple of seconds and became silent. He looked at the unblinking red dot. Jackie was coming to town. A Scotch was definitely in order, he thought getting off the chair.

That was one reunion he dreaded. In the eleven months that he had been divorced he hadn't spoke to Alison more than two or three times, and then always in some detached way, about some legal matter or other that needed to be resolved. She had never asked how he was doing, or anything personal; like if he was some unknown entity that uncontrollable circumstances made it necessary to get in touch with. Rebuffed and ignored, he had acted in the same way. A reunion with their daughter would be awkward and difficult, to say the least.

He fixed the drink on the living room portable bar, turned the stereo on to a local station that played a mixture of Latin and American music from the sixties and went back to his study. He opened the black notebook to the page where the man known as Martin Brown had probably written his last testament, and looked at it again.

SIESNEC. Findoc. MM 54/53

KCB 15 circ 1123

R12 L31 r23 L13

UndCRPT – BIG clst

He read it a couple of times and couldn't make any sense out of it. The third line looked like a safe combination, but the lower case R could mean something else. Maybe it was some kind of file on a computer. The word 'Findoc.' looked like some kind of computer file, but there were millions of computers with zillions of files. Was Siesnec some kind of business, or corporation?

The phone rang, stopping his thinking process momentarily.

"Hello?"

"Mister Timberlake, theese is Josefa," the cleaning lady said. "I'm cleaning Tuesday, ees okay? No problem?"

"Perfectly all right, Josefa. You have the key, don't you?" He asked.

"Yes, I have key mister Timberlake. No problem. Need anything?"

"No, not really. Good night Josefa."

"Good night sir," the woman said.

So it was cleaning time again, he thought. He had never worried about cleaning until he had bought the apartment. When the manager discovered that he was going to be living by himself, he had brought up the issue of a cleaning lady. He never said it in so many words, but it was evident to Jack that he thought that a single male could accumulate so much filth without the help of a cleaning woman, as to jeopardize the integrity of his beloved building. He had gone along with the man's recommendation mostly to get him out of his hair, and it had turned out to be the right move. Cleaning the place up was not his idea of having fun and he had never considered it. The particular woman had been recommended to him as extremely reliable and honest. People just gave her the key to their apartments, the manager had said, so she could go in when she wouldn't be on the way.

He pushed Josefa and the cleaning problem out of his mind and tried to concentrate again on the note before him, but he couldn't make any sense out of it. It was like a riddle, it didn't offer any useful information that he could see. He ripped the page off the black notebook and put it inside his wallet. He walked back to the living room, fixed himself another drink, flopped down on the sofa and read the newspaper article one more time.

Maybe the reporter, Suarez-Smith or whatever his name was, knew more about what was going on than what he had written on the article. Reporters usually did. If some information smelled as good news but couldn't be proved, they would hold on to it, until it was really news.

He would call the Herald on Monday and try to meet with the guy. Maybe together they could figure out what had happened. If he could sell his bizarre story to the man, that is. Anybody in his right senses would be skeptical at his explanation of why he was in there in the first place. He would try anyway. He felt he owed it to the old man.

He felt better now that he had some kind of plan. Questions were still unanswered and might forever be, but at least he had a starting point. If it came to the worst and he couldn't find any answers, well, that would be the end of it. He didn't have any real commitment, just the lingering feeling that he should at least try. The man called Martin Brown, didn't have any right to burden him with some private, and what now looked like a very dangerous secret anyway.

He really was feeling drowsy now, after the second Scotch. He decided it was time to fire up the microwave, eat whatever surprise he had on the freezer, and get into bed with a good book, his latest nightly companion. He had a sales meeting first thing in the morning and he didn't want to look hung over.

EIGHT

MONDAY MORNING'S MEETING was a mess. He had to chew Stanley Pruett's ass in front of everybody, something he didn't care to do in a sales meeting.

A brilliant Electronics engineer, Stan had asked for a transfer to the sales department after a stint on Research and Development, and he had approved the movement. He knew that the young engineer was looking for a more remunerative field, because in R and D money was kind of elusive. The young man had a gargantuan ability to grasp technical problems and solve them, but a couple of clients had complained that they had been overwhelmed by his pushy personality regarding technical data, and hard nosed attitude regarding sales agreements. Jack was having second thoughts about the future of the young engineer in the sales department. He had the needed experience, but he lacked the finesse needed in sales; where some times the technical knowledge came seconds to salesmanship. He had counseled the man and decided to give him another chance and now he had really botched it.

He had screwed the contract he was supposed to get to upgrade the navigation equipment of a medium sized commuter airline, by calling the Vice-President ignorant. It would take the smoothest talking and best white-gloved approach of his best salesman to get that client back, if at all.

"I don't care how you look at it Stan," Jack said, "You're not discussing some mathematical equation with another peer. You're trying to sell a piece of equipment to a businessman, and to a businessman, money is at the top of his list of priorities."

"I understand that Jack," Stanley said, "but if you have a dumb bastard sitting across the table you won't be able to sell him shit."

"He's not so dumb if he owns a multimillion dollars operation, which you don't. So we better get things into perspective here, you understand what I'm saying?"

"Yes sir," Stanley said, not looking directly at Jack.

"I want signed contracts on my desk, not letters of complaint, it's that clear?"

Everybody nodded their heads.

"OK then. That will be all, gentlemen."

Back in his office he wondered if he had been too harsh with the man. Usually, if he had to reprimand somebody, he liked to do it in private, but the young engineer had given him no choice. The argument was nothing new, of course there were flocks of assholes out there, but if your intentions were to sell them your goods, you didn't tell them so to their faces. Fuck Stanley Pruett anyway, he would probably get a bigger ass chewing from the rest of the sales staff, and he had some other things on his mind.

The digital clock on his desk showed one minute after eleven. He asked his secretary to get him the number of The Miami Herald, and dial the front desk for him.

He asked for Mr. Suarez-Smith when he got an answer and was put on hold. It lasted almost two minutes.

"Suarez," a female voice said. He hesitated for a second or two.

"I would like to speak to Mr. Suarez-Smith," he said.

"Speaking to. And is Ms. not Mr. How can I help you?"

"Oh, I'm sorry," he said, "I thought . . ."

"It's okay," she interrupted, "it happens. Next time when you see a Toni with an I, you'll know the difference."

"I'll remember that," he said. "The reason I'm calling you it's because I read your article about the man that was shot in the hospital, and I think I might have some information that might interest you."

"What kind of information would that be?" She asked.

"Well, it's kind of difficult to explain over the phone. I actually came over this information by mistake. What I mean is that I was not looking for it and I don't have anything to do with it. It just happened to come across me. I don't know if you know what I mean. I . . ."

"Look, Mr . . . . ?"

"Timberlake. Jack Timberlake."

"Okay, Mr. Timberlake. What kind of information do you have?"

"Like I said, it's a little difficult to explain. I thought that maybe, if we could talk personally, I would be able to explain better."

"Look, Mr. Timberlake, I have a very busy schedule. I also get a lot of calls. If I were going to make a date to discuss every one of them, without a clue of what the call is about, . . . Well, you get the picture, don't you?" She asked, skepticism very palpable.

"I swear this is not some crank call, Ms. Suarez. I'm a senior engineer with an avionics company. I just happened to come across this bit of information." He tried to sound like a solid, thoughtful citizen. He wondered how the crank callers sounded.

She didn't answer him right away, which was maybe a good sign, he thought.

"You're familiar with Bayside?" She finally said. She didn't wait for an answer. "There's a place called The Hard Rock Café. Meet me there at six this evening."

"I know the place. I'll be there," he said. "Listen, how do I know who you are?"

"Don't worry about that. I'll recognize you. See you at six." The line went dead. No free give away clues.

What did she look like? Tall, short, thin, fat? Was she blonde, brunette, or in between? Suarez was a Spanish name, but she didn't have the slightest trace of an accent. He sighed. So, it would be Bayside at six in the evening. He didn't have any other choice, but hope that she hadn't just disregarded him as another crank call, and send him on a wild goose chase.

He knew that the place would be packed with shoppers and the after office hours crowd, cramming every watering hole in the vast water front shopping mall, but he didn't have any choice. Trying to identify her on that sea of people was impossible. He would have to play it by ear, and hope for the best.

He turned to the stack of papers on his desk, and pushed Toni Suarez-Smith into a corner of his mind for the time being.

He arrived fifteen minutes earlier, but waited until six o'clock sharp before stepping into The Hard Rock Café. As he had predicted the place was full to the hilt with people enjoying themselves with total abandon. Office types in suits and smart dresses, mingled with the tee shirts and jeans. They were three deep at the bar and all the tables were taken. He walked slowly through the crowd, trying to spot somebody that looked like a woman reporter.

"Mr. Timberlake?" A pretty waitress, holding a tray full of drinks, asked him.

"Yes?", he said a little surprised at the mention of his name.

"This way please," she said smiling, threading her way toward the back of the place.

Where the L shaped bar ended against the glass wall overlooking the bay, were several small tables for two. "Over there," the waitress said, motioning with her chin to the last table on the row. He tried to ask her something, but she melted back into the crowd disappearing from his view. He looked toward where she had pointed. On the chair against the back wall, a woman sat looking him over. On the small table was a half-full bottle of Corona. The other chair was empty, apparently the only one on the place. He approached the table slowly, trying to read from her features something about the woman he was about to meet. She was on her late thirties or early forties he guessed, with black hair chopped short and worn in no particular fashion. Dark brown eyes, he noticed when he got closer, were scrutinizing him inch by inch.

"Mr. Timberlake," she said. "Please sit down."

"I'm impressed Ms. Suarez. How did the waitress know who I was?" He said sitting down.

"She didn't. She asked the same question to three others before you."

He laughed. She smiled back, showing a perfect row of white teeth like the ones you see on toothpaste's commercials. "I'm doubled impressed Ms. Suarez," he said.

"Would you care for a drink?" A waitress that looked remarkably like the one before, asked him.

"Yes please. Black Label on ice, and another Corona for the lady." The waitress disappeared

"Well, Mr. Timberlake. What about that piece of information you say you have?" The smile was gone, and she looked all business.

"Like I told you before, it's kind of difficult to explain. I spoke to the man probably a few minutes before he was shot, maybe half an hour. He was feeling all right about the operation. While I was there, he got a phone call. When he hung up, he told me that maybe he wouldn't make it out of the hospital. He didn't explain why. At the particular time I didn't think it was important."

He wasn't sure he was getting his point across. The woman sipped her beer and didn't say anything, like waiting for him to continue.

"Well, . . ." He waited for the waitress to set the drinks on the table. "Don't you think it's odd what he said? After the circumstances, I mean."

She guzzled down some beer straight from the fresh bottle, her eyes never leaving his. "Mr. Timberlake," she said looking at the bottle, "you're not telling me the whole story. What you just told me doesn't mean shit. You're holding something back." She took another gulp from the bottle and looked at him. "You're wasting my time."

He tore his eyes from hers and looked at the dock. The party boat that took sightseers around Biscayne Bay was leaving, full of tourists eager to take a look at the backyard of the homes of the rich and famous. He wondered how much he could trust the woman reporter. Media people were a strange breed. He could get in a lot of trouble real easy, and wondered if he shouldn't go home and forget that the whole episode had ever happened.

He looked back at her. She was resting her chin on her cupped hands. The brown eyes had lost some of its fieriness. He gulped down the rest of his drink.

"Let me tell you a story," he said. And he told her everything; except for the page he had torn off his notebook.

She didn't say anything when he finished, just stared at him for a few seconds. She barely shook her head, and pulled a crumpled pack of cigarettes from the bag hanging from her chair's back. She fished one out of the pack with her teeth, and lighted it with a plastic butane lighter.

"You're crazy," she said, blowing smoke at the ceiling. "You don't look dumb so you must be crazy."

"Care for another drink?" The waitress asked.

"Yes, please," he said.

"Not for me Vicky," she said. The waitress left.

"I guess it looks kind of crazy now," he said pulling a cigarette out of the pack she had dropped on the table. "It didn't look so at the beginning. It was just a bet." She had the lighter on her hand and didn't offer to light his cigarette. There were no matches on the table either. He fiddled with it, not really wanting to ask for a light.

"My God. Two grown up men playing games like that," she said. "I imagine you realize all the kind of troubles you could have got into if you had been caught?" She asked. She didn't offer to light his cigarette, or hand him the lighter. He was starting to get pissed.

"Look Ms. Suarez," he said leaning over the table and lowering his voice, "I wanted to tell you what I know because I thought it might help you somehow. I can do without the preaching."

"Listen Mr. Timberlake," she said pulling her chair closer to the table and also lowering her voice, "I didn't ask you for your help. If you're so concerned, why didn't you go to the police?" Their faces were just a few inches apart. He looked into her eyes for a fraction of a second, and then pushed himself back into his chair, the unlighted cigarette still on his hand. "For the obvious reasons," he said almost to himself.

"What?" She asked. He shrugged. The noise of the music and people screaming at each other, trying to be heard over the crazy cacophony had increased, making normal conversation almost impossible.

"Let's leave," she said standing up.

"Let me get the check," he said getting up.

"Don't worry. My treat." She got off the chair and started walking toward the entrance. He got up and followed her. Nobody came after him trying to collect the tab.

"In your article you mentioned that the man had evidence of corruption at the higher levels of local government," he said, almost quoting her. "I would think that's the kind of story a reporter would like to get his hands on."

They were walking along the wide promenade that tunneled between the myriad of stores. "Several agencies were waiting to hear that evidence, according to your article. He was supposed to be an important witness," he said looking at her, but she kept looking straight ahead, both hands pushed into the pockets of her jacket, the big bag slung over her shoulder. "I'm not a reporter or a detective," he continued, "but I have watched my share of TV shows. Usually, in a case like this, some agency protects the witness. At least on TV they do. There's always an officer sitting by the door, and only certain people are allowed in."

He looked at her again, she wasn't really paying any attention to what he was saying, he thought. Just walking along with a nut case, until he decided to disappear. He decided that if he had come this far he would push his point to the end.

"In this case," he went on, "I went into the room, not once, but twice. Not even a real doctor, and nobody ever stopped me. Do you get my point?"

She didn't say anything and they kept on walking. She lighted a cigarette, and turned around to face him. "Lets seat," she said when they came across an empty bench. She crossed her legs. Very long legs, clad in jeans. She must be at least five-nine or so, he thought. The shabby brown coat hid most of her figure, but the legs looked pretty good on the tight jeans. He tore his eyes away from her legs, and looked at her face.

"Yes, I see your point." She puffed on her cigarette, and then pushed it into the sand of the barrel-like ashtray.

"You think that he was deliberately left without protection, so whoever wanted him out of the way could get to him?" She asked.

"In your article you mentioned that the information he had involved high officials in the local government. That could include law enforcement officials. Am I correct?" He asked her.

She looked at him and shook her head.

"Would you mind showing me some I.D., Mr. Timberlake?"

"No, of course not," he said handing her his wallet.

She went trough all his licenses and cards and handed the wallet back to him.

"It appears that you are who you say you are," she said, "but somehow I don't quite believe you. You're either lying or concealing something. If you're trying to pry some information from me, you're barking up the wrong tree. If you are from Internal Affairs from one of the enforcement agencies, you should know that by law you have to tell me so. In other words we're really wasting our time out here."

"I'm not involved in anything and I'm not from any agency. I just thought that maybe I could help you, but you don't believe me."

"Why should I? You're an impostor. You said so yourself."

"I'm not an impostor, I was an impersonator, and I didn't hurt anybody," he said. "I have some information in writing that proves that I'm not lying."

"Well, let me see it."

"I can't do that now," he replied.

"Good bye Mr. Timberlake," she said getting up, "it was a waste of time meeting you, but it was interesting to a point."

"Wait," he said. He handed her one of his business cards. "You can call me at any of those numbers if you change your mind."

She looked at the card, smiled at him, and walked down toward the parking garage. He started walking on the opposite direction.

When she was far enough from him, she pulled a cellular phone from her bag and dialed a number.

"Let me talk to Captain Ambrosse," she said when the operator at the City of Miami Police Department answered the phone. She listened for a couple of seconds. "Tell him is Toni Suarez-Smith from the Miami Herald, and that it's very important.

He knew he was making a mistake if he said what he had in mind, but he said it anyway. "What I told you, is not all the information I have. I have some more, in writing as a matter of fact, but I don't trust you enough yet." He walked away, looking for an exit from the mall to the parking lot. She waited until he was far away enough, then pulled a cellular phone from her bag and dialed a number.

"Let me talk to Captain Ambrosse," she said when the operator at the City of Miami Police Department, answered. She listened for a few seconds. "Tell him is Toni Suarez-Smith, from the Miami Herald, and that it's very important please."

NINE

H E POURED AN inch of Black Label over ice cubes and stirred it with his finger. Damn woman had some attitude, he thought. She had acted like if she didn't believe a word of what he had told her. He had gone to the meeting expecting a warm and thankful reception about the information he had to give, and instead he had gotten a very cold shoulder. Maybe news reporters didn't react the way he thought they would.

He walked across the living room and pulled the blinds open. The whole twenty-foot breath of the living room was glass, with an eight-foot wide sliding door in the middle that opened into a terrace. The view of the Bay was awesome, and it was worth every penny of the bundle he had paid for the condo. Nobody to share it with was what missing. He contemplated the huge expanse of water that separated his terrace from the Bahamas Islands and the Atlantic Ocean beyond. The pessimistic side of his brain wondered what would happen if the next hurricane decided to come his way instead of swerving down south toward Homestead. The optimistic side didn't want to think about it.

He turned around sipping his drink and thought about his encounter with the woman reporter. He couldn't blame her too much, he thought. When told to a stranger, the story about the bet he and Dave had made would look kind of weird, to say the least. Under the circumstances, the credibility and intentions of the information he was giving could raise some serious questions in the mind of any reporter, no matter how eager he was to grab a first page story. He had done his best to show that he was an honest, solid citizen trying to help out, but he knew that no matter how hard he tried, whoever listened to the crazy story would take it with a grain of salt. He knew he was taking a risk. She might turn him over to the authorities instead of contacting him again, but he was counting on a reporter's curiosity to get to the bottom of a story.

He sipped his drink and walked toward his study. The red light of the answering machine was blinking. He wondered if it was Jackie again, hopefully canceling her trip. He sat on his chair and pressed the button.

"Jack, this is Fred at Piper. It's six-thirty in the eve. I know this is a bummer, but we developed some glitches on the navigation receiver of the prototype and I'm pressed. I have a spare, but need your mind ASAP to check both of them. Call me at home."

He punched the erase button and leaned back on his chair.

Shit, he thought. Fred Hoffer from Piper Aircraft, his biggest account. He looked at his watch. A quarter to nine. Arrow Aviation was surely closed by now. He looked up Milton's home number in his Rolodex, and dialed it. His wife answered the phone and told him that Milton was taking a shower. Would he like to leave a message or call back later? No, he said, he would wait on the line.

"What's up, Jack?" Milton said after several minutes.

"Milt, I have to go to Vero Beach tomorrow morning. Can you have my plane ready by eight o'clock? Preflight and flight plan ready?"

"No problem, Jack. Destination the Piper Aircraft strip, right?" He asked.

"You got it Milt, thanks." He hung up and dialed Fred's home number in a suburb of Vero Beach. He told him he would be there before eleven, which would give him plenty of time, in case he ran into some weather or any other problem.

He went to the kitchen and emptied what was left of the Scotch in the sink. No sense in drinking himself blind if he had to fly the next day. He opened the freezer side of the refrigerator, looked at the stack of instant dinners ready to be electrocuted in minutes into an unsavory meal, and wondered what Ms. Suarez was having for dinner that night.

On the way back from Vero Beach he decided to take the longer route and fly down over the ocean paralleling the coast, instead of the straight course he had flown in the morning. To his left, the Atlantic Ocean changed to different tones of blues, depending on the depth. From his right window, he looked down at all the beaches that made the East coast of Florida an almost continuos stretch of blinding white sand. The view was impressive, and at twenty-eight hundred feet over the calm waters, the docile Cessna flew by itself, making it a very pleasurable journey.

The glitch at Piper had turned out to be a wrong setting in that particular instrument. He had fixed that, and they had tested the other one. Both of them had worked beautifully. Fred and Charlie Bowen, Piper's chief test pilot, had relaxed and everybody was happy. Reason enough to enjoy a relaxing trip back home.

South of Key Biscayne, he banked right and started loosing altitude for a straight in approach to Tamiami Airport's runway 27 Left. At five-thirty-eight in the evening, the plane tire's came gently in contact with concrete again, the engine ticking sweetly, like if it had come out of the factory the day before. When he got clearance from Ground Control he taxied to Arrow Aviation's apron and parked the airplane. Putting everything in perspective, it had been a very gratifying day, he thought.

TEN

T HE SMELL ASSAULTED him the moment he unlocked the door to his apartment. It made his mind jump back to when he was about twelve years old. He had come back from school and had gone to the shack on the backyard where they were keeping King; the old Collier his grandfather had given him as a present for his first birthday. The dog had died sometime during the day, and the smell had shocked him when he opened the door. This was about the same kind of smell. Urine and feces, mixed with another that was kind of coopery sweet, but repulsive. The air conditioning was off and it was stifling hot inside, which made the smell almost touchable.

He walked in slowly. The blinds that covered the big glass sliding door; which he had left closed to keep the sun out, were wide open. He reached the opening to the kitchen on his right. The cabinets' doors were open and the drawers pulled out. Even stuff from the refrigerator was lying on the floor. The stench got worst as he walked further in. He walked slowly to the end of the small hallway and peered carefully into the living room from the edge of the wall. Lying on her back, halfway between the sofa and the TV set, was Josefa, the cleaning lady. Her face was bloated. The half closed eyes, just showing the white seemed to stare at him. From her open mouth, part of her inflamed tongue stuck out. The two front teeth were missing, showing a grotesque gap on top of the purplish tongue. The skirt of her light blue uniform was up to her groin, and one foot was missing its shoe. She had soiled herself, and all kind of body fluids had made a wide, dark stain around her. The fingers of her left hand were curled into a claw, and her right one was bent at the wrist at an impossible angle.

He carefully walked around her and went into his study. It was a complete mess. Desk drawers and file cabinets open. Papers, books and documents all over the floor. He couldn't tell if anything had been taken, but his camera case was open and apparently all the cameras and lenses were still inside.

He went into the bedroom and found the same mess. Clothes thrown about, his chest of drawers wrecked, the mattress on the bed had been pushed halfway off to one side. His 9 mm. Beretta, and the spare clip were inside the opened drawer of the night table, though. Reason enough to rule out robbery as the reason for the break in. He walked out of the room, stepped around the foul smelling corpse of poor Josefa, and dialed 911 from the kitchen phone.

Detective Sergeant Rick Lopez was in charge of the investigation. He was in his mid thirties, with wavy brown hair cropped short. He looked trim and strong, not like a body builder, but like people who play sports do. He wore a sport jacket over a shirt open at the collar and blue jeans with cowboy boots. On his left hip, Jack had noticed a square, black automatic, with the butt toward the front.

He had the annoying habit of looking straight into your eyes for several seconds before he uttered a word. Jack guessed he did it on purpose, to make people uncomfortable and get them on the defensive. It probably was standard police procedure he thought, but quite annoying nevertheless.

He had walked all over the apartment, looking at everything and drilling him with a hundred questions at the same time, stopping now and then to talk into a two way radio. After half an hour a couple dozen people had invaded his apartment. The detective made him seat on one of the easy chairs closest to the terrace, kind of out of the way, while he talked to people coming in and out. He sat still just watching, as camera lights flashed, people took measurements with tapes and talked into hand held recorders and brushed walls and furniture with funny looking brushes. Once in a while somebody would ask him a question that seemed to him completely irrelevant. He longed for a stiff drink, but somehow felt like if he was a prisoner of the chair he was sitting on.

After what looked like an eternity, people started leaving. Josefa's body was placed on some kind of stretcher, covered with a white sheet and rolled out of the apartment. He watched as the shoe she had kicked off, and a partial denture that had been her two front teeth's, were placed inside plastic bags. After three and a half hours, the herd of people that had invaded his apartment was gone. Only Detective Lopez and a couple of uniformed cops remained, one of them outside on the hallway to keep nosy tenants away.

Jack got off the chair he had been sitting on and stretched. His back hurt after sitting on the same position for so long. "I need a drink Sergeant," he said, "you don't mind, do you?" He said pouring an inch and a half of Scotch on a tumbler. "Can I offer you one?"

"No, thank you," the man said, following him into the kitchen where he went to get some ice. He added a little tap water to the glass, and stirred the drink with his finger.

"Do you have a cigarette Sergeant," he asked.

"I'm sorry, I don't smoke," he said.

"You can have one of mine," the uniform said, "they're menthol though," he said as an after thought.

"I don't care," Jack said accepting a Salem and a light. The cool sensation on his lungs felt just fine.

"What happens now Sergeant?" he asked, looking over the counter top at the big stain Josefa had left on his carpet. The stench of death was strong on his nostrils, but apparently didn't bother the two other men. It sure bothered him; sleeping on the place was out of the question. As a matter of fact, he would probably get rid of it.

"It depends," the man said. "I don't see you as a suspect on the murder case. That leaves the breaking and entering problem," he said switching back to his obnoxious stare. "Are you sure nothing has been taken, Mr. Timberlake."

"As far as I can tell Sergeant. There's not much here to steal," he said motioning around with his hand. "My briefcase, where I keep my personal stuff, is in the study. My camera case, there's over five thousand dollars worth of equipment in it, it's also on my study." He took a small sip of his drink, just for appearance sake. He actually felt like swallowing the whole thing and fix himself another one. "I think that whoever came in here had the wrong address. Hell, even my pistol is in there," he said motioning toward his bedroom. "Any robber would take that, don't you think?"

"Yes, I would imagine so. Do you have a permit for that weapon?" he asked.

"No, I don't. I don't really need one, do I?" He responded. He knew where he was standing now, and he wasn't going to let the detective bullshit him.

"No. Not really. Unless you want to carry it around concealed, that is."

Jack smiled. The roundabout way of not asking a straight question, he thought. The detective was really wondering why a fifty year old, law abiding, electronics engineer was keeping a nasty piece that carried thirteen rounds in the magazine, instead of the more civilized five shot, .32 caliber revolver.

"No sergeant, I don't carry it around concealed. I like to do some target shooting, once in a while," he said instead.

"Uhu. No problem there, then. You can't think of anybody that would need something you could have in here? Do you have any technical information that could warrant this?"

"No, not really sergeant." He answered again. "We deal in avionics. Just aircraft navigation and communication equipment, no big sophisticated stuff of national security importance." He took a last drag of the Salem, and dropped it into the garbage disposal. "That's why I think that whoever came in here had his wires crossed somehow."

"I see," the Sergeant said and gave him the long stare one more time. Jack locked eyes with him for what looked like infinity. "We'll have to talk to you again, but I don't see any reason to take you downtown right now. You're not leaving the area, are you?"

"No, of course not. But I'm not staying here tonight."

"Yeah, I don't blame you. We can contact you at your office if we need to, but let me know if you're going to make some permanent move, OK?" All of a sudden the man seemed more sympathetic.

"I'll give you my cellular number in case you need to reach me in a hurry. Sometimes I'm out on the road, not at the office," he said and went to his study to get a business card. When he came back out, the uniform was gone, and Detective Lopez was in front of the open sliding glass door, looking at the bay. "Nice view," he said when he sensed Jack.

"Yes, it sure is," he said handing him a business card with his cellular number scrawled on it.

"Okay, Mr. Timberlake," he said taking it. "We'll be in touch. Don't dwell too much over this. There's nothing you could have done to prevent it." He turned and walked toward the front door of the apartment. Jack followed him. "It's there anything else I can do Sergeant?" he asked.

The man turned and eyed him with his particular stare.

"Not at this time," he said, "unless you decide to tell me some little terrible secret you haven't confided on me yet."

"No Sergeant, I don't have any little terrible secret to tell," he said. He did have trouble holding the stare of the younger man. They finally broke eye contact and the Sergeant handed him a card. "You can reach me here if you suddenly remember something, or if you find yourself in some kind of trouble." He let himself out of the apartment and closed the door quietly behind him. Jack stood in the middle of the foyer looking at the closed door. He sensed that this was not the last time he would meet Sergeant Rick Lopez. He had a gut feeling that he was in some deep shit.

He walked back into the apartment, looking at the mess surrounding him. He didn't feel like start organizing everything back into shape. What he felt was like having another drink. He stood at the kitchen counter, sipping slowly and looking at the spot in the living room where Josefa had emptied her bowls on his carpet. He thought about calling Dave, but it was almost midnight already. He finished the drink and went into the bedroom to get his overnight bag. He stuffed some clothes, his electric razor and some toiletries inside the bag. He was about to step out of the room, when he remembered the automatic. He pulled it out of the half opened drawer, and dropped it with the spare clip inside the bag.

He went into the living room and closed the sliding glass door, pulling the curtains shut. He walked into the kitchen to pick up his briefcase off the counter where he had left it when he had first come in, what now looked like ages ago. He switched the kitchen light off, hesitated for a moment, grabbed the bottle of Scotch and put it inside the bag. He let himself out of the apartment and locked the door.

The Holiday Inn was just a few blocks down Brickell Avenue from his place. His room on the third floor was drab, but it was clean. It had a window from where you could see the traffic going into Key Biscayne.

He took a shower, and then dropped the stuff he had packed on one of the twin beds. There was no ice on the ice bucket. He wrapped a towel around his middle and opened the door a crack. There was nobody on the corridor. He ran to the end where the ice machine was, filled the bucket and ran back into his room. He switched the TV on, and changed channels while fixing a drink. It was past the late news time. He hadn't realized it was so late.

He laid back on one of the twin beds nursing his drink and tried to put what had happened into focus. He couldn't come up with any reasonable explanation. Only one person was responsible for what had happened, and that was the woman reporter. The only other person that knew that he had met the man called Martin Brown was Dave.

She had probably talked to somebody, mentioned his name and the fact that he had some information. That had leaked somehow to the people that wanted Mr. Brown dead. They had broken into his apartment looking for that piece of information and they hadn't found it. Josefa happened to be there and they had snuffed her, which told him something about the personalities of the people looking for that information. At this point they must have realized that if really there was some information, the big mouth should be interrogated, and that would be *him*. In all probability they were looking for him at this very moment, to have a little talk.

He laughed aloud. He was getting paranoid and drunk at the same time, and he knew it. His perception of the situation belonged on a cheap detective thriller, he thought. Nothing like this should be happening to him.

'*Then how do you explain what happened today, asshole?* he asked himself, '*it's childish to try to dismiss it as a chance burglary attempt. No nickel and dime burglar could get to the seventh floor of a high rise, enter an apartment without breaking any door down, leave hundreds of dollars in valuables behind, and strangle a cleaning lady as an encore.*' Whoever his visitors had been, they were professionals.

He swallowed the rest of the Scotch. He had to talk to that woman reporter; she held the key to what had happened. He was asleep when the glass slipped from his hand and fell to the floor.

ELEVEN

CAPTAIN TIMOTHY AMBROSE had three phones on his desk. Two of them were of the office variety, full of little push buttons and capable of taking several calls on different lines. The third one was a slim black handset, with a number that was privy to just a few people. He was going through some paper work at a quarter to ten in the morning, when the third phone rang. He picked it up before the second ring. "Ambrose," he said into the mouthpiece.

"Tim, Joe here," a gruffly voice said. "We need to talk."

"When?"

"Right away. My office." The line went dead.

Ambrose sat the slim hand set back on its cradle and changed position on his black, leather swivel chair. The damn thing creaked again under his two hundred plus pounds. He cursed to himself. He needed a new chair. This one was about to fall apart. Goddammit. He knew that Joe would be calling; he just had hoped it wouldn't be this early.

He leaned over and punched the intercom button on the first phone to his left.

"Marlene, I have to go out. You can reach me on my cellular, but only if it's a real emergency. You got that?"

"Yes sir, don't worry," his secretary said.

He got off the chair and gave it a kick with his right foot, sending the damn thing rolling on its coasters until it banged against a bookshelf and stopped, leaning a little bit to the left side. He looked at it with disgust as he picked his coat off one of the chairs facing his desk and struggled into it. He didn't even say goodbye to Marlene as he stormed out of his office to catch the elevator that would take him down to the parking garage.

All by himself inside the cab going down to the parking garage, he realized that he was trying to get rid of his frustrations the wrong way. He took a deep breath, and composed himself. It wasn't the time for tantrums about things gone wrong. Any mistake could be fixed, or so he hoped. When the elevator doors opened, he hurried to his unmarked car and drove out of the building.

It was a fairly short drive from Police headquarters to City Hall, on Dinner Key. Too short to sort everything he had on his mind, he thought. Payday had arrived, he reckoned. It had been nice while it lasted, with hardly anything to do. Now he would really have to perform, because things were getting really serious. He could smell what was coming from a mile away, and it really stank. He had known that he would regret somewhere along the line the action he had taken, but he had just pushed it to the far reaches of his mind and ignored it, while he relished on the benefits. Down deep inside he knew it had all been wishful thinking. Reality would catch up with him sooner or later to claim its dues, and now that it had it was not the moment to start banging his head against the wall and wishing that he hadn't taken that road.

Bending the law a little bit now and then didn't look like the biggest crime. He was the only jerk that was not doing it, anyway. A City commissioner, not some two-bit gangster, was who had approached him. A pillar of the community, or a civil servant, as you might want to call it, but nevertheless somebody up in the political process, which just needed a little favor now and then. It had been real easy at the beginning, throwing in a towel here and there. It had escalated a bit after some time, but as he had already crossed the line, he had no choice but to go along with the tide. He had been compelled to recruit some help, to make sure that a couple of cops would be at a certain place at a certain time, and he had done it without too much difficulty. He praised himself in having a knack for spotting a crooked cop if he saw one. He had recruited a couple of men he could really rely on. The money was good, and he really needed it. He had three children, which he intended to put through a college education, come tide or high water. They were going to have a better opportunity than he had had, no matter the cost. A lot of people on higher places were involved in the same shitty business, in one way or another, and whether they wanted to hide behind the more respectable titles of investors, or money management consultants, it didn't make any difference to him. They were really as low and dirty as the pusher that sold nickel bags on dark street corners, and he included himself in the category, he wasn't kidding himself. In his book they were all equal, no matter how hard they tried to keep their feet dry. He had lost some of his self-respect, and every day regretted the time when the vision of some wealth had obscured his other vision, but also everyday he had less patience for people that considered themselves above him because he was the one doing the dirty work. The last few days had been a catalyst. He was responsible for a couple of corpses that really didn't belong on the war casualty list. He wanted out, but wasn't sure how he could do it, maybe it was too late.

He made a left turn on South Bayshore Drive, and drove to the end of the road where the City Hall two-story building sat, just in front of the huge marina. He parked in an empty space reserved for the chief of staff of somebody, hoping that the son of a bitch, whoever he was, would show up and find his place taken. He locked his car and went into the building.

The security officer just nodded at him as he hurried to City Commissioner Joseph Aldridge's office on the second floor. He pulled the door open harder that he had intended and let it slam shut behind him.

"Just go ahead on in Captain, the Commissioner is waiting for you," Adele told him when he entered the anteroom, twisting her mouth in what she thought was a smile. Her little piggy eyes full of contempt, bored through him over the half moon glasses, the message they conveyed was the same every time he visited the office. The words were never uttered but the eyes said it all-'You're just another crooked piece of shit, so just don't try to impress me with your Police Captain crap' – She was as old or maybe older than commissioner Aldridge, and was the only secretary he had ever had. She painted her lips bright red, and covered her face with some kind of white powder, which always reminded him of the face of a clown. Ambrose knew that if she could be tortured, she would spit out enough shit about her boss of the last twenty years to make Miami ashamed of its civil servants for another twenty years. Aldridge was single and so was her, and he was sure that they had something going on. The idea of those two cavorting together was enough to make anybody puke, he thought.

He knocked two times on the solid door nevertheless, out of courtesy, before opening it and stepping in.

"Good morning my dear Tim," Aldridge bellowed from behind his huge desk, "come on in and close the door, please."

Aldridge was a big man by all means. At least six two or three, and two hundred and sixty pounds easily. He didn't have his coat on, his shirt sleeves were rolled up to the elbows, the knot of his tie pulled down a couple of inches; all together the image of the hard working public servant, Timothy thought. He had big jowls that tried to cover his shirt collar, and a very rotund nose. He perspired copiously and always kept a handkerchief on his hand to mop his purple face. The most striking feature of the man as far as Ambrose was concerned, were his ears. They were big and stuck out to the side, not to the back, like in a normal person. They looked like if they might start flapping at any time like Dumbo's. Whatever had kept Joseph Aldridge in office for so long, definitely were not his looks.

Ambrose had hoped for a private chat with Aldridge, but apparently it was not going to be so. On one of the two big leather armchairs fronting his desk, sat City Commissioner Andy Ruiz. Ambrose had met the young Commissioner before in other meetings with Aldridge, but had always wondered what the relationship was. He knew how Aldridge clicked, and the young man somehow didn't seem to fit into the scheme of things. Why he had been present in a few meetings him and Aldridge have had was beyond him. He personally didn't like him, or trust him.

"C'mon in Tim, take a seat," Aldridge said motioning to the empty armchair. "You fucked up real good last night, didn't you boy?" He said without another preamble.

Ambrose stopped halfway across the room, and looked around. "Don't you worry," Aldridge said, "this room is sound insulated, and swept twice a week for bugs. We can talk freely here. Take a seat please." He motioned to the empty armchair. Ambrose sat and crossed his legs.

"What do you mean, fuck up?" he asked.

"I mean the fuck up at that man's apartment yesterday. For chrissakes. A cleaning woman strangled to death. What kind of operation are you running here, Tim?"

That particular issue he had hoped they wouldn't have to discuss. A casualty of war, as Scott had put it, was not enough for him, but then, Scott was kind of callous. Ambrose had always tried to stay as far away as possible from the actual handling of any operation; he just gave his men the instructions, and then tried to forget about it. They were dealing with crooks anyway. Sometimes somebody ended on the bottom of the Miami River, or on a lonely canal on the Everglades. He understood that it was an occupational hazard, but when he was informed of the gruesome outcome of some operation, he stored it on a secret compartment on the back of his mind, and slammed the door shut.

This time it had been different. Innocent civilian victims, especially women, he couldn't stomach, and it had happened. He had been trying to ignore it, and now Joe was bringing it back up.

"For what I was told this Jarol character got carried away, and Scott couldn't stop him on time. That man is a psycho, and it's hard to keep on a leash," he said.

"Why do you use him then?" Aldridge asked.

"Be real, Joe," he said. "Why do you think? He's muscle borrowed from your Colombian friends. I have only two men that I can count on, or do you think that half my force will go along with this bullshit?"

"Maybe you need to exert more control over your people," Andy Ruiz said. "Get some new talent, if you know what I mean."

Ambrose looked at the younger man. He thoroughly disliked the Cuban-American commissioner, with his air of superiority and his flashy playboy clothes. He somehow didn't fit with an old corrupted politician, like Joe Aldridge. What their common bond was he didn't know, and couldn't care less at this point.

"What do you propose?" he asked instead. "Maybe run an add in the paper? 'Experienced hit man needed, must not be too crazy, apply in person at the City of Miami Police Department.' Do you think that'll do?"

"Okay Tim," Joe said, "we can do without the sarcasm. We have a problem here. You said that this asshole had some evidence in writing. That could be trouble, with a big T. How are we going to solve that?"

"I told the men to search the apartment, and look for anything that could look incriminating. Scotty was handling that part. He's good at that. The other two were just muscle. He couldn't find anything, he tells me. It would have looked like a robbery attempt, and I could have taken care of that. This crazy mother fucker screwed the whole operation," he said.

"There're some sick people out there Tim," Joe said, "it's a pity we have to deal with them from time to time."

Ambrose shook his head.

"It can't be that bad, Joe," Andy Ruiz said, tugging on the French cuffs of his immaculate white shirt to keep them the regulatory one inch off the end of his expensive Italian suit coat. "If that chick at the Miami Herald is telling it like it is, this guy was in the room just for a few minutes, and by chance at that. We know that Charlie didn't have anything in his possession on the room. What the hell could he have passed on?"

"Don't be naïve Andy," Joe said. His tone of voice was condescending, like if he was talking to some retarded child. "He could have given this man information on where to go look for whatever he had been hiding. We're not playing games here, son. You better pay more attention to what the fuck's going on."

He shook his head, opened a side drawer on his desk, and pulled a fat cigar out of it. He ripped the cellophane wrapping, and lighted it with the big silver lighter sitting on his desk. He didn't offer one to any to his companions, and more or less ignored them as he puffed smoke toward the ceiling.

"Best tobacco in the world," he said rolling the fat cigar on his fingers. "From Cuba," he said looking at Andy, "Illegal as hell in this country," he said smiling.

Andy smiled back, not sure of how he should take that. Ambrose crossed his legs one more time, and hated the wimp some more.

"We thought that we had solved a problem," Joe said. "We thought that whatever information Martin had, was about six feet under ground along with his body. Apparently that is not so. We have to look into this twist in circumstances real carefully." He puffed furiously on the cigar, filling the office with smoke, and the sweet smell of the fine cigar. Ambrose felt it was up to him to give some kind of input.

"I learned from the guys in narcotics that apparently this Martin guy was in possession of a shitload of information," Ambrose said. "Names, numbers, dates, the whole shebang. I found about that as a matter of shoptalk. You know that I can't ask too many questions, it could look kind of suspicious if I showed too much interest in this case."

"I know Tim, don't push it too much if you're not sure who you're talking to," Joe said. He pointed the cigar at both of them. "The old goat was feeling the narcs, that I know for a fact. The more immunity they would give him, the more crap he would deliver." He paused for effect, and looked at the tip of the perfectly burning cigar, ignoring his audience, that was supposed to be enthralled by his wisdom and his grasp of the whole situation. Ambrose couldn't help the smile. The old fart sure deserved an A plus in Political Bullshitting 101. "I don't have to tell you that the people on the other side, are quite nervous. This is not the Medellin, or Cali Cartel, those were mere country thugs pushing their weight around. These are very nice people, on very high places, on both sides, that are involved in this little operation because they love the money, and as you know, money makes the world go around." He looked at the cigar again, and decided to tap the inch-long ash on the big crystal ashtray. "They are intelligent, resourceful and sitting on high places, which means that their arms have a very long reach. We have to be very careful, because they are not the usual bunch of greedy dumb farmers with their little dirty hands on a couple of K's of coke, that you can double talk and outsmart. The only similitude," he said, and looked at Andy smiling condescendly, "the only similitude, like I said, between these people and their dumber brethren is their nastiness. We all here," he said making a circular motion with the tip of his cigar, "are at the end of a chain, which means that we're quite expendable. We fuck off and we're history. We perform, and there's a very bright light at the end of the tunnel. So," he said puffing on his cigar again, "we better get our shit together."

The three of them sat silently for a little while.

"Why don't we bump the guy, and get it over with." Andy blurted. Ambrose looked at him like if he had discovered a roach creeping up his pant leg.

"Don't be stupid Andy," he said. "We don't know for sure if he really has any incriminating evidence, but he doesn't look like a nut case. If he really has something he might have passed it on to somebody else. We bump him and the whole thing can surface again, from another quarter. We have to pry it out of him." He turned to Aldridge. "Joe, I think we should put a little pressure on this guy, just to see if he's for real. Maybe he doesn't have shit, and we're all on a wild goose chase," he said.

"I agree with you Tim," Aldridge said looking at the tip of his cigar, "although I must say that if we're on a wild goose chase, it's all your fault. You're the one that brought the whole thing up, to start with."

"I thought I should tell you when I got the information," he said.

"A very nice thought Tim, but I need hard facts," Aldridge said. "I already conveyed the information you gave me to other interested parties, and to say that they are really pissed, is to put it mildly. Lot of bad news, without a hint of how they are going to be taken care of, naturally makes people nervous, if you know what I mean." He tipped some more ash off the tip of the big cigar into the big ashtray. "You know how the saying goes Tim-One thing will lead to another-and I understand the reasoning. Because your boys blundered, we now have a little murder investigation on our hands. Which, God forbids, could backfire and point a finger in our direction. For your sake I hope it wont, because right now my boy, your ass is out on a sling." He inhaled deeply on the cigar, making the end glow to a deep red. He laid his arms on top of his desk, and looked at Ambrose. "I understand that this prick Lopez is handling the murder case. It's there any way you can handle him?"

"Not a chance," Ambrose said. "He's a straight arrow and very sharp. If he smells a rat he wont stop until he gets to the bottom of it. Trust me on this."

Aldridge took a deep breath, and rested his head against the back of his chair, closing his eyes. He stayed like that for a few moments, cigar on his left hand, right hand pressing his forehead. Another histrionic display, Ambrose thought. Finally he opened his eyes and sat straight on his chair. "Me and Andy have a meeting in fifteen minutes, Tim." He said, without looking at him, all his attention focused on putting out the cigar on the bottom of the ashtray. He raised his eyes and met Ambrose stare. "You have been riding the gravy train for how long?" He paused again. "About a year and a half, right?" He asked. Ambrose just looked at him. *Gravy train?*"

"Well," he gave Ambrose his crooked grin, "now you're going to have to deliver. That's why we hired you for, boy."

Ambrose swallowed hard. If the old bastard called him boy one more time, he might loose his cool. Andy Ruiz looked at his manicured fingernails, not wanting any part of it. He got off the armchair.

"I'll see what I can do." He didn't even recognize his own voice.

"I know we can count on you," Joe said still smiling. He turned and headed for the door.

"Oh Tim, one last thing." Aldridge called after him. He turned around to look at the man.

"Try to hold your gangsters from going on a killing spree. Let's keep the elimination process to the absolute minimum, you hear?"

He couldn't respond, he just opened the door and slammed it shut behind him.

"Have a nice day, Captain," Adele said as he walked past her. Yeah, he thought. He didn't even look at her.

TWELVE

I T TOOK HIM a few seconds to recognize his surroundings. He had slept through the night without waking up one single time, just a long stretch of dreamless void. Slowly the previous day started filtering back. He had a tremendous hang over and a foul taste in his mouth. A growling empty stomach didn't help any.

He looked at his wrist. Eight o'clock already. He struggled out of bed, and went into the bathroom. After a shave and a long hot shower he felt a little better. He had to do something about his stomach real quick, but the place didn't have room service. He dressed casually in jeans and a polo shirt, and stepped on his loafers. He hadn't brought any socks from the apartment. He checked the cellular phone, and found that the battery was dead. He used the room phone to call his office, and told his secretary that he would be out on the road all day. She had some questions, but he cut her short and told her he would call back later. He picked up the cell phone, the agenda and his wallet, and looked around wondering what to do with the automatic. There wasn't really a safe place to hide it, and it could be a temptation to a cleaning crew. He pulled it out of the bag and tucked it on his waistband on the small of his back, covering it with his shirt like he had seen it done on the movies. He stepped out on the hallway, made sure the door was locked behind him, and took the elevator down to the lobby. At the front desk, he told the girl that he would be keeping the room for at least two more days, and walked out to the parking lot.

He needed to figure things out. The night before he had contemplated the idea of getting rid of the apartment and buying another one. Today the idea didn't seem so plausible, it would probably become quite expensive. He would call the realtor that handled the sales and rentals on the building anyway, and ask him what the odds were. In the meantime he had to put some food in his stomach, before he developed an ulcer. He drove toward the area called Little Havana just a few blocks away, where he had discovered several Cuban restaurants that served very large breakfasts for a very fair price.

Two hours later he unlocked the door to his apartment, and pushed it open against the stop with his left hand. He really didn't know what to expect. He had been told at the desk downstairs that nobody had come around asking about him, but then, whoever had paid him a visit the day before hadn't asked any questions either. The floor was empty, the yellow crime scene tapes were gone, and there wasn't a flock of police officers ready to rush the place if something went wrong.

He stepped in and let the door close behind him, pulling the Beretta out of his waist band, realizing that if somebody was waiting for him inside the apartment he didn't have a chance, whether he had a gun on his hand or not. He resigned himself to whatever could happen and walked slowly in, the automatic pointed to the front, the safety off. Some sunshine filtered in trough the blinds he hadn't closed so tight the night before. He reached them without been maimed, and pulled them fully open, inundating the area with bright sunshine. Holding the gun with both hands in front of him, he walked the rest of the apartment but didn't find anybody lurking on a corner ready to shoot him. He walked back to the living room, and looked down at the place where he had found Josefa. The foul smell of the night before was gone, but if he looked carefully at a certain spot on the carpet, he could detect a stain. There was no way he would live with that reminder. If he couldn't get rid of the apartment, he would at least get rid of the carpet. He snapped the safety on, laid the gun on the coffee table and walked into the kitchen.

The place was a mess, but now it didn't look as bad as it had looked last night. Things were strewn around, but apparently nothing was missing or badly damaged. The only broken piece was a bed lamp on the master bedroom, the worst place was the room he called his den, actually the second bedroom, which he had converted into an office. He pulled a beer out of the refrigerator and went into the room. He sat on his swivel chair, twisted the cap off the bottle and took a long gulp, looking at the mess that surrounded him. All his books had been pulled off the shelves and were scattered all over the floor. The drawers of his desk and the filing cabinets had been emptied, the contents all over the floor also, but apparently nothing was missing as far as he could tell. A couple of very expensive pens were sitting on his desk, his camera bag was open, but both Nikons, and all the other gadgets were inside, about four thousand dollars worth of goodies, just on one bag. Scratch robbery. Definitely, whoever had broken into his place wasn't looking for something to steal. He needed some advice. He reached for the telephone on his desk, and noticed that the answering machine red light was blinking. He pressed the button.

'Jack, I heard there was some commotion at your place last night,' Dave's voice said, 'give me a call and let me know what the scoop is.' There was a beep, and then another voice came off the speaker. 'Mr. Timberlake, this is Toni Suarez. Your office won't give me your cellular number. Please call me, I need to talk to you.' The machine beeped one more time, and the blinking light changed to a steady red. Jack looked at the unblinking red dot. 'And I sure want to talk to you lady,' he told himself. He took a swig of his beer, and sat the bottle on the desk. She had leaked what he had told her to somebody. Who that somebody could be he didn't know, but he had to find out, because it was somehow linked to whoever had eliminated the man called Martin Brown. Besides Dave, she was the only person that knew of his conversation with the murdered man. Trying to convince the police that it had been a robbery attempt was one thing, but trying to convince himself was not only foolish, it was downright suicidal. It all could be a mammoth case of unrelated incidents and unlucky chance circumstances, but he didn't quite believe it was so. Somebody broke into his apartment searching for the information he had told the woman he had in writing, and if the events of the last twenty-four hours were any sign, they had a rather drastic way of dealing with people while they conducted their search.

He pulled the card she had given him out of his wallet, and dialed her extension at the Miami Herald.

"Suarez," she said after the second ring.

"Ms. Suarez, Jack Timberlake here," he said.

"Mr. Timberlake, I have been trying to contact you," she said. "Listen, I need to talk to you about what happened last night, it's really important. Could we meet somehow, maybe for lunch?"

He looked around at the mess that surrounded him. He didn't feel like meeting on some restaurant, among a lot of people, just in case some heated argument erupted.

"Ahh, I'm kind of busy right now straightening this mess, and really don't feel like going out right now," he told her. He waited a couple of seconds to let the idea sink in. "Maybe you could stop by my place, and we could talk here?" he said, "if you get real hungry, I'm sure I can throw something together."

She didn't hesitate answering. "That'll be fine. You want me to bring anything?"

"No, no, that won't be necessary. Do you know where I live?" He asked, knowing that his business card didn't have his address.

"Yes, of course," she said. Meaning that she had done some homework.

"I'll call downstairs then, and tell them I'm expecting you. They'll show you up right away," he said.

"That'll be fine, I should be there in a little while," she said and hung up the phone. He looked at the dead instrument on his hand, and sat it slowly on its cradle.

So she knew what his address was, not because he had told her, though. Probably finding addresses was not a big deal for a crime reporter. On the other hand, Dave also knew that something had happened where he lived, and the only way he could have found out was through the news. He could picture on his mind the possible scenario.

A TV reporter standing in front of the building with a very concerned look on her face, a microphone on one hand, motioning toward her back with the other one. "Right on this building behind me," she probably had said, and the cameraman had zoomed in on the building entrance, which showed prominently the name on gold letters affixed to a man made piece of rock, bathed by a phony cascade. Bingo. Dave would have picked it up right there. His ex, if she had been watching the news, wasn't as perceptive as Dave, or didn't give a fuck. He tended to favor the second option. No call from her to find out what had happened, but then, she probably had forgotten where he lived. He took a sip of beer and looked at the mess that surrounded him, when something clicked on his mind. Dave knew where he lived, the woman reporter didn't. If she had been watching the news, there was no reason for her to associate him with what had happened. She definitely was into something, and he decided to leave everything as it was, to watch her reaction when she saw the place.

He started dialing the building management offices, when the doorbell rang. He hung up, and went to answer the door. He wasn't prepared for what he saw, when he opened it.

Ms. Suarez-Smith looked strikingly different from the last time they had met. She might had been tired, or worried, or pissed at something, but the impression he remembered was somebody aloft, not particularly good looking, with a pair of long good looking legs, and not too interested in what he was trying to tell her.

Today's image was different. She looked fresh and alert, like somebody that had just stepped out of a good shower. She wore black pants that hugged her thighs, and a brown blouse under a white sports jacket. The black sandals, with two-inch heels, made her look almost as tall as he was. The short black hair was combed on the sides, behind the small ears. "May I come in?" She asked.

He realized he had been gawking like a stupid sixteen years old kid. "Yes, of course. C'mon in," he said.

She walked in cautiously, like somebody that is not sure what to expect. "This way please," he said to her back, forcing her into the living room. She looked around, taking everything in, and then turned to look at him. "I'm sorry about what happened yesterday," she said.

"You should be," he said looking at her.

"Me personally? Why is that so?"

"Because you pointed a finger at me, that's why."

"It's not what you think," she said looking straight at him. She turned to one side. "I guess it's my time to say that it's kind of hard to explain."

"Why don't we go to my study, and talk this thing over," he said leading the way. She looked at the pistol lying on the coffee table, but didn't say anything and followed him to the studio.

"Oh shit," she said standing at the entrance, looking at the ransacked room. "They really worked the place over, didn't they," it was more a statement than a question.

He ignored her comment, which was not what he had been expecting anyway, and sat on his chair, motioning her to one of the canvas chairs he kept for visitors. "Quite a mess," she said sitting down and pulling a cigarette out of her bag. She lighted it without asking for permission. She looked around taking everything in. "This is a very nice room you have here Mr. Timberlake. Cozy. Look at all those pictures. Are you really a pilot?" She said, getting off her chair to look more closely at a black and white photo of him strapped on the cockpit of a biplane.

"Yes, I am. Look Ms. Suarez, we have to talk."

"Of course we do, but first let's fix this room, I can't stand this mess. Let me help you," she said taking her jacket off. The flimsy material of the blouse stretched across some very good-looking breasts, Jack noticed.

"You take care of all those folders and files, and I'll take care of the books," she said. "Do you want them on the bookshelves in any particular order?" She asked kneeling down and starting picking up books.

He didn't have any other choice but to get off his chair, and start gathering papers. He felt he was loosing the upper hand on the confrontation he was looking for. "Don't worry," he was forced to say, "just get them off the floor and into the book shelves."

She worked fast, stopping only one time to put her cigarette out on the ashtray. He just crammed papers into folders and files, without really checking them, and sneaking side glances at the woman. It would take a lot of time to classify everything and make sure that each piece of paper was on the right file, but he would take care of that some time in the future. At the moment, all he wanted was to have a good chat with the woman. She kept picking up books and stacking them on the bookshelves. Sometimes she would pick one up, and open it to read the inside cover jacket, or turn it around to read the back cover. "I hate it when people mistreat books," she said, not particularly addressing him. He didn't answer, just sneaked a side-glance at her, kneeling on the floor, stacking books in different piles, maybe making some cataloguing by herself.

In about an hour, his study looked like it had before. She sat on the canvas chair, and lighted another cigarette. "It wasn't that bad, was it?" She asked. "In a situation like this the best thing is to tackle it and put everything back together, not to sit around wondering why it happened to me, and indulging in some self pity," she said puffing on her cigarette.

He stayed on his feet, looking down at her. She was very good at giving advice, he thought. He was beginning to get a little bit irritated. "Have you ever had somebody break into your place, and turn everything upside down?" He asked.

"Yes. Twice, as a matter of fact," she said. "It's the worst feeling, short of being raped, I guess. Your privacy is invaded by some asshole you can't get your hands on. Your personal book has been opened and read by somebody you don't care about. The frustration is intense. I know."

Her answer surprised him, and the little speech he had more or less concocted, didn't apply. "Would you like a beer?" He asked instead. "It's not Corona, though."

"A beer would be most welcome," she said. "I don't care what kind."

He went to the kitchen to get the beer. The woman sure had some way of speaking her mind, he thought. He grabbed a couple of bottles of Budweiser and returned to the study. She was standing in front of one of the bookcases, the cigarette on her right hand. He handed her one of the bottles, walked around his desk, and sat on his chair again.

"Hemingway, Thoreau, Dos Passos," she recited looking at the books she had stacked on the shelves herself. She took a gulp from the bottle. "Updike, Stephen King and Elmore Leonard. Quite a smorgasbord." She turned around to face him. "And then some more. Not the stuff I thought I would find on an engineer's library."

He shrugged his shoulders. "I get enough of the technical stuff on an every day basis," he said.

"We have a lot on common regarding literature, Mr. Timberlake," she said smiling in that particular way of her, that smiled more with the eyes than with the lips.

"Cut the bullshit, Miss Suarez," he said, "I have some questions that need some answers."

"I guess I ought you an explanation," she said, becoming serious. She drank some more beer, and fumbled on her pack for another cigarette. It was empty. He offered her one from the old pack he had found on the bottom drawer of his desk, and lighted it for her.

"I guess it is 'Show me yours and I'll show you mine', time," she said.

"As long as you show me yours, first," he said.

Ten miles away, Timothy Ambrose dialed a number on his private phone. Somebody answered on the third ring.

"Scott, check our friend again," he said, "he looks like a dud to me, but I have to make sure. Don't let your friend over do it, okay? Just try to get some info, but don't let any bodies around. Do you copy?"

"I do chief. I'll take care of it tonight."

THIRTEEN

"I'M GOING TO be completely honest with you," she said putting out her cigarette and looking at him. "I did a background check on you. Try to understand that it was nothing personal. I just had to make sure you were for real, not some kind of nut, or freak . . ."

"Wait," he said interrupting her, "wait just one second." He shook his head in disbelief. "What kind of a background check?"

"The usual," she said looking at her fingernails.

"Pardon me, Miss Suarez," he said leaning over his desk to get a little closer to her, "but I really don't know what *the usual* is. Maybe you can enlighten me?"

She shrugged her shoulders, and looked at the beer bottle as if trying to pry a secret out of it.

"It isn't a big deal," she finally said. "As you must know, most everything today is kept on some kind of data bank or other. If you know which keys to punch, it becomes an open book."

"Don't bullshit me Miss Suarez," he said. "Who do you think you're talking to?"

She finished the beer and put the empty bottle on top of his desk. She took a deep breath, and looked at him.

"I'm not saying that you have to know certain people on the right places, to do that. I'm telling you this because I want to help you. If I hadn't tell you, you wouldn't be any wiser anyway," she said.

He snickered at her answer. "C'mon lady," he said. "Aren't you breaking some kind of law doing that?"

She looked up at the ceiling and slightly shook her head, like some superior being that has to put up with some lesser intelligence. "Look Mr. Timberlake," she said in a condescending tone, "I thought we were going to talk. In a real world kind of way. I'm not sure if I broke some law, or not, I'm not a lawyer. I'm telling you this because I feel I owe you one. You're in some deep shit, if you don't know it, and I think it might have been my fault."

She fished a cigarette out of his pack, and lighted it.

"Do you smoke like this all the time?" he asked, "you're driving me nuts."

"I'm sorry," she said smashing the cigarette out on the ashtray, "I'm trying to quit."

"I can see that," he said. She didn't answer him, just sat there, staring at the wall across from her. He didn't know what to say next. According to her, he was in some kind of deep shit, whatever that meant, and apparently she knew what it was all about. Time to reconcile.

"I'm sorry if I snapped at you. Would you care for another beer?" he asked. "And by the way, call me Jack. Mr. Timberlake makes me feel old." She turned and smiled at him. Her face changed completely when she smiled. The hard look disappeared, and the brown eyes sparkled mischievously. "Another beer would be fine," she said. "And how old are you, Jack?"

"Fifty," he said getting off the chair to go to the kitchen, "but I'll bet you know that already."

He came back with two bottles, placed one in front of her, and sat back on his chair. "What else do you know about me?" He asked her. She started to turn serious again, and he smiled to give her confidence. "Not a whole lot," she said. "Where you work, your political party affiliation, your driving record, your marital status, things like that."

"I won't ask you how you found that out," he said.

"But I'll tell you anyway," she said. "It's not that hard, it's just a matter of knowing somebody that can access that data. To tell you the truth, it's not very legal. That's how I did it."

They stared at each other over the bottles of beer for a while, without saying anything. "I might have gotten you in some kind of trouble, Jack," she finally said.

"How's that," he asked. She told him about her call to captain Ambrose, and asking him to check him out, because he had claimed he had some information.

"Then, this captain friend of yours is involved somehow. It's that what you're trying to tell me?" he said.

"No, not him. I have known Timothy for some years. He's one of these cops that have worked his way up, against the odds. He's good and he's honest. He's also black. He went up the ranks on merits alone. I can vouch for him." She swallowed some of the beer. "He's on the Burglary division, so he probably went to other department to ask questions, and somebody's curiosity got picked." She looked at him. "One way or the other, it's my fault. Somebody is interested in you now, that's what I wanted to tell you."

He was stunned. It was senseless. Some people that had killed two times were interested in him? Would they come back? They had searched his apartment, and found nothing. Was that enough for them, or would they come back to ask him personally? What were his options? Who were they, for that matter?

"Well, Ms. Suarez, I can't say that you have made my day any happier."

"I know. It's Toni, anyway, cut the Ms. Suarez crap."

"Okay Toni, since we are now in this cozy, first name relationship, do you have any recommendations? Do you think I should get a lawyer?" He asked.

"A lawyer? A bodyguard more likely," she said smiling.

He looked at her with surprise, and didn't smile. "You have some weird sense of humor, lady."

"I'm sorry," she said, but the smile lingered on her face. "That's not a funny joke."

"You're goddamm right it isn't. There're a couple of bodies lying around, and the people responsible for them are interested in me? Do you think that's funny?"

"Okay, I said I was sorry," she said fumbling another cigarette from the old pack, and lighting it.

"What then?" He asked her. "What the hell do you think I'm facing?"

"Obviously you're facing some very dangerous people, that goes without saying. Apparently they need to get their hands on some kind of information very important to them. They tried to get it out of that man on the hospital, and you saw what happened." She blew smoke toward the ceiling, and he waited for her to continue. "Then you show up, and tell me that you have something in writing. I try to do a little investigating, and somehow that information fell into the wrong hands, which resulted into this mess you have here." She smashed the cigarette out on the ashtray, and looked at him. "Maybe I didn't handle the situation very professionally this time, but what's done it's done, and I'm sorry about that. That's why I'm trying to help you as much as I can." She finished the beer, and planted the bottle on top of his desk.

He twirled his own bottle without looking at her, the contents sloshing around and forming a funnel-like whirlwind, into which he wished he could dive to emerge unscathed at the other end, several days back on time.

"What's the bottom line," he asked setting his bottle down on the desk, "as far as you can tell."

"The bottom line?" she repeated. She avoided his eyes, and looked at the ceiling. "I really don't know, Jack. I don't want to get melodramatic, but I don't want you to sit on your laurels either. I have been a crime reporter for a few years now, and I have seen a lot of shit. Most of it after the facts, but nevertheless, you pick up some clues along the way." She turned and looked at him. "I would say, that sooner or later, these people will want to have a chat with you. Just to make sure that you have something they need, or that you're just bullshitting. The outcome of that meeting could be anybody's guess."

"Hmm. Doesn't look too promising, does it?"

She shrugged her shoulders.

"Any suggestions?"

"You told me you had some more information, in writing. Maybe if I could see it, I could give you some ideas," she said.

So that was it, he thought. She wanted to know what was on the note. He wondered if she was playing straight, or was some kind of plant. The first attempt to find the note had failed and ended in an ugly mess, so the second was made on a more subtle way, his brain told him. If he showed it to her, what could happen? The note itself was a riddle. If she was playing it straight, she might help him out in figuring what it meant. If, on the other hand, she was working with the other side, she might tell them that he didn't have shit, and get the dogs off of his back. He decided to trust her, and pulled the folded piece of paper out of his wallet. He unfolded it in front of him, and she got off her chair and came around the desk to stand by his side to look at it.

SIESNEC. FINDOC. IN
MM 54/53 KCB
15 circ 1123
R12 L31 r23 L13
Und Carpt Clset.

Both of them read it in silence a couple of times. He had looked at it a couple of times before, without really paying too much attention. "It could be a file in some computer," he said after a while. "What do you think?"

"It looks like it. FINDOC. really looks like a file. The rest doesn't make too much sense. What did he say, when he gave you that piece of paper?" She asked.

He thought back, and tried to remember the exact words. "Can't say exactly. More or less, that if something happened I would know what to do with it. Something along those lines."

She walked back around the desk, and sat again on the canvas chair. She just sat there, and looked at the pictures hanging on the wall across from her. "Can I get a copy of that note?" She asked after a while.

"What for," he said. "To show it to some of your friends?"

"No. Not to show it to anybody, just to study it by myself," she snapped back. She stood up, and picked up her coat. "It's okay. You have the right not to trust me too much."

"Sit down," he said not too gently. "I need some help, anyway. Let's talk this over." He started copying what was on the note on a legal pad. She sat back down, holding her coat and her bag. "Make sure you copy it exactly as it is on the note," she said.

He looked up at her. "Of course. If it's some kind of code, the spacing and the capital and lower letters could mean something, right?"

She gave him her disarming smile. "You're learning Jack."

"Not fast enough." He ripped the page off the pad, and turned it around, so it would face her. "Do you have any ideas?"

Her eyes roamed up and down the page in deep concentration, her unkempt eyebrows almost touching each other. "The fourth line really looks like a safe combination. The lower case letter R could be a mistake or something completely different. I don't know Jack. Something like this has to be read time and time again, until something clicks," she said.

"Do you have any experience along these lines?"

She shrugged her shoulders. "I wouldn't call it experience," she said, "when I majored in journalism, my minor was psychology. I like to dwell in the human behavior now and then. Just as a hobby though." She returned her gaze to the page in front of her. "I think this man wanted to give you some kind of information, in case something happened to him. Not to clear, just in case he did make it, scrambled enough not to make any sense at first sight, especially to somebody not related to his problems, but decipherable with a little work. Kind of a last testament under pressure." She had talked without raising her eyes from the paper. He kept staring at her, until she raised her eyes.

"I never thought about it that way," he said, leaning back on his chair. "For an amateur psychologist you're doing pretty good. At least we have a start." He stood up and grabbed both empty bottles by the neck. "I ran out of beer, but I've got some pretty good Scotch. Let me fix you one."

"Scotch? I don't know. What time is it anyway?" She asked looking at her watch. "My God, almost seven. I didn't realize it was this late."

"Stay put," he said, "just one drink." He walked around the desk. "We can talk about something else, forget about this mess for a minute. Then I'll make you a proposition."

"I hope you're not getting carried away, Jack," she said seriously, but her eyes were teasing him.

He went to the kitchen to fix the drinks. He couldn't help a smile while he poured Scotch over ice into two tumblers. He distrusted the woman, but there was something in her that attracted him. She was, he wasn't sure how to put it; different, he guessed the word was. Compared to Alison, that is. Alison had always been so conventional, so *unaware*. This woman was so different, he thought. For God's sake, they were discussing matters of life and death, not what color a particular wall should be painted. He felt he was navigating toward some weather he hadn't experienced before. Whether it was going to be good flying or not, he wasn't sure yet, but it sure was exciting.

He wrapped the tumblers on paper napkins and went back to his study. He handed her one of the glasses, and sat behind his desk one more time.

She sipped the drink and made a face. "I hope you're not trying to get me drunk, Jack. I would like to hear what kind of proposition you have in mind, before I sprint out of here."

He smiled and took a sip of his drink. He liked the way she pronounced his name.

"A very innocent one, Ms. Suarez," he said. "I was thinking about having dinner together. Montie's sounds good to you? We can sit outside, enjoy the view, and the food is very good."

She looked at him for several seconds. "Okay, that sounds good to me," she finally said. He wondered if he shouldn't have been a little more aggressive on his proposition, and a fraction of a second later realized that he was getting carried away. "Finish your drink," he said getting off his chair, "let me get a coat."

She was standing on the living room, looking at the bay, when he came out of the bedroom struggling into a blue blazer. He picked up the automatic off the coffee table and pushed it under the waistband, on the small of his back. "One piece of advice, Jack," she said before stepping out of the apartment, "Get a real chair for your office. My butt is sore of sitting on that damn canvas chair of yours." He smiled, made a mental note, and locked the door behind him.

They rode to Montie's in separate cars, as each one would go different ways after dinner. It was still too early for the usual crowd, so they had their pick of a table, and Jack choose one out on the deck, right by the water edge. The restaurant deck butted out over the sea wall, the calm waters of Biscayne Bay slapping the rocks gently just a few feet under it. Ironically, the restaurant was next door to the City of Miami City Hall. From where they were sitting, they could watch the window of Commissioner Joe Eldridge's office on the second floor, had they wished to do so. The panoramic view of the bay, with all the sailboats at anchor, was more entertaining though, even if they had known about the Commissioner's interest in him.

Jack ordered wine, and both of them took the hint from the waitress and decided on the smoked swordfish.

They talked about inconsequential matters for a while, and exchanged bits of information about their personal lives. She was demure at first about her own personal life, but after he openly told her about his strange divorce and the daughter that apparently didn't give a shit about family life, she opened up a little more. He learned that she had been married to one time City Commissioner Stanford Smith. After his stint in local politics, Stanford had gone back to his private law practice, which was more profitable. She had never dropped her maiden name, but incorporated the Smith, when she got married. After a couple of years he had insisted that she quit her position as a reporter for the Herald and become a full time housewife. She wouldn't do it, and finally they had split. She had kept her byline at the paper as Suarez-Smith, because it was five years old, and already recognized. They had no children, and the separation had been painless.

The swordfish arrived just in time, because the place was starting to fill up at an alarming rate. The noise level kept going up a few decibels every a few minutes, as most of the crowd greeted each other, like if one half hadn't seen the other half in years, which of course was not the case. Jack looked around him at a happy, party-ready crowd.

"I must be getting old, because I don't know how they do it," he said. "It's the middle of the week, and they're starting to party. I would say most of them have to go to work tomorrow morning. God knows at what time this partying is going to end."

"It's just that we're not spring chickens anymore," Toni said. "I'll bet that when you were that age you did the same thing. Maybe a different setting, but still the same."

He poured the last of the wine on their glasses, and smiled to himself. "I guess I missed half the fun. When I had that age I already had a family, two part-time jobs, and was going to school at night trying to get a degree in engineering. That didn't leave too much room to party." She didn't say anything for a while, just stared at the tables around them. She finished her wine and looked at him.

"I like this place," he said, and it sounded like an excuse. "The food is great, the view superb, and it's close to home." He raised his hand to call the waitress attention. "Next time I would like to take you to a place that you might really enjoy. It's a little far though, down on the Keys. Do you like going down to the Keys?" He asked.

"Of course," she said, "we used to have a place in Tavernier when I was married. I love to go fishing."

"This place I'm talking about is a little bit down south, around mile marker 62, or so. Not too many people know about the place, and the owners want to keep it that way. Not as trendy as this, more of a back to basics place, but I think that you would like it," he said.

"I'm sure I would, Jack," Toni said. "Maybe some other time. I thank you for the dinner, it was delicious, but I must go. Lots of paper work waiting for me, I hate to say."

He suddenly ran out of conversation. Lack of practice, he guessed it was. It had been too many years talking to business associates about work, and women that were married to his friends. He had lost the ability to talk to a woman that didn't have any relationship with either his work or his social life. The waitress appeared back with the little tray, and he welcomed the interruption. He signed the receipt, and the girl turned and disappeared into the multitude.

"Yes, of course," he said getting up, "I have some work to do myself."

They walked slowly across the packed parking lot to their cars. He waited until she unlocked the door, and held the door open for her. She turned around to face him.

"I know somebody that works for the DEA. I'm going to try to get some information about this guy Martin, or whatever his real name is. If I get to know more about him, it might be easier to decipher what he wrote on that note." She opened her bag, and rummaged inside. She pulled a business card, and handed it to him. "That's my address and home phone number. If something comes up, you can reach me here if I'm not at the office. If something interesting comes up, I'll give you a call. Thanks again for dinner."

She lowered herself into the seat of the small sports car. He closed the door for her. She started the engine and lowered the electric window.

"Jack," she said, "remember to keep your eyes open. Okay?"

He just nodded. He waited until her car pulled out of the parking lot and then walked to his Explorer a few feet away. Unreal, he thought as he opened the door of his car.

FOURTEEN

IT WAS ALMOST midnight by the time he drove into the parking lot of the Holiday Inn. He reached automatically for his cellular phone, and realized that the battery had been dead since the day before. He opened the center console compartment and pulled the phone car-charger out. He didn't have any choice but to leave the phone charging on the car. He picked the hotel room key and locked the car.

Maybe the woman was right, he thought while walking to the front entrance. If she could get some background on the man, it could be some help. The other option was to turn the damn piece of paper to the police and forget about the whole thing. If it fell on the wrong hands, that was not his problem. He wasn't in any crusade to clean up local politics. On the other hand, the old man had confided something on him, as Toni had put it, like some kind of last will and testament under pressure. It was kind of stupid though, to pick up somebody else's grudge as your own. Especially if that somebody else didn't mean anything to you and his antagonists didn't care about leaving a corpse here and there.

He walked down the hallway of the third floor to his room, opened the door and stepped in. The room was in complete darkness; just a very thin slit between the closed heavy curtains at the other end of the room let some glow from the parking lights filter in. The door closed behind him automatically on its own spring-loaded hinges with a definite clack. He ran his left hand along the wall feeling for the switch he knew was there. He found it, flipped it up and nothing happened. It was incredible how dark it could get inside this hotel rooms when all the lights were out. The bathroom door was just a couple of feet away, he remembered, and there was a light switch right inside it. Suddenly a chilling sensation ran down his spine. "Keep your eyes open," the woman had said. He ran his left hand along the wall until he found the doorjamb and groped desperately around trying to find the light switch while trying to reach the butt of the automatic under his coat.

Cold fingers wrapped around his wrist in a vise grip, twisting it and pushing his arm up his back. Pain rushed through his arm, exploding at the tip of the fingers. He couldn't help the anguished cry, as the ligaments on his shoulder were stretched to the limit. His face hit the folding doors of the closet, as the force behind him pushed him across the narrow hallway. A cold piece of steel pressed against the nape of his neck, forcing his face against the plastic closet curtain.

"Just relax, Mr. Timberlake. I just want to have a little talk with you," somebody said from behind him, and the pressure on his arm relaxed some. "If you're going to be sensible I won't hurt you," the man said, pushing back on the arm again. He winced in pain, his face scrapping the rough material of the closet curtain. "Are you going to be sensible?" The man asked. He grunted in agreement. "Good," the man said letting go of his arm, but increasing the pressure on the nape of his neck. With his other hand he searched him, found the pistol on his waistband, and pulled it out.

"Let's take a seat," he said, pushing him forward. His arm was still halfway down his back, but he couldn't make it come to his side, it stayed on his back, like an appendage that didn't belong to him. He didn't have any control over his shoulder joint. The lamp on top of the dresser came on, and he saw another man at the end of the room. He was dressed all in black and somehow looked familiar. With one hand he picked one of the two flimsy chairs sitting against the wall, and positioned it between the cheap dresser and one of the twin beds. On the other hand he had a long black tube that he kept against his thigh.

"Sit down," the man behind him said, grabbing his right arm and pulling, bringing it to his side. The pain shot through his brain and he bit his lower lip. He turned around and sat on the chair, holding his right arm with his left hand, and faced the man with the low voice. He sat on the edge of one of the twin beds; legs spread apart, both hands holding a black automatic with a long, fat cylinder on its end, which he assumed was a silencer. He held the gun between his legs, pointed at the floor. His face was round and very pale, and he had a receding hairline. The hair was almost as pale as the face, and the eyes didn't have any color at all. They were almost translucent.

"I have a little problem here, Mr. Timberlake. You have something that doesn't belong to you, and all I want is for you to hand it over to me." The thin slit of a mouth curved at the ends, trying to give the impression of a smile.

"I really don't know what you're talking about," he said.

The translucent eyes moved from his face to some point above his head. The impact of the blow across his upper shoulders and just under his neck took off his wind and knocked him off the chair. He hit the floor, face first and gasped for air that didn't want to go into his lungs fast enough.

He was picked up and dropped back on the chair. His vision was blurred, and he had difficulty breathing. His right arm was still numb, and now a new pain spread down his back.

"As I was saying, Mr. Timberlake. We can make this as easy as possible, or as hard as you can endure it, it's up to you."

"You have the wrong person," he gasped.

Strong hands grabbed him under the armpits and pulled him up on his feet. The next blow hit him on the right kidney and he felt hot urine run down his legs. He twisted, and another blow struck the small of his back, sending him back to the floor again.

"Search him," he thought he heard, but was not sure. Bile and pieces of swordfish were trying to choke him. He felt hands going through his pockets, pulling his wallet and all the contents out. His coat was ripped off him, twisting his right arm one more time. Vomit erupted from his mouth, making a pool under his head and seeping into his nostrils, almost choking him. He lifted his face a bit and turned it to the other side, trying to get it out of the mess, and pull some air into his lungs. A big, black, pointed shoe was just inches from his nose.

"Don't," he heard a voice say from far away. "Let's go."

He could hear scrapping sounds of feet moving around. He moved his eyes on its sockets, to take a look. The man closing the door had a long, slick ponytail. He closed his eyes and laid his face against the carpet.

Captain Timothy Ambrose kept his cellular phone and his beeper, on his night table along with the regular house telephone, when he went to bed. When either one of them went off in the middle of the night, he never knew for sure which one was the one ringing. He picked the regular one first, hung up and then picked up the cellular. "Hello?"

"I'm out, boss. No dice," the soft voice said.

"Are you sure?"

"Yep. Checked the car too, nothing. He was packing the Beretta, though. I lifted it."

"Nothing at all?" Ambrose asked.

"Boss, I really don't know what I'm looking for. No big bundle of papers, or anything like that. There was a piece of paper in his wallet with some notes that don't make any sense. It was the only thing out of the ordinary, looks like something personal, but I've got it anyway. He spent quite some time today with that woman from the paper. Maybe he gave it to her. You want me to check her out?"

"No, no, leave her alone. I'll talk to her. Maybe he's been bullshitting all along."

"You want me to keep a tail on him?"

"Nah. This might be a dude. I'll let you know tomorrow. Hold on to that piece of paper and bring it to me in the morning, I want to take a look at it."

"Will do," the voice said and the line went dead.

He had been sitting on the edge of the bed. He lay back down again, and pulled the covers up to his chest. His wife was lying on her side, her back to him. "I hope that when you make Major, there'll be enough Captains around to take care of middle of the night calls," she said. He didn't know she had been listening. "I'll make sure of that babe," he said, but wondered what would happen if the shit really hit the fan.

Jack opened his eyes, and blinked several times before he could focus them. There was a crumpled pack of cigarettes, and what looked like a road map under the bed. He tried to pull himself up on his elbows, and the muscles on his back screamed in pain. He dropped his head on the carpet again. Slowly he rolled into his back, took a deep breath and looked at the ceiling of the room, which kept swinging from side to side.

He raised his right leg, grabbed his knee with his left hand and pulled himself up to a sitting position. He hurt all over and stank like hell. Grabbing the dresser, he pulled himself up on wobbly legs and faced himself on the mirror. He looked like shit, with vomit caked all over his face. He walked to the bathroom, turned the shower on, and stepped into the bathtub with all his clothes on.

After half an hour he stepped out of the shower, and looked at himself in the bath mirror. Not too much improvement, he thought. There were dark marks across his shoulders and his midriff. His right arm hurt at the joint with the shoulder, but it worked. He walked naked back into the room, and stood in front of the dresser. His wallet was open on top of it. Credit cards, driver and pilot licenses, plus other stuff he had kept on it, were scattered all over it. The notebook page was missing.

He pulled some clothes out of his overnight bag and got dressed. He looked at his watch and found that it was only a quarter after six in the morning. He collected his wet, soiled clothes, off the bathroom floor and pushed them into a plastic bag. He zipped the overnight bag close and looked one more time around to make sure he wasn't leaving anything behind. He stepped out on the corridor and let the door click shut behind him.

Instead of taking the elevator, he walked down the service stairs to the ground floor. As he had thought, there was a door at the bottom floor opening into the back of the hotel. A long, metal trash bin was parked alongside the wall of what looked like some service entrance. He flipped the plastic bag containing his soiled clothes into the bin, and walked back the corridor toward the front desk.

He went through the motions of checking out, and assured the half asleep young man behind the counter that his stay had been great, and of course he would be back some time soon.

The sliding doors swished close behind him, and he walked into a quite warm parking lot, even at this early hour in the morning. He looked up at the clear blue sky. There was hardly a cloud on the sky, and those few were above thirty thousand feet, he estimated. Beautiful flying weather, he thought, trying to keep somehow the nightmare of a few hours before, out of his mind.

When he reached his car, he noticed that the door lock was missing. There was just a hole where the lock should have been. No real damage, just the edge of the metal slightly bent out, like if the whole lock had been sucked out. It was some professional job, not just kids breaking into a car.

He pulled the door open and looked inside. Everything seemed to be in order. The cellular phone was in place on its charger. The speed radar buster was still attached to the windshield. He tossed his baggage on the back seat and climbed into the driver's seat.

The brief moment of sky gazing he had experimented was gone. The beating of the night before, and the realization that some people knew exactly all of his movements, brought him down to earth at a faster rate that he could ever dive one of his airplanes.

He switched the cellular phone on and dialed Dave's home phone number.

FIFTEEN

THEY SAT ACROSS from each other at the breakfast table. Dave nursed his grapefruit juice and Jack swallowed some painkiller pills with orange juice. Camille was in the kitchen fixing their breakfast. The breakfast room was tuck on one side of the immense kitchen, in front of a bay window from where you could see the swimming pool and part of the backyard. The blue water in the pool sparkled under the early morning sun, unhindered by any aluminum and wire mesh enclosure. The lush landscaping surrounding the keystone deck made it look like a little oasis.

"The first thing you should do it's go see your doctor," Dave said. He was showered and shaved, but still wearing a silk robe. "Maybe you have some internal injury, or a broken bone."

Jack shook his head, swallowing two more pills. "Nothing's broken Dave. I'm just sore as hell. They knew what they were doing. They could have broke a bone if they had wanted to."

"You think they were police?" He asked.

"I don't know. How can you tell between a police officer and a hoodlum, in something like this? They both know the tricks. The man was using a rubber hose, or something of the kind. They just wanted to work me over, don't kill me."

Camille came from the kitchen with a big tray that she planted between them. Scrambled eggs, sausage and Canadian bacon, toasts and muffins, and a big coffee pot.

"Enjoy yourselves guys," she said.

"You're not going to join us?" Jack asked her.

"No, my darling. Half a grapefruit, and a bowl of cereal for me. I have to go, I have a heavy day." She kissed Jack on the cheek. "I'll be late tonight Dave. I must attend that art show on the Grove. Have dinner at the Club, will you?" She wiggled her fingers and disappeared.

They dumped food on their plates, and started eating. "You know Jack," Dave said with his mouth full of scrambled eggs, "if I wanted to cheat on Camille, it would be so easy. I've so much leeway."

Jack looked at him, and smiled.

"I know what you're thinking asshole," he said swallowing, "but I doubt it. She just loves all this art bullshit, and there are not enough shows to satisfy her." He drank some coffee. "It helps her business anyway."

Jack helped himself to the last sausage, and took a sip of coffee.

"Dave, I need you to loan me a gun," he said.

"That's not quite the answer, Jack." Dave said wiping his lips with a napkin. He pushed his chair back and pulled a pack of cigarettes from his robe pocket. Jack motioned with his fingers to get one. Dave lighted both cigarettes. "I can go in front of a Judge and ask for police protection. You've been threatened enough."

"I don't think so, Dave. I would have to explain everything. It's all not that legal, and you know it."

"Well, you can take that chance, but you'll feel safer."

"I'm not so sure about that. That might backfire. Let me do it my way. I just want to dig a little deeper into this. If I run into some real legal problem I'll let you know."

They smoked in silence for a few minutes. "We really fucked up with that bet, didn't we Jack?" Dave said.

"Not *we*, Dave. This is my problem. You don't have to get involved in this shit."

"How couldn't I? We're still friends, aren't we?"

"Okay, we are. So just loan me a fucking gun."

"This is so ridiculous that I can't believe it. Impersonating a doctor is one thing, Jack. Playing with guns with the big boys is another. Have you lost your mind?"

"So you're not going to lend me one of your guns?"

Dave got off the chair and straightened his bathrobe. "Yeah. I'm going to loan you one. The one you talked me into buying a couple of years ago to keep on the boat. I never put it on the boat and I had never used it."

They went into his study, and Dave pulled a case from the bottom drawer of his desk. "You told me that if I ever ran into any problem in the high seas, I could sink a boat with this baby. Desert Eagle, .44 Magnum. Never used."

Jack smiled. "I like it," he said. He picked up the weapon and hefted it in his hand. It was the ten-inch barrel version; it was heavy and it looked mean. There were two clips and a box of ammunition inside the case. He loaded both clips and pushed one into the butt of the automatic. "I don't think you realize what you're getting into, Jack. If you are so determined to push this on, why don't you hire a private detective. Let him take the risks. That's what they get paid for."

"I just might impersonate one," Jack said smiling.

"This is no funny stuff, Jack," Dave said very seriously. "Anyway, as soon as I get to the office I'm going to open a dossier on you, and start preparing a case. I have the feeling you'll be needing legal advice pretty soon."

"You do that Dave. That'll give me some peace of mind. Just don't start charging me yet." Jack stuck the big gun in his waistband on the small of his back, and covered it with the polo shirt. He dropped the other magazine in his right pocket. "I have to go. I'll keep in touch."

"You better, asshole."

The first thing he had to do, he thought when he pulled out of Dave's driveway, was to get everything into perspective and into some kind of logical order. The people that wanted to find out what it was that he had in writing, knew about his movements. They had been waiting for him in the hotel. They knew the car he was driving, so probably he was been followed. He had to get another car, and make sure he wasn't watched doing so. He also had to stay away from his apartment, because maybe they were keeping an eye on it.

He turned into Old Cutler Road and fell in line with the flowing traffic, keeping an eye on the rear view mirror. It was hard to tell if he was been followed. It could be any car anywhere. For sure they wouldn't be riding his bumper so he could recognize the faces. He kept driving, trying to pinpoint something out of the ordinary. Some cars veered off the road, and others turned into it. A blue Volvo, several cars behind him, caught his attention because it had been there since he had turned into the road. There was a big intersection just two blocks ahead. It was a complete circle, where four roads converged. At a quarter turn on the right, was the private entrance to Cocoplum, an upper class gated community, at half the turn Le Jeune Road headed North, and at three quarters turn, Sunset Drive took you to the West. If you completed the turn, you were back on Old Cutler Road. Under normal conditions the Circle was tricky to navigate. When traffic was heavy it resembled an old, fair ride; the one where you tried to dodge all the other cars coming at you from different directions, all intent in running you over. He made the three quarters turn safely and headed west on Sunset Drive, the blue Volvo still a couple of cars behind. After a couple of miles he reached the business district of the City of South Miami, and the Volvo was still behind him. On the left hand side of the road was a small business complex that housed a convenience store, a cleaner and a couple of other stores. Just before the light he made a sharp left turn into the convenience store parking lot. He watched several cars drive by, and then the blue Volvo passed by. There was a young woman at the wheel, talking animatedly to two young kids on the back. The light changed to green, and they moved along.

He picked up the cellular phone and called his office. No particular new developments, Bertha told him. He told her that he had to take care of some family business and he would be moving around, not going to the office.

"It's everything all right with you, Jack?" she asked, her voice so low he almost didn't hear her. He was surprised that she had used his first name, she never did, unless they were discussing something in private. She was not his own personal secretary, but also the secretary to two other senior engineers, and she tried to keep an even keel, with no particular preferences, although he knew that she leaned toward him.

"Of course everything's all right Bertha, what makes you think . . . ,"

"C'mon Jack," she interrupted, and her voice was almost a whisper this time. "Somebody was murdered where you live, and now all of a sudden you're taking care of family errands. Can I be of any help?"

Her restrained outburst really surprised him. How had she found out about somebody been murdered where he lived? How did she know where he lived, for that matter. Maybe he had told her the name of the place where he lived, and couldn't remember doing so. She was pretty sharp, he knew, and trying to feed her some bullshit wouldn't work now.

"Listen Bertha, and listen carefully. I'm not in any kind of trouble right now, but if you get a phone call that doesn't make any sense, or somebody that you don't know drops by asking about me, don't say anything. Whatever you hear out of the ordinary, you let me know. You can either reach me on the cellular phone or leave a message in my answering machine. You got that, sweetheart?"

"I got you, and now I know that you're in some kind of trouble. Don't bullshit me, Jack. Are you sure there's nothing else I can do?"

"I'm sure. I'll keep you posted." He paused for a minute, wondering again how she knew about the murder of his cleaning lady. A lot of questions suddenly popped up in his mind, like data downloaded on a computer monitor.

She was about ten years older than him, and they had been working together for about five. The first couple of months after his divorce, she had provided the helpful shoulder where he could cry his frustrations, and he knew that she really cared for him.

"Bertha," he said carefully, "how do you know there was this problem at my place?" He couldn't bring himself to mention the word murder.

"I just put two and two together, Jack. You told me one time how happy you were with this lady that was really taking care of all the house chores for you. They showed a picture of her on TV, and her name. I didn't know her personally, but I remembered the name you told me, and of course I know where you live. It wasn't very hard to figure that out."

That was some part of the news he had missed.

"My name was not mentioned, was it?" He almost was afraid to ask.

"No, of course not. But they mentioned the address of your building," she said. "That's how I figured it out."

"Do you think somebody else in the company knows about this?" He asked.

"No, Jack. I haven't heard anything from within. Are you sure you are all right? Let me know if I can do anything," she sounded really concerned.

"No, Bertha, don't worry. I just need a couple of days to sort things out. Like I said, I'll keep you posted."

"You do that Jack. Just call me if you need anything."

He pressed the end button, and dropped the cellular phone on the passenger seat.

He pulled the automatic from the back of his waistband, and pushed it under the driver seat. It was not really the place to carry a gun while driving around, especially not such a big one. He had done it because he had watched it done in a lot of movies. Maybe in the movies they used guns with shorter barrels. He dialed his own number, and after listening to his recorded voice, punched the code to activate the answering machine. There were no new messages. He tried to find a better position on the big bucket seat, to no avail. If he moved to one side, the sore muscles on his shoulders ached. If he moved to the other, the muscles on his chest screamed. He opened the door and stepped out of the car.

Standing up and stretching out he felt a little relief to his pain. He walked into the convenience store and bought a pack of cigarettes and a plastic lighter. He stepped back outside and lighted a cigarette, leaning against the hood of the Explorer. Traffic kept flowing by, and he couldn't spot a car that was particularly interested in him. He flexed his back muscles, trying to dissipate the soreness away and thought about the turn that his organized, methodical existence had taken in a little over six months.

At forty-five, just a little shy of half a century, he had thought he had it made. A good job, a family, a nice home, four bucks in the bank. He had tightened the belt at the right time, so his wife could fulfil her dream of getting a law degree. He had baby-sited and pinched the penny, but everything had come out all right. They were both professionals, making fairly good money and enjoying a happy life. The American dream had been reached, more or less, until six months ago.

Then, his wife of twenty-one years had divorced him for no logical reason. The family life and the comfortable home were gone. Plans for the future were shattered. The carefully planned course had been altered by a sudden and unforeseen thunderstorm, and there was no particular alternate airport close at hand.

In just two days his apartment had been ransacked and an innocent woman had been murdered in it. He had been robbed and beaten by unknown people that apparently believed he possessed some information they badly needed, and their method of getting information was not the nicest one. So now he was carrying a gun capable of blowing a car engine apart, like some movie cowboy, which he wasn't. His pleasant, organized way of living was deteriorating by the hour. He didn't know what could go wrong next, and couldn't get rid of the encroaching feeling that somebody, somewhere, was watching him and trying to anticipate his next move.

He dropped the cigarette and climbed back in the Explorer. He reached with his right hand under the seat, just to reassure himself that the big automatic hadn't somehow disappeared. He started the car and thought about his options. Whoever he was up against knew what kind of car he was driving, that was a sure bet, so the first thing to do was to dump it and get another car. And there was no better place to do it that at Miami International Airport. He scanned his mirrors again and then eased the car into the traffic flow. He turned into US 1, which at that time was a slow moving parking lot, and tried to spot somebody following him. It was impossible of course, among the hundreds of cars. He raised the volume of the radio and tried to ignore the painful signals his muscles were sending to his brain.

It took him forty-five minutes to reach Miami International Airport. It was close to the midday peak hour of departures and arrivals and the place was a mad house. The airport had been on the expand mode for years, building new access roads and extra parking spaces, but still couldn't cope with the ever growing flow of passengers going through the terminal. New construction never stopped, which made the situation more difficult. It was the place to stay away from, if you could help it. For Jack, today it was a given.

A small Toyota pick-up truck overloaded with all kinds of baggage and boxes, cut in front of him, forcing him to slam on the brakes. A young Latin kid, sitting on top of the baggage trying to hold it all together, smiled and gave Jack the finger.

Some other day he would have been pissed, today he welcomed the uncontrolled traffic jam. He made a sharp left turn at the entrance to a parking lot showing a pink Flamingo on a sign, as a means of identification. He kept riding up the ramp trying to find a spot to park, until he reached the roof level. Today he really didn't mind. He pulled his overnight bag from the back seat and the cellular phone, and walked to the elevator bank.

He got off on the third level and walked over to the walking tube that connected the parking complex with the main terminal building, three floors above ground level. He kept looking to the rear, trying to spot somebody that could be following him, but it was impossible among the myriad of people moving around him. At least he couldn't spot the faces he knew.

When he reached the end of the moving walkway somebody bumped into him and something pointed touched his spine at his waistline. He whirled around, slashing back with his right arm.

The shopping bag with the umbrella across the top of it flew off the woman's hand and hit the side of the corridor wall. Little packages spilled from it and the woman fell to the floor.

"Hijo de puta," she cried. He knew what that meant in Spanish, but he ignored it, while he pushed the little wrapped presents back into the shopping bag and helped the woman up.

"I'm sorry," he said, "here's your bag. I thought it was . . ." he stopped. How could he explain? "I'm sorry," he said again. People kept going by, hardly paying any attention to their little encounter. "I'm really sorry," he said again and started walking toward the elevators.

"Gringo hijo 'e puta," she cried to his back.

He ignored it and kept on walking. Most of the people milling and moving around didn't pay any attention either. The elevator doors opened, he pressed himself into the filled cab, and rode down to the underground level, where international arrivals were located.

When the doors opened, the people inside the elevator cab had actually to fight their way out against the human horde trying to get inside. He had forgotten what Miami International was like at peak hour, especially at the international arrivals gate. Chaos was a very mild word to describe the activity. The tired and frustrated crowd that had sweated the interminable immigration and customs procedures, was spitted out of the glass enclosed cage and exploded into the hysterical and anxious crowd of friends and relatives that had been waiting for hours, pulling and dragging immense amounts of luggage. Dozens of airport baggage handlers pushed their carts at over-speed limits, with complete disregard for ankles and toes. Drop on top of that a stream of travelers running late to catch their national connecting flights, which they didn't have the slightest idea from which level or concourse they were taking off, and you have the last place in Dade County where you wanted to be.

He leaned against the side of the elevator well for a few seconds to get his bearings. Rest rooms and car rentals were to his right, a sign said, and he pushed that way through the sea of humanity. He forgot about somebody following him and concentrated in holding on to his carry bag. Around him, people pushed and pulled, cried and laughed, all in a rush to hit the exit doors, like if the building was on fire.

He reached the car rental aisle, and it was like coming out of a storm-ravaged sea into a calm waters bay. In distance it was just a few feet. Emotionally, it was eons.

He leaned against the Avis counter, and the pretty girl gave him an understanding smile. After a few words, she took his plastic card and processed his rental agreement, rapidly and efficiently. She told him that he would have to step out to the concourse ramp outside customs, and wait for the mini-bus that would take him to the company parking lot on Le Jeune Road, where his car would be waiting. He braced himself again, and battled his way out of the building.

SIXTEEN

H E DROVE THE gray Ford Taurus out of the rental agency car park, and headed south on Le Jeune road. He reached for the cell phone and dialed his apartment number. He waited for the answering machine to kick in, and punched the code. No new messages whatsoever. He hung up and dialed Toni Suarez number.

He was about to hang up after ten rings, when a voice that sounded out of breath answered.

"Toni? It's that you? This is Jack," he said.

"Of course it's me . . . listen, I was going to call you anyway . . . ,"

"Are you all right?" he interrupted. "You don't sound too good."

"It's okay, . . . I'm just out of breath. I rushed out of the shower to get to the phone. Listen . . ."

"You don't have any clothes on?" he interrupted again.

"I . . . ah, . . . how the hell did you know?"

He laughed. "I'm just kidding. It was just a guess."

There was silence from the other end for a few seconds.

"That was not nice," she said.

"I'm sorry. Forget it." Suddenly he felt embarrassed. He realized that his comment could have sounded a little bit too intimate. She didn't answer right away, and he waited a few seconds.

"Hello," he said, "are you still there?"

"Yes I am," she finally said, "I'm getting my bathrobe on, in case your fucking sick mind it's still wondering."

He decided not to comment.

"You were going to tell me something?" he asked.

"Yes," she finally said, "I have some new information that might be helpful, but I don't have time to discuss it now. I have to go to my office. Maybe we can talk about it later on tonight."

His hopes went up a notch when he heard the news. New information that could be helpful meant a lot to him. Maybe the whole mess could be solved and he could return to his regular life.

"I also have some news that are going to really interest you," he said. "Just tell me where and when can we meet."

"I should be home by seven tonight," she said, "give half an hour or so, just in case. Let's meet here at seven-thirty. Write down my address."

"Hold one," he said. He looked around for something to write with. In the glove compartment were a couple of maps, two cheap plastic pens and some candy, all courtesy of the rental agency. He grabbed a Dade County map, and wrote down the address she gave him on the cover flap. It was somewhere in Coconut Grove, but he would have to use the map to find it, the place was a jigsaw puzzle if you were not really familiar with it.

"I've got it," he said. "I'll see you at seven-thirty then." He punched the end button and dropped the cell phone on the passenger seat. The dashboard clock showed one forty-eight. He needed a place to rest for a while, he couldn't just drive around until seven thirty at night. His body was sore and his mind needed some rest after being on override for the last seventy-two hours.

The strangers that had entered his life in the last few hours had catapulted an organized, peaceful existence into chaos. He made a left turn in the next intersection, and headed East with no particular place to go on mind. He felt confident that if he had been followed, he had lost them at the airport, but kept an eye on the rear view mirror just in case.

Violence was really getting close, he thought. Maybe Dave was right, this game was not on his league. These were the Majors and he still was playing in High School. The problem was that it didn't look like a game to him. He couldn't say, 'I quit. I don't want to play anymore.' He was stuck. If he could change things around, he would be in Patagonia chasing butterflies, or whatever they did down there, but this was not the case. He had some mean people chasing him and he wondered what would he do if it really came to a confrontation. Shooting at paper targets was one thing, blowing away a human being was another. Welcome to Real Life 101, he thought.

The sign was what caught his eye. He slammed on the brakes a few inches short of rear-ending the car in front of him. On his left was another Holiday Inn. When the traffic started moving again, he stepped on the gas and made an unlawful left turn in the middle of the busy street. It produced a cacophony of horn blasts and some tire screeching, but he made it safely into the ramp, and parked under the hotel canopy. He pulled his overnight bag from the back seat, and an attendant gave him a ticket and drove his car away.

He registered in at the front desk and was given a room on the fourth floor. At the gift shop on the lobby he paid a ridiculous amount of money for a black polyester brief bag. It had a lot of compartments and a detachable shoulder strap. It would handle all the stuff he didn't want to leave behind in a hotel room, including the large automatic. He also bought a bottle of Tylenol.

The room was almost a replica of the previous one. The furniture was newer and a little more modern, otherwise it was the same. He dropped the overnighter and the new bag on one of the beds and pulled the heavy curtains apart. The view was nothing to linger on.

He picked up the room telephone and dialed his own number again. He punched in the code to listen to messages. There was one from Mr. Lamartino. The carpet boys had taken the measurements and would be installing carpet on Friday. The other one was from his daughter Jackie. She would be arriving Friday at five thirty-five PM on American. Not to worry, she would take a cab to Mommie's place and get in touch with him later on, she said. End of messages the machine told him. He hung up, and lay down on the bed. He would have to keep Jackie away from him until the situation cleared, one way or the other. He wanted to take a shower, but didn't feel like getting off the bed. He swallowed a couple of Tylenols without the benefit of any water. He felt like if he was sinking deeper and deeper on the mattress and closed his eyes.

He woke up with the jolt that the dream where the stairs suddenly disappear from under you, produce. He felt disoriented for a moment, and then looked at his watch. Twenty after seven already. He would be late for his meeting with Toni. He rushed into the shower and then dressed in new fresh clothes. He dug from his carryall the stuff he didn't want to leave behind in the hotel, including the automatic, and stuffed it into his new brief bag, which he slung over his shoulder. He stepped out into the hallway and let the door click shut behind him.

As he had thought, he had to use the map to find Toni Suarez address. It was in the old part of the Grove, where short streets dead-ended sometimes just after a few blocks. The vegetation on this part was lush, to put it mildly. The narrow streets had been just trails in the old times, and the only difference now was that they were paved. Still, some of them twisted and circled in order not to bother the old trees that had made this part their home, long before any human had decided to settle in. In the old part of Coconut Grove you didn't knock down and old oak tree just because a street should be straight. Some residences were set so far back into the vegetation, that you couldn't see them from the street. For people who liked to live on a wild frontier setting, but just fifteen minutes from the modern maelstrom that was downtown Miami, Coconut Grove was the place; if you were willing to pay the price of a modern bay-front condo for an eighty years old cottage.

He finally found Toni Suarez place. Not because he saw the number, but because he spotted her bright red Mitsubishi with the 'Save the Manatee' tag, parked under a kind of carport, that was actually not a carport, but some kind of wood trellis structure covered by vines.

Eucalyptus and Frangipani trees enveloped the cottage style house, isolating it from its neighbors. In front of the house, half out on the street and half on the tiny front lawn was a white Ford Crown Victoria. There was no place to park. Jack backed up a little and angle-parked against the back bumper of the Mitsubishi, leaving part of the rear end of the Taurus sticking out into the street. He grabbed his brief bag, and walked to the front door.

He looked around the frame of the front door for a bell push button and couldn't find one. He was about to knock on the door when he heard some muffled voices and what sounded like a small cry. He put his hand on the doorknob and tried to turn it, but it wouldn't budge. He put his ear to the door and heard voices, but couldn't make out what they were saying. The tone didn't sound like if they were having some party, though.

He looked around. There had to be another entrance to the house. He walked over to the funny looking carport. From the end of it, a path of loose concrete slabs led to the back of the property. He walked down the path trying not to make any noise. Something wrong was going on inside the house, he could feel it. He reached a narrow side door, the old, wood frame and glass louvers kind, which nobody in Miami dared to keep anymore, because it was so easy to break through. The bracket light by the door was out, but he could see that no glass had been broken. He grabbed the doorknob and turned it. The door opened to his surprise. He put the brief bag on the concrete steps, zipped it open and pulled the Desert Eagle out. He worked the slide chambering a round, and carefully let the hammer fall back to the half-cocked position. He pulled the door open slowly, hopping the hinges were not rusty and would scream in alarm, and walked in.

He stepped into a small kitchen that opened on the other side into a hallway. He quietly sat the brief bag on the floor, holding the automatic on his right hand, and slowly stuck his head out peering into the hallway. To his right, a door opened into a bathroom. Across the hallway there were two doors. One was closed, the other one was half open, some light coming out from inside. It looked like a bedroom. To his left the hallway extended for several feet into what he guessed was the living area. He could just see part of it; what looked like a dinning room, at right angles to the left. He could hear voices clearly now, somewhere to the right off the end of the hallway.

" . . . don't want to hurt you real bad." He heard a muffled voice say. A female voice whined something intelligible. He heard the unmistakable sound of an open hand striking flesh.

He walked down the corridor, his back against the wall, his right hand holding the automatic against his thigh. When he reached the end he peered out, not knowing what to expect.

Toni Suarez was sitting on a sofa, a man by her side holding both arms at her back in a wrestler grip. There was a piece of duct tape across her mouth. Sitting on the coffee table across from her was another man. Both men were wearing black ski masks.

"Just be sensible and you'll make it easier on yourself," the man sitting on the coffee table said. "Just nod if you're going to be sensible and I'll take that tape off and then we can talk." He then matter of factly slapped the side of her face again. Her head bounced to one side under the impact.

"I can make it very painful my dear, it's up to you," the man said. Jack froze where he was, unsure of what to do next.

He couldn't just burst into the room like James Bond. These people were professionals and he didn't know how they were going to react, the whole thing could turn into a blood bath. On the other hand, he couldn't stay on the hallway forever while they beat the shit out of Toni. He had never been very religious, but he took a deep breath and crossed himself with his left hand.

"Let her go," he said stepping out of the corner of the hallway, his right hand holding the gun, still pointed to the floor. The man sitting on the coffee table turned toward him in surprise, his right hand diving under his coat. The man holding Toni reacted even faster. He pushed her away with a swift motion of his left hand, while on the other appeared something black pointed at him. Jack recoiled back into the hallway. He didn't hear a sound, but chunks of plaster and wood exploded just inches above his head. Instinct made him drop to his knees. Across his face on the other side of the hallway three holes suddenly erupted. He dropped into his belly and embraced the floor. The light fixture in the ceiling shattered and small glass shards rained on his back. Still, no ear shattering explosions like in the movies, they were using silenced guns. He raised himself a little on his left elbow, hoped that Toni was hugging the floor, aimed his pistol in the general direction of the sofa and squeezed the trigger. A real explosion shook the small house. He was awed by the power of the big gun. From his prone position he saw the front door open. He got off the floor and ran toward it. He hesitated a moment leaning against the doorframe and then jumped outside. As he did, a white Ford was pulling out, tires screeching. He held the big automatic with both hands, sighted on the back of the car and pulled the trigger. The recoil pushed both his hands up to a forty-five degree angle and heard the incredible explosion again. The rear window of the Ford disintegrated, but the car kept on going and disappeared around a bend in the street. He felt like keeping his finger on the trigger, blasting away at something. Adrenaline had taken over and fear and surprise had disappeared. He looked around, surprised that nobody had come out to investigate the commotion, and then realized that the only sound had been his single shot out on the street, that probably had been lost among the dense vegetation or otherwise mistaken for a car backfire. The only person in sight was Toni Suarez standing at the front door of her home, looking at him. He pushed the safe lever of the automatic to on and tucked it in the waistband on his back. He walked back to the house and looked at her. A nice bruise was developing on the left side of her face.

"Are you okay?" he asked.

She didn't utter a word, just nodded and wrapped her arms around his neck, resting her face against his chest.

Her sudden reaction took him by surprise, and he felt at a lost about what to do next. For sure he looked stupid with a woman hanging to his neck while both his arms were hanging by his side. Slowly he wrapped his arms around her back. It had been a while since he had held a woman this close to his body, he realized. She was warm and soft to the touch, and her hair, just under his nostrils smelled of some kind of flower he couldn't remember the name. The tingle on his loins told him that he was going to be so obvious in a minute that he would look like a sex fiend.

"It's okay," he said, "they're gone. Everything it's going to be all right. We better go inside."

She unwrapped her arms and turned around and he followed her inside and closed the door behind them. "Shit!", she said running both her hands trough her hair, her back to him, walking toward the kitchen. He followed her. She flipped the light switch on and noticed his black brief bag on the floor. "They came in through this door Jack. Look what they left," she said pointing to his bag.

"That's not theirs," he said, "that's my bag."

She stared at him, a puzzled look on her face for a moment that dissolved into a smile in the next. "You also came in through here, of course." She opened the door of one of the top cabinets and pulled out a bottle of Cutty Sark, which she sat on the counter. "We need a drink Jack," she said, pulling out two tumblers. He opened the bottle and poured an inch of whisky on each glass. "Thank you," she said raising her glass, "you saved my life. I ought you one."

They downed their drinks in one gulp. "Let me tell you one thing Jack," she said, "those creeps really scared the hell out of me."

He walked past her and locked the side door. He noticed a security chain hanging from the doorjamb. "Don't you use this thing," he said jangling the chain. "If it had been in place they wouldn't have been able to open the door that easy."

She stared at the chain like if it was something she had never seen before. "Yes, of course I always set the chain. I guess I forgot today after I put the garbage out."

He slammed the end of the chain into its slot and checked one more time to make sure the door lock was on. He turned around and faced her. "Get some clothes, a couple of days worth at least, and whatever else you feel you don't want to leave behind," he said, "we have to get the hell out of here right now."

"Why?"

"Because they might be back any minute for one thing. The other is that maybe a neighbor has already called the police. I recognized those characters. I'll explain later."

She went into the bedroom across the hall. He followed her and leaned against the doorjamb. She had opened a closet and looked bewildered. "Something comfortable, Toni," he said, "you're on the run now."

She turned around and looked at him, uncertainty and fear written all over her face. He pulled himself off the door and walked into the kitchen. He poured another half inch of Scotch in his glass and downed it in one gulp.

He shook his head in disbelief. Was he being real, or was he loosing it somehow? 'You're on the run now', indeed. Like if that didn't sound like a script line from a third grade cowboy movie. If you add a few gunshots that had almost wrecked her house, and a couple of slaps on the face by two masked men, it was no wonder that the woman looked bewildered.

He was the one on the run, and now he was going to drag somebody else along? Why didn't he tell her to go to her mother, or sister, or whoever? For sure she must have a relative or friend where she could safely go. He didn't need the extra baggage to start with. Or was it maybe that he wanted her close, so he could keep an eye on her? No matter how scared he had been, he had recognized the two men. Black ski mask or not, he could tell they were the same men that had paid him a visit at the Holiday Inn. They hadn't bothered to show him their faces, why the ski masks now? They had come through the unlocked back door, that apparently she had forgotten to lock after she took the garbage out in the morning. Something that in this city, people very seldom forgot to do. Not everything was clicking the way it should. Some people evidently thought that he was the recipient of some information they very badly wanted. Why they hadn't tried to torture it out of him at the Holiday Inn he wasn't sure of, but a good guess would be that they were hopping he would lead them somewhere, or to somebody. That he had loosed them somehow, had been pure luck on his part, and now they had come to the next link on the chain, to pry from her what it was or to find out where he was. Either way, it meant that those people, whoever they were, had very long ears stuck in places where they shouldn't be. The only way you could do that was if you carried some real power, he figured.

The whole situation was getting more out of hand by the minute. How, or to whom, could he explain that he didn't have anything to do with the man that had been shot in the hospital? They were out on a wild goose chase, where he was the goose, and they were carrying guns to kill the goose. He didn't want to think about a big conspiracy in which the woman had some part, because that was kind of stupid, he wasn't that important. He kind of liked her, and wanted to give her the benefit of the doubt. Still, the masked men and how they had come into the house bothered him. The bruises on Toni's cheek were real enough, but then, there was no major damage, and they would disappear in a few days.

"I'm ready," she said. She was standing on the corridor, a three-foot long duffel bag on her left hand and a large brown leather brief hanging from her right shoulder. "Where the hell are we going?"

He reached down, picked his brief bag off the floor and slung it over his left shoulder. "I have a room in the Holiday Inn in Coral Gables," he said, "I think that would be safe enough for a while."

"Jack, I hope you didn't put this show together just to get me into a hotel room," she said. He was going to give her some answer, when he noticed the smile and the teasing on the eyes. He flipped the kitchen light off, and on a second thought grabbed the bottle of Scotch and put it under his left arm. "Let's get out of here," he said, giving her a little push on the back. "Turn all the lights out."

He walked to the front door and pulled the automatic out of his back with his right hand. With the house in complete darkness, he pushed the door open with his left hand, holding the bottle under his armpit at the same time.

"Jack, this is so dramatic," she said in a very low voice.

"Those bullet holes on the wall are dramatic enough for me," he said. He stepped outside and looked around, but the street was as dark and quiet as it could be. "Just lock the door and walk over to that car behind yours." She obeyed, and he walked behind her, expecting the white Ford to come crashing toward them at any time. Nothing happened and he unlocked the car and both of them got in.

He started the car, backed up, and turned around to leave on the same way he had come in. He didn't want to find any surprises at the other end of the street, where the white Ford had disappeared.

"I have some new information about the man that was killed in the hospital, that might explain a few things," she said in the same low tone of voice she had used when they were leaving the house. After a couple of turns he finally found Main Highway, and turned toward the center of Coconut Grove business district. He would have to back track to go to the hotel, but at the moment, driving down a busy road toward a bustling, very well lighted area, gave him a sense of security. Nobody would try any funny business in front of hundreds of people, in one of the busiest places in Miami at night. He started relaxing and feeling more comfortable. He then thought about the low voice, conspiring tone she had used to talk to him, and couldn't help it but to start laughing. It wasn't that funny, maybe it was just a release of the tension that he felt was dissolving, but he couldn't help it. The more he thought about it, the harder he laughed. "What the hell's so funny," she asked.

"You don't have to talk like that," he said mimicking her low, conniving tone, "nobody can hear us anyway." He cracked up laughing again. She just turned her face to the side window and didn't say anything.

He drove all the way down to the Dinner Key Marina, keeping an eye on the rear view mirror for a big, white Ford. He made a U turn on South Bayshore drive, and returned toward 27 Avenue. He never paid any attention to the brown, ten years old, Toyota station wagon four cars behind him.

SEVENTEEN

"SHIT!," HE HEARD her muffled scream through the closed bathroom door, "look at what those creeps did to my face."

He was sitting on a chair alongside the piece of furniture that functioned as dresser, desk, and whatever else you wanted to do on top of it. He had in front of him several yellow pages, full of notes made by Toni and he was trying to make some sense out of them.

They had come to his room in the Holiday Inn in Coral Gables, after some circumvolutions around Coconut Grove to make sure that the white Ford was not following them. After he had assured her that the room was equipped with two single beds she had agreed to spend the night, so they could talk and try to put everything into perspective.

She had handed him a sheaf of papers when they had arrived at the room, so he could look them over while she took a shower.

She came out of the bathroom wearing a Miami Dolphins T-shirt that reached halfway to her thighs and nothing else that he could see. He wondered if . . . She raised both arms to push her hair back with her hands, the T-shirt raised with the motion, and he noticed the ragged edges of cutoff jeans. His wondering came to a sudden halt.

"Did you see this?" she asked, indicating her left cheek with her hand.

He nodded. It had started to turn purple and it would be black by tomorrow, he was sure.

"It will look worst tomorrow," he said, "but it will disappear in a couple of days. You don't have anything broken, so don't worry too much."

She pulled the other chair and sat across from him. "I have to worry, it's my face not yours," she said. "Anyway, did you read my notes? What do you think?"

"Well," he said, "that the man called Martin Brown was a Colombian citizen surprised me. We knew that the name was an assumed one, but that he was Colombian? I never suspected that he wasn't American. He didn't have the slightest accent, and didn't look Latin either." He lighted a cigarette, picked one of the written pages and read from it.

"Carlos M. Hidalgo-Arzon. Born in Cali, Colombia on February 17, 1929. Graduated from Harvard Business School in 1951, with a degree in Economics. Held positions in the banking industry until January 13, 1992, when he was fired from 'Banco Industrial de Bogota' for embezzlement. Never convicted. Recruited by his grandnephew, Andres Hidalgo Santor, sometime in 1994. Andres Hidalgo Santor is suspected to be the head of a fairly new, very sophisticated Colombian drug cartel, in which are involved top echelon officers in banking, industry and the government. These high level officials are in close association with their same counterparts in the US, especially in the Miami area. These are not gun totting cocaine cowboys. These are community pillars and civic leaders. Carlos M. Hidalgo-Arzon was supposed to have all the information needed to crack open the Miami end of the operation," he finished reading. "Where did you get this information?" he asked her.

"Confidentially Jack, just between us," she said, "I got it from a friend that works for the DEA."

He looked at her, surprise and incredulity on his eyes.

"Why the hell would somebody working for the DEA, give you some secret, confidential information Toni?"

She rolled her eyes back and pulled a cigarette out of his pack. She waited a few seconds, and when she realized he was not going to light it for her, grabbed the Bic and lighted it herself.

"I met this guy, professionally I mean, about two years ago, while doing a piece for the paper. He took a liking of me I guess, kind of a crush, if you know what I mean." She tapped some ash off her cigarette on the ashtray between them. "I looked better two years ago," she said smiling, but he didn't smile back. "Anyway," she said crossing her legs, "I agreed to a dinner date later this month, and I guess his testosterone overwhelmed his better judgement." He still looked at her without smiling.

"He probably doesn't consider this information so confidential anymore Jack," she said. "After all, the man is dead and whatever information he was supposed to have is lost. Or at least that's what he thinks."

He didn't know what to make out of the whole situation. He wanted desperately to trust her, because he needed somebody to help him out. On the other hand his real problems had started since he had confided on her. So many things didn't look right. She had forgotten to lock the side door in her house, making it very easy for the two men to get in. The whole thing could had been a little act; she had been slapped a couple of times but there was no real harm done. The shots had been very real though. Now she had come up with some information from a DEA agent, something that was hard to believe. He imagined that Federal agents didn't go around divulging sensitive information, just to crawl into bed with somebody. Then again, this was the real world. If the agent in question thought that the information wasn't so sensitive any more, and he really carried a hard on for that particular piece, who knows. If she was part of some confabulation trying to pry some information from him, which he didn't have, what was the point? She knew about the whole thing as much as he did. Maybe she was just trying to pull a big story out of the whole thing. He decided to go ahead and trust her, and told her about the visit he had had the night before.

"I'm almost sure that the men that were at your house are the same that paid me the visit," he said, "I saw pale blonde hair sticking out from that sky mask."

She had listened to his story in silence, without interrupting. Now she stood up and walked over to the night table where he had left the bottle of Scotch, and grabbed it by the neck. She dropped back on her chair and put the bottle on top of the dresser between them. "I need a good drink," she said, "do we have any ice?"

There was an ice bucket on the dresser, but it was empty. He shook his head no.

"Did you read the rest of my notes," she asked.

"I scanned through them, but they're not easy to understand. Bunch of arrows pointing here and there, and your handwriting it's not very intelligible," he said. "I concentrated on the notes with the information about this man Brown, or whatever his name is. How come those notes are real clear and readable?"

"Because those I copied from the fax Jerry sent me, which he made me promise I would destroy right away. That information I wanted word by word. The rest are notes of ideas I got while thinking about this whole thing." She dragged deep on her cigarette. "I know that my hand writing it's not the best on the world. I type most of the time anyway."

"Who's Jerry?" he asked.

"Jerry's the guy I know that works for the DEA," she said. She rolled back her eyes again in that way of hers, which was beginning to annoy him.

"Oh Jack," she said raising her hands and dropping them again to her lap, like when somebody has lost all hope of trying to communicate, "you feel so uncomfortable. You're questioning and doubting everything I tell you. You don't trust me at all, so what's the use?"

He got off his chair, and walked to the window. He parted the heavy curtains and looked down. No bright inspiration came with the view, just a bird's eye view of several cars on the hotel parking lot. The heavy wooded street concealed whatever could be lurking there. He let the drapes fall and turned around to face her.

"I might feel or look a little uncomfortable as you say Toni, but maybe I have some reasons to be so," he walked back to his chair and sat down facing her. "You see, I made this bet with a friend that I could impersonate a Doctor, make some rounds in a hospital, and get away with it. Stupid, unrealistic, unconceivable for a man of my age and position, whatever you want to call it. I realize that. But what's done it's done, and that's beside the point. During this impersonation, if you want to call it that, I came into a situation. A situation, that if I kept it to myself, nobody on this earth would be the wiser. After reading your article on the Herald, I decided that maybe I could be of some help to right a wrong, and I contacted you. Since I talked to you, the only person in which I have confided, it's been one big clusterfuck." He spread the fingers of his left hand. "My apartment was ransacked," he said curling down one of his fingers, "my cleaning lady was murdered, some people were waiting for me on a place that nobody was supposed to know I was, and beat the shit out of me, and then," he said curling all his fingers into a fist, "at your house they tried to shoot me. Now, you tell me if I shouldn't feel a little uncomfortable, or doubtful, or plain paranoid when I'm around you. I really don't know what your part in all this is, or on which side you're on, but let me tell you something, if somebody tries to break into this room tonight, we're going to have the latest version of the fight at the OK Corral right here. Whoever they are, they pushed me as far as they are going to push me. I just don't give a fuck anymore." He poured some scotch in one of the plastic tumblers, and tossed it down in one gulp. "Do we understand each other?" he said placing the plastic cup carefully between them.

She stared at him in awe when he finished his speech.

"Paranoid Jack, paranoid is the word," she said. "You're not uncomfortable or doubtful, you're fucking paranoid. I really need a drink now. Cool down for a second and listen to what I have to say, and then make up your mind. And by the way, cut all that OK Corral bullshit. You're not the type." She stood up. "Do you have a map of the Florida Keys in here?" She asked him, changing the subject so suddenly, that it took him by surprise.

"We have to get some ice," she said grabbing the ice bucket, "I'll try to find some. There should be an ice machine on this floor or the next. Why don't you go down to the lobby and get a map of the Keys?"

He got off his chair and walked to the night table between the twin beds. He pulled the Desert Eagle from the top drawer and stuck on the front of his trousers, covering the gun butt with the bottom of his Polo shirt. He picked up the plastic card that served as a room key, from the dresser, and touched her elbow.

"Why don't we go together in this little errand."

"Paranoid Jack, just paranoid you are," she said smiling at him. He smiled back, opened the door, and let her step into the hallway ahead of him.

He felt kind of foolish when they got back to the room. Nobody had assaulted them at the ice machine or in the lobby, where he had to pay $3.00 for a map of the Florida Keys. 'Sorry, they're not free anymore,' the girl at the reception desk had said. He dropped the automatic back into the top drawer of the night table, while she poured Scotch over ice into two glasses at the dresser.

"Okay Jack, come over here, sit down and listen to me for a few minutes," she patted the chair next to her. "There's your drink. Relax. Open your mind and just cope with me for a while. Remember this is just a hunch, but let me finish before you start throwing objections around, okay?"

"I'm all ears ma'am. I already feel like if I'm in some psychiatrist office. I would lay down if it wasn't for the drink."

"Laugh all you want," she said. "Let's start at the very beginning." She pushed the page of yellow stationary he had given her two days before, to the front of the desk. "What does it says?"

He looked at the piece of paper.

SIESNEC.FINDOC.IN
MM 54/53 KCB
15 CIR. 1123
R12 L31 r23 L13
Und crpt. Clset.

"The same thing it always said, as far as I can recall."

"Read the first line aloud to me please," she said. He looked at her and was going to make a smart remark, but her face was so serious that he decided against it. "What do you mean by reading it aloud?" He asked her.

"Just that, Jack. Just read the first line like if you were reading to yourself, whatever comes to your mind, but said it aloud," she replied exasperated.

He looked at the piece of paper again.

"Siesnec dot findoc dot in," he said aloud.

"Exactly!" She said beaming at him, a look of triumph on her face.

"Exactly what?"

"That's exactly how you read it the first time you saw that note, and that's how I also read it the first time I saw it. The clue is that it is not 'dot', it's 'period'. Don't you see it? You probably don't, because you don't speak Spanish," she answered herself right away, she was so wound up. "Don't blame yourself Jack, it's not that you are dumber than me. I figured it out when I found out that the man was Hispanic. You see, 'siesnec.', could be a contraction of 'si es necesario', which in Spanish means 'if it's necessary'. A contraction would have a period at the end. The rest of the line I assume it says, 'find document in', and then the rest. Some of it written in Spanish, some in English. Why? Because the man didn't want to go all out and give some stranger some very delicate information. On the other hand, if his worst fears came true, he was leaving behind some clues that might, they just might, nail down his assassins. It was a last resort option, Jack. Don't you see it?"

He was amazed by all the conclusions she had come to. He tried to rationalize all the information she had thrown at him in a couple of minutes. If you wanted to take a long shot, it might make some sense, now that they knew that the man could express himself in both English and Spanish. Still it was a long shot.

"It looks like you really did some home work Toni," he said smiling. "What's next?"

She raised her glass and took a little sip of her drink. He drank the rest of his, and fixed himself another one. "I can't wait to hear the rest of it," he said, and couldn't help himself if it sounded a little skeptical.

"This part is the one that's really a hunch, Jack. It's about the second line of the note. But before we go into that, let me ask you something," she said.

He turned around on the chair, and rested his left elbow on top of the dresser. There was no comfortable position on the hard chair. He resigned himself to receive whatever conclusions she had come to, on a piecemeal basis. The Scotch was starting to mellow him, and he realized that he didn't care if he spent the whole night answering ubiquitous questions.

"Go ahead Toni, ask," he said.

"What's the address of that place in the Keys, the one hardly anybody knows and serves such good food. The one you said you would like to take me?"

"Oh, . . . 'The Sand Piper'. I don't know the exact address. It's on the Bay side, on mile marker 62. Why?"

She gave him again a triumphant smile. Something like, I told you so; but didn't say a word, instead she took her own sweet time to refresh her drink and light a cigarette.

"People on the Keys refer to addresses according to which mile marker they are on," she said blowing smoke toward the ceiling. "What does the second line of the note says?"

He looked at her and then down at the sheet of yellow paper,

MM 54/53 KCB

"It's a hunch Jack, I don't want to look at the map. You look it up yourself," she said crossing her fingers like when people make a wish.

He opened the Florida Keys map, and started scanning down mile markers with his index finger. His finger froze between mile marker 54 and 53. A causeway led from the Overseas Highway, or US 1, to a private community called Key Colony Beach. KCB. It was a small island with its private golf course, and slashed by canals, so every house could have a back yard dock and access to the ocean. The streets were numbered, and in one corner of the island one of the streets was called 15 Circ. The place was just one mile from the Marathon airport, a general facility airport he had used more times that he cared to remember.

He looked at Toni. She still had her fingers crossed and had closed her eyes. It was unbelievable. It had been so clear all the time. Very clear now, but he hadn't been able to figure it out. He had to give credit to the woman.

"It looks like you hit pay dirt lady," he said.

She opened her eyes and jumped off her chair. "Let me see that," she screamed. He pointed the area on the map to her. "Shit!, I knew it," she screamed again, "I knew it Jack." She danced around the room, "Hooray", she sang. She stopped in front of him and pointed a finger at him. "I know what the rest means, Jack. The numbers are a safe combination, and that safe is 'under the carpet in a closet'. I'll bet my life on it."

Her enthusiasm was contagious, and he let it carry him away. Her hunch had paid out pretty good, if everything she had told him was true. He couldn't get rid of the idea that she was not been really truthful with him, that somehow she was hiding something, and he was been taken for a ride. He shook his suspicions into some recess of his mind, and analyzed everything as objectively as he could. Apparently she had been really working on trying to break the riddle of the note. He pushed suspicions away, and let euphoria creep in. He refilled both their glasses, and handed one to her. "Let's drink to a very good piece of detective work," he said touching his glass to hers.

He sat back, grabbed the sheaf of papers and looked at them one more time. He took a sip of whiskey and dropped them on the table. "It really wasn't that hard to figure it out," he said.

"What?" She asked.

"The riddle, or mysterious code, or whatever you want to call it," he said. "It was in plain sight and kind of dumb in a way. It's actually a message to somebody."

She looked at him, a surprised look on her face. "What was so dumb and in plain sight?" she asked.

"All that information," he said.

"Why didn't you figure it out yourself then?"

"I don't speak Spanish," he answered.

"Oh man," she said slamming her plastic cup on the table, "you really have an answer for everything, don't you?"

"I try to," he said, "we still don't know if what you think is true."

"You're still skeptical Jack, but I know I'm right."

"There's only one way to prove it, isn't?" He asked.

"Yeah? Which way it's that?"

"We're going to take a little trip to the Keys tomorrow and find out by ourselves," he said.

She smiled and raised her right hand up in the high five fashion. He slapped it. "I knew you'll go along with it Jack. I love it. It might even be dangerous," she said.

"I hope not," he said. "We should leave early in the morning, I think we should hit the sack." He finished his drink. "Are you going to sleep like that, or are you going to slip into something more comfortable?" he asked.

She looked at herself. "You're right, I should change. Don't worry about me Jack, you just relax and go to bed." She picked up her bag and walked to the bathroom. When she closed the door, he turned off the wall lights and crawled into one of the beds, leaving on the little lamp on the night table between the two single beds. He pulled the bed covers up to his chest, and rested on his side. After a while the bathroom door opened and the light went out. She walked into the room wearing a two-piece pajama, and sat on the far end of the other single bed.

"You call that comfortable?" he asked.

She turned around and looked at him. "Jack, I thought you were already asleep." She crawled into her bed, and pulled the covers up to her chin. "Yes, these are really comfortable for me," she said. She turned to his side and reached for the light switch of the small table lamp. "Don't even think about it, Jack," she said, and flipped the light switch off.

EIGHTEEN

H E WOKE UP with a slight headache and a sour taste in his mouth, which he credited to the few whiskies of the night before, but other way, fine enough. Even the aches and sourness produced by the beating had all but disappeared. The room was enveloped in almost complete darkness. He could tell it was a new day, because of the thin slice of sunlight creeping in through the small crack where the heavy drapes didn't quite overlap. Otherwise you couldn't tell the difference whether it was day or night outside. He looked at his watch and then at the prone figure of the woman lying on the bed next to his. His watch told him that it was sixteen minutes after eight in the morning. The peaceful breathing figure on the other bed, told him much more. She was lying on her side, her back to him, and even covered by the heavy hotel blanket, he could notice the curves of her hips and thighs. He realized how long it had been since he had possessed a woman. Really possessed. He missed Allison like one misses something that had been taken for granted, and suddenly disappears. Their sexual relationship in the later years had been good, especially after a party or other get together, where their libidos had been aroused by a few drinks or the companionship of other people. The rest of the time it had been just a matter of fact. When he thought about it, he realized that their divorce had hit him more in his organizational chart, than in his heart. He had lost the family environment, with all of its normal accoutrements; the love story part had been lost somewhere along the way. He regretted it somehow, because he considered it as some kind of failure on his part, the untold, unspoken, deep down inside bred consciousness, that a man should create a family and hold on to it, until he was no more. He regretted it because he had been the one that had been dumped, and not the other way around. When Allison had told him that she didn't want him any more, that she wanted some freedom, it had hurt; because he had always assumed that he was needed.

Anyway . . .

He looked at the sleeping form on the other bed. Maybe she was playing hard to get, feigning sleep, just waiting for him to crawl under the blankets and embrace her from behind.

But what could happen if she wasn't? All hell might break loose. He had too much at stake, and he needed her at least until he could find if her assumptions were right or wrong. He threw his covers to one side, got out of bed, and walked to the bathroom.

"I thought that you were going to spend the rest of your life in there," she said as soon as he opened the door, "get out of my way, I have to pee." She slammed the door shut behind her, almost before he had cleared the way. He didn't have time to even say 'Good morning'. He shook his head, dropped the towel he had wrapped around his middle, and changed into blue jeans and a loose fitting white, cotton shirt. He was finishing packing his stuff, including the Scotch bottle, when she stuck her head out of the bathroom door. "Jack, will you handle me my bag please," she said. He picked the bag off the floor and tried to push the door open to handle it to her, but she just stuck her arm out and reached for it. "Thank you Jack," she said and pushed the door close. He went to the night table, pulled the automatic out of the drawer and dropped it inside his brief bag.

His stomach gave an ominous grumble, trying to remind him that it had been fed nothing but whiskey in more than twelve hours. He put his ear against the bathroom door, and could hear the shower going on along with some humming. Apparently she sang while showering. He stepped out into the hall and went to the far end. He had noticed an instant coffee machine in the little room at the end, among the soft drinks and ice machine. It was probably stale and bitter, but it should be hot. When he returned to the room, she was still in the shower. He opened the heavy curtains, and sat on one of the uncomfortable chairs, sipping the black concoction and smoking a cigarette. Then his cellular phone chirped. He flipped it open and looked at the display that showed the number that was making the call. It was Dave's.

"Hello Dave," he said.

"I've been watching the news on TV and reading the papers. I even read the obituaries, but I can't find your name. Where the fuck have you been hiding Jack?" the voice said.

"Lots of shit going on, Dave," he said. "I really don't want to go over the whole deal over the phone right now."

"Don't you think it's time you quit the cowboy wars and we sit together and look at this situation in a sensible way?"

"You're probably right Dave, I just need a few more hours, and then I'm sure I'm going to need your advice," he said.

"C'mon Jack, don't be a fool."

"I promise I'll call you either tonight or tomorrow. I'll give you something where you can really sink your teeth into."

"You haven't shot anybody yet Jack?" The tone of voice had a hint of sarcasm in it.

"As a matter of fact Dave, I tried," he said, "but I missed."

"You're kidding me. C'mon Jack, tell me about it."

"Talk to you latter Dave," he said and punched the end button. The phone started ringing again immediately, but he ignored it.

"Who was that," she asked. She had come out of the bathroom and he hadn't noticed. "Friend of mine," he said. She was wearing blue jeans and a flower print blouse, the tails of which she had tied in a knot around her waist. She was barefooted.

"I was going to tell you to dress into something comfortable, because we . . ." She raised her hand interrupting him, and walked to where he was sitting, until she was close enough to look down at him.

"I swear Jack. You keep on telling me to get into something comfortable, and one of these days I'm going to slip into something really comfortable, just to see what the hell you're going to do about it," she said looking straight down into his eyes.

He didn't know how to respond, so he just showed a sheepish grin. "I got you some coffee," he said nodding toward the other cup of instant coffee. She smiled back, and took a sip of the coffee. "Shoot," she said setting the cardboard cup back on the dresser, "we need a good breakfast Jack." She grabbed her bag and sat on the edge of her bed. She pulled out a pair of canvas sneakers, stepped into them, and zipped the bag close. "I'm ready to go any time you are," she said.

He nosed the front end of the Taurus to the edge of the parking lot exit ramp as far as he dared, and a Metro-Dade bus zipped by, barely missing his front bumper. He had to go south, but that was out of the question. Just trying to make a right turn was going to be risky enough. The ornamental trees and shrubbery planted in front of the hotel canopied entrance made it almost impossible to see the traffic coming up, and at this time in the morning traffic was all but hectic. He turned the wheel and rode on top of the sidewalk, so he could look out his side window. Half a block down a traffic light turned to red, he waited until the three cars that ran it passed, and then stepped on the gas.

"There's a Burger King half a block down," he said, "we could have walked there."

"Forget about Burger King," she said, "I'm going to take you to a Cuban cafeteria, so you can have a good breakfast. Just keep on going on Le Jeune until you get to Southwest eight street, and then make a right. I'll show you."

He followed her instructions and pulled into a parking lot that was full. He rode around a couple of times, but nobody was pulling out. In some places cars were doubled parked. "Right in there, Jack," she said pointing, "hurry, before somebody grabs it." He looked at the spot she was pointing.

"In front of the fire hydrant, where it says no parking?" he asked.

"Sure, everybody parks in there, don't worry. This parking lot belongs to the cafeteria."

"No matter who it belongs to, it's still a not parking area," he said.

She shook her head, raised her eyebrows and let out a deep sigh. "Just park in there, please, before somebody else takes our place." He swung the car into the no parking yellow zone, just in time to cut off another car that was aiming for the same spot. He got off the car, opened the rear door and pulled his brief bag out.

"You don't need that," she said from the other side of the car.

"I don't want to leave it inside in case they tow the car away," he said.

"Don't worry Jack," she said walking to the door of the restaurant, "it won't be towed away. Orlando won't let it happen."

"And who's Orlando?" he asked catching up with her.

"The owner of the place, Jack." She said as a matter of fact. Like explaining something to a little child. He held the door open for her, and walked into the place. The sudden smell of coffee, fresh bread, cooking eggs, fried bacon and some other smells he couldn't identify, suddenly engulfed him. His stomach churned and groaned, and his mouth filled with water. He couldn't remember a time when he had been so hungry. They had to stand behind three people that were also waiting for a table. He salivated and swallowed a couple of times. Right by his elbow there was a counter, behind which a couple of young women were dispensing orders to go, through a small window that faced the street. One of them placed a demitasse of Cuban coffee in front of him. "Courtesy of the house while you wait," she said with a smile. He drank the strong brew in one gulp. Toni looked at him and smiled, but didn't say a word.

The three men in front of them were led away by a waitress, and five minutes later another waitress showed them to a table way back, in the innards of the vast place.

He figured that the distance from the cafeteria to Marathon Key was just a bit over one hundred miles, but the trek west on Eight Street, the hub of Cuban small businesses in Miami, was taking forever. It was late morning, but the traffic jam resembled the five o'clock rush hour. He should have gone either north or south on Le Jeune Road, to avoid the mess, but it was too late now. There was no easy way out of the mess, until he could get to the North-South bound Palmetto expressway, which was probably a parking lot at this time anyhow.

He had never before really been exposed to too much of the Cuban presence in the City. He read the papers and watched TV, but until today he hadn't been to a place where he hadn't heard one word in English and eaten such an immense breakfast.

"What it's that you call those sausages, Toni?" He asked while waiting for the old woman in front of him, that had both lanes blocked trying to make a left turn on the middle of the street, either got run over or finally made it. Horns blared and people shouted, but she ignored everybody while pushing the front end of the old Mercedes in front of the oncoming traffic. She finally made into the parking lot, and traffic crawled again.

Toni was looking at the whole situation and grinning to herself, the brown leather portfolio, where she had been making notes, open on her lap. "Some of our old people will never adapt," she said almost to herself and shaking her head. "Those sausages are called *chorizoz*, Jack. Real Spanish sausages," she said looking at him.

"I loved them, they're delicious."

"Yes they are, but you don't want to make it a habit. Your cholesterol level might make the eleven o'clock news, if you do," she turned back to the notes she had been making on the yellow pad of the agenda.

"Do you always breakfast like that?" he asked her.

She stopped making notes, and looked back at him. "Are you crazy?" she said, "I never do. I just had a Cuban toast and a cup of *café con leche*, in case you didn't notice."

"Why did you push all that food into me then?"

"I didn't pushed it, I suggested it, and you wolfed it down," she said smiling. "You were hungry, and I just wanted to show off what Cuban cuisine can do for a hungry man."

He shook his head, and they fell silent, she engrossed in whatever she was writing, and he wishing he had a helicopter and could fly over the mass of cars still in front of him.

NINETEEN

THE PALMETTO EXPRESSWAY was busy, but not as clogged as he thought it would be. After twenty-five minutes, he swung south and entered Florida's Turnpike. The four southbound lanes, with almost no traffic to account for, looked like paradise after the hour of stop and go misery. He floored the Taurus, and the car shoot forward. He lighted a cigarette, cracked the window down a bit, and relaxed back against the seat.

He took side-glances at her now and then. Sometimes she was writing on her pad, and some other times she was resting her head against the seat, eyes closed, the pen held in her fingers, like if she was asleep. He slowed down to take the sharp turn exiting the Turnpike and going into Florida City, and stopped at the traffic light.

"What are you writing? An article for the 'Herald'?" he asked.

She stretched her arms fingers entwined, palms out, and cracked her knuckles. It came out as a little series of small snapping sounds.

"No, not really. It's just that when I'm thinking something out I find it easier if I write down notes. Like a question and answer quiz, you know. What would be the reaction to this action, that kind of thing, you know. Some people talk to themselves aloud. I prefer to write it down." She lighted a cigarette, and slid her window down. "Of course, it could be used as reference if a story develops. But that you never know."

"I see," he said. The light changed to green, and he stepped on it. "You want anything to drink, or take a leak or something before we hit the Overseas Highway? It's a long way to Key Largo."

She thought about it for a moment.

"Well, maybe a beer."

"A beer?"

"Why not? Look around you. It's a beautiful day, not a cloud in the sky. We're going to the Keys. I feel like I'm on vacation or going on a fishing trip."

"A beer it is then. But remember that this is no fishing trip."

He swung off the main highway into the parking lot of a place called 'Jack's'. It advertised cold beer, bait, tackle, and anything else you might need on a trip to the Keys.

"I'll check the girls room while we're here," she said. He went to the beer cooler, and pulled two Budweiser long necks out.

"We have beautiful live shrimps and fresh minnows," the grizzly of a man behind the counter said.

"No. Not today, I'm afraid," Jack said, "I'll take a pack of Marlboroughs though."

He stepped out on the false wooden sidewalk, and uncapped one of the bottles. It was a splendid day indeed. Not a cloud on a light blue sky, a slight breeze and the humidity wasn't even perceptible. He took a long swallow from the bottle, and remembered that his daughter Jackie was arriving that same day, sometime in the evening.

"Ready," she said. She was standing by his elbow. He handed her the other bottle, and they walked to the car. He wondered what he should tell Jackie, or if he should tell her anything at all.

"You're not supposed to drink while you're driving," she said, opening her door.

"I know," he said, "we're not supposed to do a lot of things we're planning to do either, are we?"

She shrugged her shoulders, and got into the car.

He got back on US-1 and headed south. They kept silent for the best part of twenty minutes. She went back to scribbling on her note pad, and he concentrated on driving. Traffic was heavy on account of being a Friday. The regular caravan of weekend fishermen, with their boats in tow, clogged the road. Passing cars was out of the question on the two-lane highway, at least not until you got to the especial passing areas.

The vast green expanse that was the Everglades saw-grass beds fell behind, giving way to the other green expanse that was the shallow waters of the Card Sound on his left, and Black Sound on his right. 'PATIENCE, PAYS, JUST THREE MILES, TO NEXT, PASSING AREA'. The evenly spaced signs read. He finally got to the passing area. Slower traffic swung to the right, and he stepped on the accelerator, overtaking about eight or ten cars, before falling behind another slow crawling line of cars towing boats.

He swung his hand back over the back of the front seat, and dropped the empty beer bottle. He carefully nosed the car around the end of the big sailboat in front of him, into the oncoming lane to take a peek, and saw an expanse of empty highway. He floored the Ford and started overtaking the traffic, on the wrong side of the road. The line of cars was longer than he had figured. Toni came out of her slouch, and sat bolt upright on the seat.

"Shit Jack, if something comes out of that curve we don't have any place to go!" she screamed.

He glanced at his left. Nothing but rocks, a heavy wall of mangroves, and the shallow waters of the Sound beyond them. He had grossly miscalculated the distance to overtake all the traffic. He pushed his foot against the floorboard, but the engine just didn't have any more juice on it. To hit the brakes now was suicide. He hunched over the steering wheel, trying to push the car forward with pure mental power. The tractor-trailer showed its snout around the bend and bored down on him. It's headlights switched from low to high beam frantically, and he could hear the air horn blaring. He pushed harder on the gas pedal, which was all the way against the floor. In a frantic swirl of screeching brakes, air horn blasts, bright red paint and chrome coming towards his windshield, he managed to barely squeeze his car between the left fender of the big truck, and the front end of a Chevy van. He was going way too fast.

He hit the hump of the Jewfish Creek drawbridge, at over one hundred miles per hour. The Taurus went airborne for a moment, and then landed again on the road, its rear end screaming loudly, its bottom scratching sparks off the pavement. He coasted down the road along Lake Surprise, foot off the gas pedal, and both hands gripping the steering wheel hard, so Toni wouldn't notice them shaking.

She wouldn't have anyway, because she was curled on the seat, both hands over her head, the beer bottle forgotten, rolling around and spilling beer on the floor of the car.

"We're in Key Largo," he said after a few seconds, as a matter of fact, like if nothing had happened, driving along at a relaxed forty-five miles an hour. She sat back straight on the seat. "I have to use a bathroom," she said noncommittally.

"Sure," he said turning into a gas station. "They have clean rest rooms in here," he added, parking on the side of the building in front of two doors, one with a man sign and the other with a woman sign.

"How the fuck would you know that?" she asked angrily.

He shrugged his shoulders. "I'm just guessing. It looks pretty neat from outside," he said.

She got out of the car, and slammed the door so hard that he thought it would fall off its hinges. Apparently the woman was angry and pissed. He lowered his window and lighted a cigarette. Maybe she had a right to be. It had been a close call, to say the least, and she probably was scared. What the hell, *he* was still scared.

He wondered what had come over him. He had always been a meticulous individual. He was not prone to take unnecessary risks, like the one he had just taken on the highway. He was not just a car driver, he was also a pilot. Pilots didn't take anything for granted, and planned everything ahead of time. Anyway, besides the pilot and engineering training, it had been a matter of personality. He had never been a risk taker before. The 'devil-may-care-I-don't give a shit what happens' attitude had never been his. And now he was carrying a gun, drinking while driving, taking stupid risks on the road, running with a woman he didn't know anything about, toward a confrontation he was not prepared for. Something indeed had come over him, and it had all started with that stupid bet to impersonate a doctor, something that wouldn't have even crossed his mind a year ago. The whole mess has developed into murder, beatings, shoot-outs, and a situation that he didn't know how it would explode. Because explode was the word. This was not a bad dream that would disappear in the morning. This was real and here to stay, until it exploded one way or the other.

Toni came out of the manager office carrying a key at the end of a long piece of wood. She ignored him as she walked past the car. He watched her struggle with the key, trying to open the men's room door. He smiled, as the thought of a smart remark crossed his mind, but he refrained from saying it. He didn't want to piss her off more than she already was. "Maybe if you try the other door you'll have better luck," he said instead. Apparently that was smart enough for her, because she tried to vaporize him with her eyes.

Maybe his sense of humor was also changing, he thought. To the darker kind, that is. He backed the car, swung around and parked in front of the main door of the station, to wait for her. He thought about how he would get in touch with Jackie, he didn't have Allison's home phone number. He would have to wait until she got in touch with him.

Toni got into the car and slammed the door again with more than the necessary force. "Ready now?" he asked trying to sound completely neutral.

"Goddammit!" she screamed when she stepped into the spilled beer on the floor. "You couldn't clean this up?"

"Sorry. I forgot about it. Wait a minute."

"Forget it," she said stepping out of the car again.

She pulled a bunch of paper towels from the courtesy bin, swept the floor and dropped them and the empty bottle into the trashcan. She slammed the door still one more time. He pulled out of the service station.

"I don't know why you're so mad all of a sudden," he said after a few minutes.

"Goddamn car stinks," she said.

"It will go away, let's keep the windows open for a while."

He zigzagged trying to avoid the slower traffic. The two lanes helped a lot, but at the end of Key Largo he would hit the one lane road again until they reached Isla Morada.

"Maybe you have a death wish, but I don't. If you're going to drive like a maniac let me know, and I will get the fuck out right here," she said in a low voice.

For a woman, and a journalist at that, she sure had a colorful choice of words, he thought.

"I'll admit that it was kind of close," he said, trying to play it down, "but I'll bet that you have had close calls driving before. Especially if you drive a lot on Southwest Eight Street," he said smiling.

She ignored the intended pun at how Cubans drove.

"Not that close, Jack. Not that fucking close." She shook her head. "I swear, I thought . . ." She didn't finish, just kept looking straight ahead. He thought it was better to leave the issue along, and fiddled with the radio, trying to get a Keys station to tune to.

She went back to her notes and he concentrated on driving once more. Traffic was lighter and moving at a faster clip. For some reason that he had never been able to put his finger on, traffic was always heavier between Florida City and Key Largo. After Key Largo it always got better, even if the road between the keys was the same two-lane road. After leaving Isla Morada the keys were more spaced out, and the long spans of bridge offered an unlimited view of the ocean on one side, and Florida Bay on the other.

The sharp smell of open-ocean salt water, mixed with the sweet and sour one of coastal vegetation and rotting wood, engulfed the car through the open windows, wiping out the sour one of spilled beer. He turned to her to make a commentary, but her head was lying back on the seat, eyes closed. She had fallen asleep, he guessed, or she was faking it so she wouldn't have to talk to him. He shrugged, and kept on driving, enjoying the smells and the sights.

Thirty-five minutes later, he slowed down and made a left turn into a broad causeway. Suddenly she was awake and looking around. "Where are we?" she asked him.

"On Key Colony," he answered, "this is the main road going in."

The road was a straight causeway. He slowed to forty-five miles an hour. There was a broad canal on his right, with big houses on the other side, their back to the canal. Most of them had expensive sport fishermen tied to individual docks. Toni grabbed the map lying on the seat between them. A narrower canal appeared on his left, almost a replica of the other side.

"Make a right on Ocean Drive," she said, "it's before the end of the road."

He slowed down to thirty-five, and made the turn. Across the street was a building with a sign that said City Hall. He followed the road, which made a sharp right turn, and drove to the end, where it curved on a one hundred and eighty degrees turn. It had a street sign that said 15 Circle. These were two-story townhouses, not single-family homes, and they were in clusters. Some of the clusters had two townhouses, some had three. The first townhouse of the second cluster had the number 1123 etched in tiles on the small wall that separated it from the next one. He stopped the car by the curb, and put it on park.

"Bingo," Toni said in a whisper, looking at him. "What do we do now?"

He killed the engine and looked at the number. The woman had been right so far with her assumptions. They had to corroborate the other part of her assumption though, and that part looked real tricky.

"I don't know," he said. "I guess we step to the door, ring the bell, and see what happens."

They got out of the car, went to the front door, and rang the bell several times. They could hear the chime going off inside, but nobody answered the door. "Let's go around to the back," Jack said. He looked around. There were no cars parked at the curb, or on the two car parking spaces in front of each townhouse, the only visible car was about a block away. Across the street was a wood pier running along a narrow channel, but there were no boats tied to it. It looked like a common pier for the owners of the townhouses. He imagined that the properties on 15 Circle, at the end of the island, were for the less than filthy wealthy.

There were no fences to speak of, just thirty feet of grass separated on cluster from the other. They walked to the back of the building. There was a small concrete terrace, on which two sliding doors opened. A slanting block wall, about seven feet high, separated one unit from its neighbor, to give it a little privacy. Against the wall was a gas BBQ.

Three-inch wide vertical blinds covered the sliding windows from the inside. The first one was not completely closed and he could tell it was a living area. The second one he assumed led to a bedroom, but it was closed so tight that it was impossible to see inside. He knocked several times on the first sliding glass door with his wedding band, the one he should have taken off six months ago.

He tried to spot some kind of security system contact on the inside of the door, like the ones he had installed on his house, but it was impossible from the outside.

"What do you think?" Toni asked him.

He looked across the expanse of grass at the rear of the other row of townhouses, the ones facing the other side of the circle. They all looked deserted like this one.

"I don't know," he said pulling a bit on one frame of the sliding door. "Definitely there's nobody here, but the electricity it's on. I can probably pry one of these doors open, but if there is some kind of alarm we're in trouble. Usually there's a sign you know, like protected by such and such. But that doesn't mean shit. Some people don't like to advertise they have an alarm system."

He looked around again. No nosy neighbor had stepped out in the backyard to see what was going on at 1123. That in itself was a good sign.

"Are we going to break in now?" She asked.

He looked at his watch. "No, no, of course not, not yet. Like they say in the military, we should retreat and regroup."

"Were you in the military, Jack?" She asked.

"No, I wasn't, but I have watched a lot of movies." He grabbed her hand. "Let's go."

He pulled her along. When he turned around the corner of the building he froze on his tracks. Parked front end to front end with his car was a police cruiser. The officer sitting at the wheel was looking at them from behind dark, wrap around glasses.

TWENTY

"HI THERE FOLKS. Can I be of any help?" the voice was friendly, and Jack relaxed a bit. He started walking again, pulling Toni along, which seemed stuck to the ground. The biceps and forearm resting on the open window of the cruiser reminded him of those Virginia hams they hang from the ceiling in some stores.

"Maybe you can officer," he said stopping a couple of feet from the open window. "Some friends in Miami told us that this property was for sale, but I rang the bell and apparently there's nobody in. We were just walking around, looking it up. Do you know the owner by any chance?"

"No, I really don't. Most of these places are owned by people from up North. They just come down when they get snowed out, if you know what I mean."

"I sure do officer," Jack said smiling and trying to look real friendly. "Snow birds that come down here for just a couple of months to make our lives difficult," he said in a just-between-you-and-me tone.

"You got it," the officer said smiling, and immediately turned dead serious, like if he had caught himself making unnecessary remarks, "but we're real courteous to every tenant. It's a City policy."

"I don't doubt it officer, I don't doubt it," Jack said. He patted his pants pockets. "Darling, do you have any cigarettes on you?" he said addressing Toni.

"They're on the car dear, I'll get them for you," she said running to their car.

"I'll tell you what your best bet is," the police officer said. "You noticed a building that says City Hall at the end of the causeway?"

Jack nodded.

"There's an office there that handles all the sales and rentals. They can tell you if this property is for sale."

Toni ran up with the pack of cigarettes and a lighter. Jack offered one to the officer. "Nah," he said raising a hand that looked like a catchers mitt, "that stuff will kill you man."

He and Toni lighted up, making sure they didn't blow any smoke on the young man's face. They looked like two chimneys, turning their faces up to blow out smoke.

"I assume that security is very tight in here," Jack said. "I can see by the sign on your cruiser that what you have here it's actually a Police force, not some Mickey Mouse security company."

Apparently he had hit the right button, because the young man inflated some more on his seat. He was on his early twenties, but could hardly fit inside the car. Jack guessed he was several inches over six feet and around two hundred and fifty pounds, and no blubber either.

"Oh yeah," he said, "we're small, but a real Police force. Just the Captain and seven of us officers, but there's always a deputy on duty. Twenty-four hours a day."

"That's very reassuring," Toni said.

"Oh yes ma'am, it really is." He raised his left wrist and signaled at a big, black, rubber watch full of buttons. "Like today?" he said signaling to his watch with a sausage size finger from his right hand, "I'm turning in at seven. As soon as I go in, another deputy is going out. Like clock work. Twenty four hours a day."

"That's great officer, that's really great," Toni said looking at the young man, all smiles. "Such security is great. The peace of mind that your property is really well protected is priceless. That's one of the first things my husband and I check when we're looking for properties to invest." Jack thought that she was kind of overdoing it, but he would be damn if the guy didn't kind of blush. He put the car on reverse, and backed into the empty driveway. He put out his massive arm and saluted. "Like we say over here folks, if you need any help, just holler."

They raised their arms and waved. He disappeared down the road. "He was very nice," Toni said, "scared the shit out of me when I first saw him though."

"You really gave him a speech about security. I hope that the next deputy is not as dedicated as him. It really could make it difficult for us to get in there."

They walked back to the Taurus and sat inside for a few minutes, Jack just looking straight ahead, lost in some thoughts. "What do we do now?" she asked.

He looked at her for several seconds, like if it was the first time he had seen her, and then nodded to himself.

"Like I said before, we regroup and we plan," he looked at his watch. "We have time. Let me take you to that place I told you about, off mile marker 62."

She shrugged her shoulders, and lighted another cigarette. He started the car and drove slowly toward the main Causeway. On US-1 he made a left turn. She looked at him, but didn't say anything. He slowed down a little when he came abreast Marathon airport. He started looking toward the hangars and parking spaces. She followed his gaze, but she couldn't tell what was going through his mind. There were just rows and rows of parked airplanes of different shapes and sizes.

"What's the problem now?" she asked.

"No problem at all," he said, switching his eyes from the airport to the highway in front him.

"I have a friend that keeps a very nice airplane here," he said, "I'm just trying to see if I can spot it."

He looked back toward the airport.

"There, there it is," he said pointing with his finger, "the white one with the wild colors."

She looked to where he was pointing. It looked to her like a white fly squatting on the ground, with some orange and red strips on its wings. "Not very impressive," she murmured.

He stepped on the gas again. About four miles down the road, he drove into a shopping center and parked in front of a hardware store. "Just wait here," he said, "I'll be back in a minute."

Fifteen minutes later he came out of the store, holding a paper bag in his right hand, which he dropped on the back seat. He pulled out of the shopping center, and headed south on US-1 again.

"What did you buy?" Toni asked.

"Oh, just some tools of the trade."

"And what trade it's that Mr. Timberlake?"

"The one you have pushed me into, Ms. Suarez."

TWENTY-ONE

WHEN THEY REACHED Little Conch Key, he made a right turn into a side street, one that was so narrow and so covered by trees on both sides that it looked more like a tunnel. Anybody that didn't know that the street was there would just drive by and never be the wisest. Toni noticed the sign that said Mango Street, half buried by the overflowing dense foliage.

They drove on the narrow asphalt road for about two hundred yards, which then turned into a gravel path scarcely wide enough for two cars. The high vegetation on both sides that met overhead, made it look like a real tunnel. After another hundred yards or so, the encroaching vegetation gave way and a clearing, maybe five hundred yards wide, materialized. There was no real parking lot, just an open area of crushed coral and sandstone that had been cleared from the surrounding wall of mangroves. Instead of bumpers, there were thick logs lying on the sandy shore, to keep cars from parking too far out and getting swamped by the high tide.

On the middle of the clearing was a low wooden structure like nothing she had seen before. Jutting halfway over the water of the bay, the structure looked like it had haphazardly been put together. It was sitting on wooden pilings that kept it a few feet above the water level. Sticking out from the top was a smaller second floor, surrounded almost completely by windows. A veranda surrounded the whole first floor, which was joined to the mainland by a rickety four feet wide plank bridge, with a thick rope for a handrail. The whole structure was painted a dull marine gray.

They stepped out of the car and she was overwhelmed by a combination of smells. On one hand was the particular smell of the shallow salt-water cove, a mixture of rotting vegetation and decaying marine life. On the other hand was the delicious smell of fresh fried seafood, coming from the strange looking building.

Toni stood by the side of the car, mesmerized by the surroundings. To their back the thick, impenetrable wall of wild vegetation excluded out the real world. The racket of traffic on US-1, just a few hundred yards away, could hardly be heard. Just the small hole on the lush vegetation that covered the gravel road was a reminder that you were not on some isolated island. Toward the west the sun was about to start its dive into the waters of the bay, and its slanted rays made the scattered little mangrove islands shine in a brighter green hue than the green of the bay.

"If you like a cold beer and some real seafood, this is the place Toni," he said. She remained speechless.

"C'mon, I'll show you in," he said putting out his hand. She grabbed it like if it was the most common thing on the world, and he led her over the rickety wood bridge.

"How the hell did you ever find this place, Jack?"

"It's a secret," he said, "just don't spread the word."

He opened the door for her and they stepped inside. To the left was a bar about fifteen feet long, with an array of mismatching stools. Four men, with the unmistakable look of the Keys captains or guides, were talking animatedly to the one behind the bar. There were several tables scattered on the saloon with no particular order. There were two middle aged couples sitting on one of them, the rest of the place was empty. In one corner was a jukebox that by any standards should be on a museum. Every body stopped chatting when they walked in. Jack raised his hand and steered Toni to the back of the room.

"Let's seat out on the terrace," he said walking toward the end of the saloon. A double door was open into a small terrace that hung over the water with no apparent means of support. There were just two tables with four chairs each. The jukebox came to life all of a sudden and Frankie Valley's 'Sea of Love' came out of speakers hung from the ceiling on the terrace. She looked at him and raised an eyebrow.

"That's an oldie," she said.

"I know, but I like it anyway."

"Does the music starts as soon as you walk in?" she asked smiling.

He didn't answer and pulled a chair for her.

They had hardly sat at the table, when a bear of a man appeared carrying two Budweiser long neck beers in one hand. He sat the bottles on the table and smiled at Jack. Toni figured he was about six feet four or five, and weighed close to three hundred pounds. He had a full black beard that reached down to the second button of his western style shirt, and wore his hair on a thick braid that was a foot and a half long.

"What ya'say Jack. Been a while pardner," he said raising his right eyebrow to an incredible position.

"Have gone trough some problems Tiny. I'll tell you about it some other time," Jack said. "Tiny, I want you to meet my friend Toni. Toni this is Tiny."

They nodded to each other.

"I have some Yellow Tails you'll want to eat the bones Jack," the man said.

"Yellow Tails will be fine Tiny," Jack said.

The man turned around and went back inside the building.

"Tiny!" Toni exclaimed in a very low voice, leaning over the table. "My God. I don't know how the whole building doesn't collapses under his weight." She sat back, sipped the beer and looked at him. "Jack, you're full of surprises. Sophisticated people like you don't drink this horse piss."

He laughed aloud. "Maybe I'm not as sophisticated as you think, Toni. I hate the taste of real strong beers," he raised his bottle, "this Bud's for me."

She shook her head and took another sip of her beer. "How did you find this marvelous place, Jack?"

He took a long gulp from his beer, and looked out toward the darkening bay. The sun had started its rapid descent. From their vantage point they could actually watch the orange ball sink into the dark waters a piece at a time.

He turned back to her. "It's a long story Toni, I might tell you about it some time." He turned around on his chair and pointed at the horizon. "Look at this Toni," he said, "something you won't be able to watch from the city."

She turned and looked. The fiery orange of the sun was just a slice over the horizon. The waters of the bay had a coopery hue on some areas. "From now on you can time the sunset in seconds," he said, "here we go."

As clockwork in a matter of three seconds, what was left of the orange ball disappeared under the horizon and the bay became a black void.

"Amazing," Toni said.

Tiny appeared balancing a metal tray on one hand and two bottles of beer held by their neck, between the huge fingers of his other hand. They each grabbed a bottle and Tiny sat two clay plates on the table. On each one was a whole Yellow Tail snapper, head and all, and some brown pieces.

"I threw in some conch fritters Jack," he said smiling, "I know the missus will like'em." He turned around, and disappeared back into the building.

Both of them attacked the fish. The skin was fried enough, but the tender meat underneath was moist and cooked to the right point.

"This fish is delicious Jack," she said taking a gulp of beer. "What are you planning to do after this?"

He squeezed some lemon juice on the meat he had pried away from the bones, took a mouthful, and looked at his watch.

"It's just a few minutes after seven," he said, "so our friend just finished his shift. We don't want to run into him again. There will be a new deputy making rounds out there that has never seen us before." He plucked both eyes of the fish with his fork, squeezed some lemon juice on them, and put them in his mouth. "I'm going to park the car on the driveway of the other townhouse. A car on a driveway doesn't draw too much attention. They don't know when an owner might show up anyway. Then we'll go to the back, and try to open the sliding door. If there is some kind of hidden alarm, we split. If it's one of the silent ones, we'll be in a lot of trouble." He wiped his lips with the napkin and finished his beer. "There are a lot of ifs, Toni. Like they say on the news, this is breaking and entering. Are you sure you want to go ahead with this?"

She pushed her chair back and looked out toward the bay for a little while.

"If we found a safe and the numbers are the right combination, it will mean that my hunch was right, doesn't it?", she said almost to herself.

"Yeah."

"If there is some real important stuff inside that safe we might have a very hot potato in our hands, don't you think?"

"Definitely."

"It's very challenging to me as a reporter Jack, but what about you? You have everything to loose and nothing to gain."

"Oh, I don't know about that."

"How so?"

"Maybe I just want to get to the bottom of this."

"We can turn the information we have to some kind of authority, the DEA, Miami Police, or whoever, and let them handle it from here on."

"Right now I'm not sure which authority I should trust."

"You're getting paranoid again."

"Maybe I am. Are you sure we haven't been followed, or are not being watched right now?"

"I . . . I never thought about that. Out here on the Keys?"

"Why not? What's the difference between your house and the Keys? All it takes is a car, and there're hundreds of them around. Those guys could be tailing us, and we'll never find out until the last minute."

"How was that fish Jack," Tiny said.

For such a big man he had a knack for materializing at your side without you noticing him coming.

"It was great Tiny," Jack said.

"It was delicious Mr. Tiny," Toni said, "really delicious."

"Glad you folks enjoyed it. Can I get you anything else Jack?"

"No Tiny. We really have to go," Jack said getting up.

The three of them walked to the front door. Toni started walking down the little bridge. Tiny grabbed Jack's arm with his huge hand. "You look troubled my friend," he said, "if you need anything, you have my number."

"I know. I'll be seeing you," he said and walked down after Toni.

"Where the hell are they going?" Jarrol said as he watched the car they have been following make a u-turn and head south again.

"Don't know, but they're not going back to Miami, that's for sure," Scott said, "make sure you don't loose them."

They were about six cars behind and Scott wanted to keep his pace and don't become too conspicuous. Jarrol was already keeping track of them trough the spotting scope.

"They changed lanes," he said, "you better hurry so we don't loose them."

"Stay cool Jarrol," Scott said, "we'll get there."

Scott made a u-turn in the same intersection. "They're way ahead, you see them?" Jarrol asked.

"I got them," Scott said, passing three cars before swinging into the right lane and slowing down. Just three cars separated them now, Scott eased down on the gas so he wouldn't get too close. Jarrol fidgeted on the right side of the seat. His right hand kept patting his left breast.

"Leave that alone Jarrol," Scott said, "you're not going to be using that piece any time soon."

The Taurus suddenly made a right turn and disappeared from view into some dense vegetation. Scott couldn't pinpoint where. Like so many streets on the Keys, the signs couldn't be spotted, and the vegetation was so dense that sometimes you wondered if there was actually a street in there.

Scott was caught a little by surprise with the sudden movement. He instinctively hit the brakes; then realized he couldn't follow them. He got off the main highway and drove along the wide gravel path paralleling the main road. He took a good look at where the Taurus had disappeared and drove slowly by. There was actually an asphalt street there, although it looked more like a tunnel than a street, the vegetation was so thick.

"Ain't you going to follow them?" Jarrol asked.

"You crazy? We'll be spotted right away, a lonely road like that."

"What we're going to do?"

Scott drove into an open area in front of a big boat dealership. It was not a regular parking lot, but a big space of crunched gravel and coral outside the fence of the dealership. He made a half turn and parked facing U.S.1.

"We seat here and wait Jarrol. We just seat and wait. You are just going to have to learn to be patient."

"They might be going away through another street."

"That's a dead end street Jarrol. Just the Bay at the very end."

"What if they have a boat waiting for them?"

"Then we're fucked Jarrol. It happens sometimes. On the other hand, if they come out and head south they'll drive by in front of us. If they decide to go back to Miami, they have to come to this intersection to make a u-turn, so relax, we have the time."

He lowered the window halfway and lighted a cigarette.

TWENTY-TWO

J ACK PARKED IN the driveway of number 1123, and killed the engine and the lights. The road was lighted by high-pressure sodium fixtures on twenty-five feet high concrete poles, spaced about one hundred feet apart.

The wooden pier across the street had its own vapor fixture on a ten feet high wood pole in front of the fish-cleaning table. The end of the pier was in darkness. The lighting was appropriate, but not extremely bright.

From the back seat he pulled his brief-bag and the paper bag with the stuff he had bought at the hardware store. He dropped his cellular phone inside the bag, and pulled out the Desert Eagle. He worked the slide back a bit to make sure there was a round on the chamber, and stuck the automatic on the front of his waistband.

"You have those combination numbers?"

"I have them here," she said patting her pocket.

From the paper bag he pulled a small flashlight, a heavy screwdriver, and a short shank pry-bar. He handed Toni the flashlight. He looked toward the main causeway, over a mile away. Nothing was moving.

"Ready?" he asked.

She nodded. She didn't look so self assured or cocky as before.

They got out of the car, and walked to the rear of the building. There were a couple of lights on the back of the townhouses on the other side of the street, but he figured they were on timers or photocells, because the units didn't show any inside lights.

He kneeled down and started prying at the bottom of the sliding door with the screwdriver, trying to raise it a little bit. If there was an alarm system it should have got off by now. He raised enough of the bottom frame of the sliding door to insert the pry bar.

"Hold on to this Toni," he said in a whisper, "keep pushing it up."

She put both hands on the bar, and he pushed the screwdriver under the lock, working it back and forth. The door slid back on its tracks after a couple of pushes. They walked inside through the vertical blinds and he slid the door back, without letting it click shut.

In front of them was a dinning table with seats for six people, and they walked around it. The rest of the space, all the way to the front door was a living area. There was a big L shaped sofa, a couple of leather easy chairs, and a big entertainment center against the left wall. A huge TV set was surrounded by all kind of electronic equipment. To the right of the front door, a stair led to the second floor. An opening between the living area and the dinning room, led into the kitchen. On the other side of the kitchen opening, and under the thick wooden steps of the stair leading to the second floor, was a closed door.

Jack grabbed Toni by the wrist and pulled her toward the closed door. He turned the knob, and it opened into a bedroom that had been made into some kind of office. To the rear was the other sliding door facing the small outside terrace. There was a desk facing away from the sliding glass door with a leather swivel chair behind it. A computer sat on a separate table to the left of the desk. There was a seven feet high wood bookcase against one wall, and a couple of gray, metal shelves against the other. They were randomly filled with books and folders, and the cardboard boxes used to store office records. On the far wall was your regular bedroom closet, with its louvered by-fold door.

"Cross your fingers girl," Jack said, "if there is a hidden safe, this should be the place."

He pushed both doors of the closet open. There were some clothes hanging from hangers, and boxes and shoes on the bottom. He pulled everything on the floor out, and started banging on the carpet with his fist. The left side didn't feel as solid as the rest.

"Hand me that pry bar," he said.

She gave it to him, and he pulled the baseboard loose. It broke in two, and he pushed it to the side. He then loosened the carpet from its retaining nails, and pulled it back with both his hands.

Flush with the concrete slab, was a two by two feet square of plywood. He inserted the screwdriver on one edge, and pulled the wood out.

"Let me have some light here," he asked.

Toni switched on the flashlight. Sure enough, there was a safe imbedded in concrete down there. It had a round cover, with a knob full of numbers on its middle, and a little twist handle to one side.

He sat down on the floor, and rested his back against the closet door. "It's your turn Toni," he said.

She held the flashlight with her left hand, and started working the black knob with her right. In a few seconds she turned the handle and pulled the cover open.

"We got it Jack," she whispered.

"What have we got?" he asked leaning on his elbow and looking inside.

She pulled a package, roughly the size of two masonry bricks held together, wrapped in some kind of heavy waxed paper and bundled with heavy rubber bands. It was moist to the touch. Then she pulled a nine by twelve, clasp envelope stuck inside a waterproof Zip Lock bag. It was also moist to the touch.

"Thank God he waterproofed everything," she said in a whisper, "apparently there's a leak on the safe."

"It's not a leak, it's condensation," Jack told her. "He knew it was going to happen, that's why he did it." He stuffed the contents of the safe inside his bag, and zipped it close.

"Don't you want to see what's in there?" she asked.

"Not here." He closed the lid of the safe, put the piece of plywood over the hole, and pushed the carpet back.

"C'mon, let's get out of here." He grabbed her wrist and pulled her up. "Turn that light off."

He walked out of the room, with her following close behind. When he got to the corner of the wall separating the kitchen from the dinning room he stopped cold and recoiled. Toni bumped into him. He pressed his back against the partition, and peered around the corner.

"What's the matter," she whispered.

"I saw a shadow. There's a man out there. He was either peeking in, or was about to let himself in," he answered in his lowest possible voice.

He closed his eyes for a moment. Everything had gone too smooth to be true, he thought. There were only two guesses at who could be out there, he knew. It could be the local Deputy, his curiosity picked by an unknown car parked in front of an apparently empty unit. Even a half-witted security guard would want to do some investigating.

On the other hand, they could have been followed by their two persistent friends, which always found the means to be on the right place at the wrong time. Either way, he was faced with a very sticky situation, he realized. He wished he could climb to the second floor, find a bedroom, and lay down until the next day.

He tried to put everything into perspective. If he walked out carrying a gun in his hand, and the man out there was a Deputy, the guy could panic and start shooting.

If it was their friends out there and he walked out unarmed, *they* might start shooting, and he wouldn't stand a chance. He considered both options, and made up his mind.

"Let me tell you what we're going to do," he said pulling the shoulder strap of the bag over his head, so it would hang on his side. "We're going to walk out through the front door. If it's the Police Deputy out there, we just turn ourselves in and see what'll happen. If it's these other guys, I swear to God I don't know what will happen." He pulled the automatic out of his waistband, and clicked the safety off. "I'm sorry I got you into this spot, but I don't see any other way out."

She just nodded.

They walked to the front door and stood in front of it for several seconds. There were two dead bolt locks on it. He turned both of them, and put his hand on the doorknob. "Whatever happens, stick close to me, okay?"

She nodded again. He opened the door, and stepped out into the tiled path leading to the sidewalk. The seven feet high ornamental wall blocked his sight to the right, but to his front and left he couldn't spot a soul.

"Hey there!" a voice said when they reached the sidewalk. He jumped at the sound of the voice and turned. A man was standing on the far side of his own car, both hands clasped together in front of his chest, like if he was going to say a prayer. He got a glimpse of short cropped, almost white hair and realized that the hands were not held up in prayer, but holding a gun with a very long and thick barrel. That meant only one thing. A silencer. Not your regular Florida Keys law enforcement stock item.

He put his left hand on Toni's shoulder and yanked the Desert Eagle out of his waistband with his right. He aimed it in the general direction of the man and squeezed the trigger. The explosion was deafening and the savage recoil took him by surprise.

"Run!" he yelled, pushing Toni ahead of him toward the wood dock that ran alongside the channel. She took off like somebody in the hundred-meter dash and he followed, crouching a little, the muscles on his back cramping into a solid knot, his shoulder blades squeezing together waiting for the impact he was sure was about to come. He pointed his arm back and squeezed the trigger again, without bothering to look. Toni was at the head of the dock running like mad. His peripheral vision caught a shadow coming out from the side of the building. He pointed his gun again in the general direction without really aiming, and fired two shots in rapid succession. He was at the head of the dock now and saw splinters of wood flying off the pole holding the light fixture, and from the fish-cleaning table.

"Jump!" he cried. They both dove into the black waters of the channel at the same time. The momentum carried him all the way to the bottom, the channel was only about seven feet deep. He pushed himself off the bottom with the hand holding the automatic, and swam underwater in the direction he assumed was away from the dock. In the complete darkness he couldn't tell if Toni was anywhere near him. He surfaced when he couldn't hold his breath any more. Heavy mangrove vegetation was just about three feet off to the right side of his head. Small water geysers sprouted about ten feet to his left, but there was no loud noise, just the click-clack of the slide of the silenced automatics. He pulled his right hand holding the Desert Eagle out of the water, and pushed himself with his feet against the mangroves. He hoped the Israeli's boast that their gun would perform under the worst field conditions, was true.

If he were going to stand erect, the water would only reach to about the middle of his chest. He was about twenty-five or thirty feet from the dock, but not in a direct line of sight. The heavy mangrove growth zigzagged, and a dense clump hid him from anybody standing on the dock. He untangled his bag from around his neck, and pushed it into some high branches of the encroaching trees. He could hear voices coming from the dock, but couldn't make what they were saying. He wondered where Toni was. She couldn't have been hit by any stray shot, unless she had swam out into the open water away from the mangroves. He heard the wailing siren of a police car approaching.

"Just jump the fuck in, Jarrol." A voice said loud enough for him to hear. "They can't be more than twenty or thirty feet away. They're hiding in those mangroves, there's no place else they can go."

"Shit Scott, there might be all kind of animals in there."

"You're a big boy Jarrol. There's a police car coming this way and I'm going to have to do some fancy talking, so just get your ass in the water," the voice on the dock said.

Something stirred the water to Jack's right. The mention of some kind of animal and the sudden disturbance made him recoil in panic.

Toni's face appeared from below some low hanging branches. She was completely submerged, only her face above the water line. He smiled at her, and she smiled back.

There was a sudden splash, somewhere to their left.

The big barracuda had been sleeping under the dock's edge, two feet off the bottom it's huge tail moving slowly sideways to compensate for the current drift. The two bodies dropping unexpectedly almost on top of it had scared the animal senseless. The primal self-preservation instinct of the huge beast had instantly kicked on, and its formidable propulsion system had hurled it from a stationary position to twenty-five miles per hour in nanoseconds.

Now it turned around, twenty feet away, to investigate the cause of such unexpected invasion of its domain. Forty-two pounds of hard bone and pure muscle writhed about, its immense jaws lined with rows of dog-like pointed teeth opening and snapping shut angrily.

Another unwelcome guest dropped noisily right on top of its preferred resting place, hit bottom and then started kicking around with its long appendages. It was all the provocation the huge fish needed. It snapped its big tail from side to side, wriggled its body, and shot forward, mouth closed until the last minute to be more aerodynamic and offer less resistance to the water. It opened its jaws just one foot away from its prey, and hit the intruder right between the long appendages at twenty-five miles per hour. Razor sharp teeth tore through cloth and tissue, blood vessels and cartilage, in just one violent pass that exploded into a crimson underwater cloud.

The fish didn't stop its mad dash until it reached the inside end of the channel, where it dropped to the bottom to masticate on its morsel.

The scream was so loud and had such a pitch, that it was almost not human. For a moment it was higher than the wail of the siren of the police car, which had shut down all of a sudden. It was pain and terror mixed in one hair-raising howl.

"Ay, Dios mio, help me! Scott! Scott, please help me. They're eating me alive!"

"Freeze!" another voice said.

"Easy officer. Just take it easy. Look here. We're with the Miami Police Department. My partner had an accident. Give me a hand here."

The splashing on the water was frantic. "Give me your fucking hand Jarrol!"

"Aghhhh!"

"Shit. He's bleeding like a stuck pig."

"We have to take him to a hospital."

"He's going to mess up my cruiser."

"Okay. We'll put him in my car. Give me a hand. You'll lead, give me lights and the siren, he's in shock."

They heard car doors slamming, tires screeching and the loud wailing of the police cruiser siren again.

In a matter of seconds the only sound that could be heard was the water slapping quietly against the shore.

"I'm not swimming over to that dock," Toni said, pushing herself as far as she could back against the mangroves.

"Me neither," Jack said, "I don't want to meet whatever it's under that dock."

It was impossible to try to climb trough the mangroves to reach solid ground, the vegetation was too thick, it's finger like branches intertwined with it each other in such a way, that only a very small animal could walk through them. The whole south end of the island was like that. To reach the main causeway they would have to wade miles hugging the mangrove line, and he didn't know how deep the water could get in some places.

His car was just fifty feet away, but swimming to the dock, after what he had heard, didn't appeal to him at all. He had discovered that he could handle a situation he had never imagined he would ever be in. He had kept his head and reacted swiftly. Most of all, he hadn't chicken out.

Swimming into a dark channel where unknown animals capable of ripping a man apart lurked, was another proposition.

He handled the pistol to Toni, and pulled his bag off the branches where he had tucked it. "Let's see if these electronic marvels work after they had been dunked in salt water," he said unzipping it, and pulling out his cellular phone. To his amazement it was dry. He punched some numbers on it, and waited for several seconds.

"Tiny? Jack here. I don't have too much time to explain now. You know where Key Colony is, right?" He listened for a few seconds.

"Exactly. I'm on the . . . lets see . . . west end of the island, on the water, holding on to the mangroves, about thirty feet from the first channel when you come around the bend. Can you come and pick me up?"

He listened for a few seconds. "No, I'm not drunk. I can't explain right now, but that's where I am." He listened some more. "I hope not," he said, "but some insurance it's always welcome. Watch out for some people on the dock." Another pause. "Yes, my cellular."

He turned to look at Toni. She was shaking badly. "Tiny it's going to pick us up," he said. She nodded her head several times. Her hands were trembling so much, that he picked the automatic off them before she dropped it on the water.

Less than thirty minutes later a twenty-four foot open fisherman came around the bend, its twin outboard engines rumbling at low speed, all lights out. A powerful quartz spotlight came on, and started sweeping the shore. He closed his eyes so he wouldn't loose his night vision. As soon as he felt the light hit his face, it was turned off. He opened his eyes and watched the boat crawl toward them.

"This is as close as I can get Jack," a gruff voice said, "you gonna have to swim over."

He dropped the pistol inside the bag, and held it above his head. "C'mon Toni," he said pushing the woman ahead of him. When they reached the boat, she was pulled out of the water like if she didn't weigh anything.

One hand grabbed his bag, and another grabbed him under the arm and pulled him over the side, like a sack of potatoes. He dropped to the deck and the boat immediately picked up speed, turning southeast toward the open waters.

"Thanks Tiny," he said picking himself up, and holding on to the grab rail around the center console.

"Don't mention it," the big man said. "You don't have to explain anything if you rather not."

There was another man on the boat, a rather skinny fellow wearing a white T-shirt, blue jeans and a cap with a Daiwa logo on it. He was spreading a thin blanket on top of Toni, and when he straightened up Jack noticed the butt of an automatic sticking from the front of his waistband. He had a dropping mustache and was wearing Polaroid glasses, even if it was as dark as it could get. He nodded to Jack and grabbed the rail on the other side of the console.

"It's a long story Tiny," Jack yelled over the roar of the twin outboards, "but I'll tell you sometime." The big man nodded. "Right now I need to go back to that dock," Jack yelled, "I have my car there and I need to pick it up."

Tiny pulled back on the throttles, and the boat started slowing down. The loud roar became just a rumble once more. "I thought you wanted to get as far from there as you could," he said.

"Yes sure, but . . . I need to get my car. I'm sure I'll be okay if I can get out of here right away. I'll explain later."

Tiny looked at him. "You mean you called me to give you a fifteen feet lift? You could have waded and you had been out of here one hour ago."

"There's some kind of strange animals under that dock Tiny," he said with a sheepish smile. "The lady is afraid."

"The lady is afraid," Tiny repeated. The man with the big mustache smiled. "Unbelievable," Tiny said.

The boat roared to life again, making a one hundred and eighty degree turn and raced back to the dock. "I hope you know what the fuck you're doing Jack," Tiny yelled, "you sure you don't need no extra help?"

Jack shook his head no. They were back at the dock in a couple of minutes. Tiny eased the boat down the channel and alongside the dock, and put the engines in neutral. The skinny guy held on to one of the wood pilings. Toni stood up, still wrapped on the thin blanket. Jack helped her jump from the gunwale onto the dock. "Thank you Tiny. I'll be talking to you soon, I promise," Jack said and jumped onto the dock himself.

"Be careful with strange animals mister," the man with the big mustache said smiling, as Tiny backed back away from the dock.

He grabbed Toni's arm, walked around a big pool of blood on the boards of the dock and they both ran to his car. He started it, backed out of the parking space and headed toward the main causeway.

TWENTY-THREE

IT TOOK A lot of willpower to keep his foot off the gas pedal and drive within the speed limits. He kept his eyes more time on the rear view mirror than looking to the front, expecting a police cruiser with lights flashing and siren blasting, to materialize behind him at any minute, but nobody chased them.

He made a right turn on US-1 and headed north, his eyes almost glued to the mirror, trying to spot something out of the ordinary. After a few minutes he realized that it was an exercise on futility. It was impossible to tell from the row of headlights behind him one car from another. And he didn't know what kind of car they could be driving to start with.

"I'm cold," Toni said, both her arms wrapped about herself. He switched the air conditioning off, and turned into a huge service station. He parked in front of the rest rooms, which were on one side of the building, killed the engine and handed her the keys.

"Get our stuff out of the trunk," he said, "we can change clothes in the rest rooms. Let me go get the keys."

He stepped out of the car, pulled the automatic out of his waistband and handed it to her. "Hold on to this too."

He walked into the facility, which was also a huge convenience store. He picked off a beer out of a cooler and walked to the counter.

"I also need the keys for the rest rooms," he said.

The guy behind the counter gave him a wary look as he gave him the change for the beer.

"I fell off the boat," he said with a sheepish smile. "I want to change."

The man was reluctant, but finally slid a key attached to a long plastic sign with MEN stenciled on it.

"I would like the Women's room also," he said.

The guy behind the counter made a big deal of looking around, like if he had lost something.

"I don't see any woman around here," he said.

"My wife's on the car," Jack told him.

"Well, tell her to come get the key herself," he said.

"You're a suspicious kind of person, aren't you?" Jack said.

"Just don't try to pull any shit on me," he said.

Jack just nodded, smiled and walked out. Toni was standing on the sidewalk by the rest rooms, both their bags by her feet. He unlocked the men rest room door, and pushed it open.

"Come in."

"Where's my key?" she asked.

"You're not getting any key, I'm lucky I got this one, make the best you can."

She looked inside through the opening. There was a urinal against one wall, a toilet against the other, and a lavatory on the right hand side.

"I'm not going in there with you to change clothes."

"No? What the hell are you going to do?"

"I'm going in by myself," she said picking up her bag from the floor, "you're going to have to stay out here."

"The attendant wasn't too happy. He might get nervous if we take too long."

"I really don't care Jack," she said pushing past him, "that would be your problem."

He held the heavy metal door for her. "Let me tell you something. You're thinking all the time that I'm trying to seduce you or assault you," he hissed, "but let me tell you the truth lady. You're not all that good looking as far as I'm concerned."

"Hah!" she said, and slammed the door shut on his face.

"Goddamn woman," he said to himself.

"What's up pal," the attendant said coming around the corner of the building.

He smiled and spread his arms. "My wife beat me to it," he said trying to make it sound like a joke.

"Your wife, ah?" Like in, 'what-the-hell's-your-wife-doing-in-the-men's-room'. "Listen bud, you better take your kinky stuff some place else. Where's the key?"

"It's not whatever you're thinking, I swear," Jack said. He knocked on the door. "Toni? Toni, hurry up, we have to go."

"Tony, ah?" the attendant said.

Oh shit, he thought. How do you explain. He banged on the door again. Toni stepped out, the bag on her left hand. "What's the problem?" she said.

He snatched the key out of her hand and walked over to the attendant, who was looking at her with his mouth open. "Here you are," he said handing over the key.

The attendant never took his eyes off Toni. "By God, he could have fooled me anytime," he said and turned around.

"Aren't you going to change?" she asked.

"You change too?" the attendant asked turning back. "I got to see this."

"Hell no," he said pushing their bags into the back seat, "it's not what you think."

"What is what I don't think?" Toni asked.

"I'm not talking to you."

"Umbelievable," the attendant said, "what are you guys called? Transvestites?"

"What? What is this creep calling us?" Toni screamed.

"I'll explain later," he said getting behind the wheel, "just give me the goddamn keys."

Fifteen minutes later he was speeding as fast as he dared on the two-lane highway. Southbound traffic was still heavy, the weekend crowd would keep it like that most of the night. Northbound it was clear, but the long stretches of unlighted road between the inhabited keys demanded complete driving concentration. Just the reflectors imbedded on the pavement, like an airport runway, gave you directions as to where you should be. It was like driving down an unlighted tunnel. His polo shirt was almost dry on account of the wind coming in through the open windows, but his pants were still wet and uncomfortable. His crotch and his ass itched, and his loafers were full of sand and other debris. Toni had been appalled when he had explained to her his encounter with the service station attendant, and then had started laughing. The tension was gone and it was like an inner explosion. The little absurd situation that had developed at the gas station had just been the catalyst. They had pulled what they had set out to do. They had walked into a life threatening trap, been shot at, scared to death, and had come out of it alive and without a scratch.

He drove for a few miles and then started laughing again. He couldn't help it.

"What the hell's so funny now," Toni asked.

He couldn't stop laughing. He slowed down because his eyes were so full of tears that he could hardly see the road.

"You know what I was thinking all the time at that gas station?" he said between spasms of laughter.

"What?"

"I thought," he wiped his eyes with the back of his hand, "I thought, this creep was going to pick up the phone, call the police and tell them-'I have a couple of drag queens here using my bathroom.'

They laughed and joked about what had happened all the way into Florida City.

By the time he was on the Turnpike their ebullient mood had mellowed down. Neither had said a word in half an hour. He knew that the whole thing was far from over. He didn't have any idea yet what was in the package and the envelope they had lifted from the safe, or what to do with it. The other interested party obviously would keep on trying to get it one way or the other, now with more reason than ever.

"What are we going to do now Jack," Toni said.

"I've been thinking about it," he told her, even if he really hadn't done so, but her question forced him to make some kind of decision. "You heard that guy on the dock cry out that he was with the City of Miami Police Department. Maybe your friend the captain could give us a hand here. We have a pretty good description of the guy. He'll probably be able to trace him down."

"You're right," she said. "I'll probably won't be able to get in touch with him until Monday, though."

"That's okay. In the meantime I'm going to call Dave. He's a criminal lawyer, he can give us some advice." He looked around the seat and then remembered. "Get my cellular, it's on my carry bag. Let's see if it's still working after the dunking."

She turned around and kneeled on the seat to find his bag on the back seat. She had changed into cut off jeans, and her butt was sticking up in the air just a couple of feet away. He had an urge to give it a slap, but she turned around and sat back again before he could make up his mind. She pressed some buttons. "Battery is gone Jack," she said.

"The charger it's there, I'm sure."

She kneeled on the seat again. This time he didn't hesitate and slapped her on the butt.

"Jack!"

"Just checking," he said smiling "I thought you had fallen asleep."

"Of course I haven't Jack," she said, "lets keep this kind of professional, OK?"

"No problem, sorry," he answered.

She sat back and plugged the charger into the cigarette lighter.

"Where the hell are we going," she asked.

"Dave's house. I hope he's home," he said.

After a few minutes she unplugged the phone. "It's ready now," she said handing it to him.

She slapped him on the shoulder. "And I'm wide awake, I'm not asleep."

He smiled while he punched Dave's number.

TWENTY-FOUR

"QUITE IMPRESSIVE," TONI said looking around, standing in front of Dave's house front door.

"Well, they make an impressive amount of money, these two," Jack said pushing the doorbell button again. He had the brief-bag slung over one shoulder and held his overnight on his left hand. The big automatic was tucked in his front waistband. Toni was carrying a small bag on her left hand.

Both of them, clad on wrinkled, salt water soaked clothes, made quite a site in the sumptuous surroundings.

"Well, well, well," Dave said opening the door himself, "what do we have here? The prodigal son has returned home," he looked at Toni, "and apparently very well accompanied. Please come on in, come on in."

He stepped to one side holding the door open and they walked into the huge foyer. "Dave, I want you to meet Toni Suarez, she's a reporter with the Herald," Jack said.

"Pleased to meet you Toni," Dave said grabbing her hand in both of him. He kicked the door shut with his right foot, "I'm very familiar with your column, it's a pleasure meeting you personally."

He turned to Jack and punched him not too hard on the stomach. "You son of a gun, I've been trying to get in touch with you. Did you actually try to shoot somebody? I want to know everything, every little bit of it," he raised his hands turning toward Toni.

"What the hell are we doing just standing here?" he said, "please come in, come in, and let's go to the Florida room." He moved between both of them, and grabbed each by an elbow. "C'mon, we have a lot to talk," he said while he led them into the huge Florida room overlooking the terrace and swimming pool behind.

"Sit down, sit down," Dave said motioning to a U-shaped white leather sofa, about twenty feet long, facing the French doors leading out to the terrace. "Let me fix you guys a drink. Jack, yours will be a tall Scotch and water, what about the lady?"

"Same for her Dave," Jack said before Toni could answer. "Where's Camille? She's not home?"

"Nah. It's Friday night. She's at one of those Coral Gables art galleries. You know, wine and cheese for the very intellectual and sophisticated souls and all the other bullshit," he turned around from the ice making machine under the bar, where he was pouring ice into an ice bucket, "sorry about that Ms. Suarez." He started fixing the drinks.

"Anyway, I called your office, left messages on your answering machine, even called Alison's office, but nobody could tell me where the hell you were. Hey," he said turning from the bar, "talking about Alison. I ran into her yesterday," he looked at Jack and seemed to change his mind. "Well, that's another story anyway. I want to hear what you've been up to," he said setting three glasses on top of the huge center table.

Jack started talking, and told Dave all he had been trough since Thursday morning. It had taken more than half an hour, with Dave asking innumerable questions, and Toni interrupting with her opinions. Dave had moved bottles, ice bucket and water decanter to the table, so he wouldn't have to be making trips to the bar. Jack had opened his bag, and the contents were also on top of the table, alongside the automatic, which he had pulled out of his waistband, and laid on one corner.

"So, this is it," Dave said looking at the envelope and the waxed paper wrapped bundle. He looked at Jack, and picked up the bottle of Johnnie Walker Blue. "I think we should refresh our drinks before we continue," he said pouring some Scotch on his glass and adding a little bit of water. "I also need you to retain me Jack," he said while dropping a couple of ice cubes on his glass.

"Uhmm? Retain what?" Jack asked refreshing his drink and Toni's.

"Just give me a dollar."

"What are you talking about?"

"Just give me a fucking dollar."

Toni dug her hand into one pocket of her jeans, and pulled out some crumpled bills. She handed a five to Dave smiling. Dave snapped the bill a couple of times, looking at it. "I have been retained by Mr. Jack Timberlake and Ms. Toni Suarez-Smith, as their defense attorney," he said to no one in particular, and pocketed the bill. "We're legal now chums," he said smiling, "let's see what we have got here."

He pulled the rubber bands off, and unwrapped the wax paper. He picked up the bundles of bills one at a time, and fanned the ends, looking at the denominations.

"I would estimate roughly about three hundred and fifty thousand dollars in one hundred dollars bills in this package," he said. "Now let's see what we have inside this envelope."

He pulled it out of the plastic bag, and ripped the top open with one finger. From inside he pulled two typewritten pages and a small micro cassette. He pushed his hand inside, but there was nothing else inside the padded manila envelope. The three of them bumped heads trying to read what was on the pages.

It was a list of names of Banks and corporations in the Bahamas and the Cayman Islands, followed by long strips of numbers and some letters. No personal names were mentioned.

"What do you make out of this Dave?" Jack said after they had been looking at the pages for a few moments.

Dave leaned back on the sofa, and rested his feet on top of the center table. He sipped some of his drink.

"Definitely Bank accounts, and probably phony corporations. They exist only in paper, I'll bet. Nobody can tell whom these accounts belong to. You know how this Banks operate. Complete secrecy, as far as who the holders are. Just like in Switzerland."

"We have to listen to the tape," Toni said.

Dave didn't answer, he just sat there holding the glass resting on his stomach with both hands, his eyes focused on some point beyond the French doors. Jack noticed that all his ebullience had suddenly disappeared, and the man looked like if he was in some kind of trance. They stayed like that for a few moments, Jack and Toni sitting on the edge of the sofa, looking at the almost supine figure of Dave.

Suddenly he sat upright, dropping his feet to the floor. He poured some more Scotch on his glass, and stared at Jack.

"Yes," he said, patting Toni unconsciously on the knee, "we're going to listen to that tape in a minute but before, I would like to have a couple of words with Jack," he smiled at Toni. "In private, if you don't mind."

Toni just shrugged her shoulders.

He got up and signaled Jack to follow him. He closed the double doors of his study and sat behind his desk, Jack took one of the chairs across it.

"What is it?" Jack asked.

Dave pulled a cigarette out of the pack lying on the desk and offered one to Jack. He lighted both with a silver lighter that resembled a Dolphin jumping out of the water. He leaned forward, both arms resting on top of the desk.

"I don't know if you have figured it out Jack, but we have a very hot potato in our hands here," he said.

"I can figure that much Dave. That's why they are after my ass with such persistence. Some very important people are involved in some very corrupt dealings."

Dave took a swig of his drink and puffed furiously on his cigarette. He smashed it on the ashtray and waved the smoke away with his hand.

"Forget about corruption, Jack. Most people are corrupt to one point or another, especially politicians, until they're caught. I'm talking about something else. I'm talking about the bank accounts."

"What about them?"

"Jack. Do you realize that there could be millions of dollars on those accounts?"

Jack looked at Dave with a blank stare.

"Do you realize that we have the account numbers and the codes to access those accounts?"

"What are you talking about Dave?"

Dave lighted another cigarette, and fidgeted with the silver lighter, not looking directly at Jack, his eyes roaming his study like if it was the first time he had saw it. He finally looked straight at Jack's eyes.

"We have known each other for a few years Jack," he said tapping some ash on the ashtray, "we like to bet on things. We bet on football games, basketball games, baseball games, almost anything, right? Whether you get seasick on my boat, or I get airsick on your airplane, we sometimes do crazy things just for the hell of it. Too crazy for our age, I recognize that. But we do it just for the challenge, just for fun, right? And we don't do it for money either. We bet fifty dollars on a football game, peanuts. We overdid it this last time with the doctor impersonation deal, but that was an exception, am I correct?"

Jack just nodded not sure of what Dave was driving at.

"Well," Dave said, "I just want to make one more bet, and this one is going to be the last bet." He pushed himself across his desk as much as he could, without actually crawling on top of it. "I'll bet half of whatever is on those banks that I can clean those accounts and put that money some place else."

Jack smiled and took a sip of his drink.

"That's the most fucked up bet I have ever heard of Dave," Jack said. "What do I loose if you win?"

Dave sank back into his leather chair, and swallowed the rest of his drink.

"Nothing," he said. "That's the beauty of it. You don't loose anything."

Jack looked at Dave and shook his head.

"This is not a real bet Dave. You're just looking for a partner in this wild scam you have just figured out."

"That's another way of looking at it," Dave said smiling.

"It's illegal as hell Dave."

"You telling me? Of course it is, I'm a lawyer remember."

Jack was silent for a few moments.

"What about Camille?" he said.

"Camille is fucking that Portuguese painter, what's-his-name? He's the hottest thing in the paint circuit. You should see his work. It's all about women with small tits and men with unbelievable large dicks."

"I didn't know that. One time you told me . . ."

"I know what I told you. What else could I tell you at the time?"

Jack shook his glass, rattling the almost melted ice cubes on the bottom. "I need a drink," he said. Dave opened a drawer on his desk, and pulled out a bottle of Jhonnie Walker Black. He poured on both their glasses. Jack took a big gulp.

"What about your practice?"

"I will retire. Stay in the firm maybe as some kind of consultant, but most of the time I would be sailing the Caribbean in the biggest sailboat I can handle," he said. He leaned forward again. "Jack, we keep all this money offshore, we can retire to the islands. I wouldn't try to bring it in. I don't want to bend the law that much. We don't have to, anyway."

"A semi retired consultant," Jack said almost to himself. "That's not a bad idea. Kind of the best of two worlds."

"You're getting the drift."

"Are you sure you can pull this off?"

"Not one hundred percent. I want to know if I have a partner."

"We have to listen to that tape," Jack said.

"We're going to," Dave said pulling a tape out of a micro cassette recorder that was sitting on his desk.

TWENTY-FIVE

T HE HOUSE WAS not as ambitious as some other in the neighborhood, but it was comfortable and spacious and more than he could have ever dreamed. He had enough money stashed away to buy something a lot better, but it was not the time yet. You could go so far on a Police Captain's salary.

Even if your wife was a real state broker and had a successful real state business, you had to be very careful. Two plus two was four. If you called attention to yourself, sooner or later an asshole would come along and dig deep enough to create a big problem. Watergate was the mother of the examples.

Timothy Ambrose sat on his very comfortable leather swivel chair, on the privacy of his den, nursing one inch of Curvoisier on the bottom of a very expensive goblet. It was almost midnight and he was still waiting for the call he knew would come.

He had told his wife to go to bed and don't wait for him, because he was working on something and might even have to go out for a little while. She had been a cop's wife long enough to understand the idiosyncrasies, and had retired long ago.

He took another sip of the cognac and looked at the two cellular phones lying on his polished desk. At six minutes to twelve one of them chirped and he picked it up.

"Hello,"

"Bad news," the voice said. "The convenience store on fifty-six. Ten minutes."

He dropped the cell phone on the desk and swallowed the rest of the cognac in one gulp. Bad news was the last thing he needed, he thought. He looked around him. The real mahogany paneled walls, the floor to ceiling custom made bookcases filled with over five thousand dollars worth of his preferred books, the gray elephant skin sofa where he liked to lay down to read. It would be a cold day in hell before he lost everything he had achieved. Bad news indeed.

He got off the chair, stuck the .45 Glock on the small of his back and picked up the keys of the City of Miami issued Cadillac ElDorado.

"Shit like that happens, you know," the man with the almost white hair said. He was eating Cheetos and drinking a beer. They were both sitting on Ambrose's Cadillac, which was parked under a small olive tree across from the convenience store. One good thing about been a cop, Ambrose realized, was that you weren't bothered by other nosey cops. A Dade County cruiser had stopped by to investigate two cars parked side by side and away from the bright lights of the overhang. He had just lowered the window and flashed his badge. The patrolwoman behind the wheel had given him a knowing wink and disappeared.

"It's fucking unbelievable," Ambrose said. "Is he going to make it?"

"I think so," the blond man said with his mouth full of Cheetos, "I called Jackson Memorial on the way over. He was on stable condition, as they say."

He smiled and popped open another beer from the six-pack between his feet. He filled his mouth with Cheetos.

"He won't be making any babies though. That fucking barracuda ripped half a pound of meat off his thigh, along with his nuts and most of his pecker." The man laughed to himself. "I would love to see his face when he comes out of shock and looks between his legs. He's gonna shit a brick."

Ambrose wished he was just having a bad dream.

"You are sick Scott, you know that?"

The man's eyes went from pale gray to a very cold colorless hue. "Maybe I am Captain," he said. "But maybe you need sick people to do your dirty work, don't you *Captain*?"

Ambrose decided to drop the issue. He realized that he was navigating very dangerous waters.

"Are you sure it was them that broke into that safe?"

The blond man pulled two beers from the six-pack and offered one to Ambrose. He took it without hesitation.

"I'm sure Chief," the man said. He opened the can and took a gulp.

"I was back there an hour at the latest. The broken baseboard, the loose carpet, the piece of plywood," he took another gulp of beer, "I know what I'm talking about. It was all fresh done. I know about these things."

"Son of a bitch," Ambrose said.

"Looks bad, ah?"

"You don't have any idea how bad it looks," Ambrose said. "I've to go to a luncheon tomorrow at Eldrige's house. I don't know who else's going to be there, but I'm going to have to answer some questions and I don't have any fucking answers."

"I don't know where to start looking for these two assholes, Chief. They could be holed up anywhere."

"I know," Ambrose said. He drummed his fingers on the steering wheel for a while.

"Tell you what I'm going to do," he said looking at Scott, "I'm going to call the paper and leave a message for the Suarez woman to contact me. Wherever she's hiding, I'll bet she keeps in touch with the paper somehow. She'll call me because she trusts me. When I get a hold of her I'll tell her that I need to meet both of them, that they are in some kind of danger or some bullshit like that. Bring them out into the open, if you know what I mean. Then you take care of them." He put both his hands on the steering wheel and looked across the parking lot at the lighted front of the store. "I don't care how you do it Scott, but this time it has to be definitive. Don't bother about trying to extract any information, just waste both of them. You understand?"

"I got it Chief."

"Who do you have for a back up, now that our friend Jarol is convalescing?" he asked.

"Nobody," Scott said opening another beer, "Mike is sitting home suspended, pending that investigation by Internal Affairs. I hate to ask Jairo for some help. That bunch of spicks he has are kind of unpredictable. They're only good for an all out war. Jarol was the best of the bunch. Even if he was hard to control sometimes."

"Call Mike, off the record," Ambrose said. "Tell him he'll get a nice bonus for this operation, but that he's on his own. If the shit hits the fan and you have to pull your badge he better be invisible. I can't go that far. You understand?"

"Completely chief."

"Okay then. I'll keep in touch."

Scott got out of the car carrying with him the paper sack with the empty beer cans.

Ambrose watched him drive away in the unmarked yellow Mustang. He then noticed the crumpled bags of Cheetos on the floor of his car.

"The son of a bitch," he said aloud.

TWENTY-SIX

"I'M SORRY MS. Suarez," Dave said when they walked back into the Florida room, "I didn't mean to leave you all by yourself for so long. It's my fault. Some personal matter I wanted to discuss with Jack and I didn't want to overwhelm you with the boring details."

Toni was sitting on the edge of her seat looking at the décor of the huge Florida room.

"It's O.K. Dave, and you can call me Toni, Ms. Suarez makes me feel kind of old," she said.

"I like that," Dave said, "that makes us like a band of old friends. Right Jack?"

"You got it Dave."

"You have quite an impressive collection of art hanging from these walls Dave," Toni said.

"I guess so," Dave said looking around like if he was noticing everything for the first time, "I am not exactly a connoisseur of art, but Camille is. She is an interior decorator, maybe Jack told you about it."

"Yes, he mentioned it," Toni said. "A very successful one from what I hear."

"Yes, I guess she is at that," he said looking around following Toni's gaze. He sat down by her side.

"We travel a lot you know, and every place we go she'll find some piece to pick up and bring home."

"It's amazing the way she mixes pieces from so different places, and makes them blend so well," Toni said.

"It is, it is," Dave said, "she sure has a knack for it. Maybe that's why people pay her those ridiculous amount of money to decorate their homes."

"I'm sure she earns every penny Dave," Toni said.

"I don't doubt it, and I sure don't question it," Dave said laughing.

"I wouldn't laugh at her year income," Jack said smiling, "I could live on her IRS return."

"Lets keep the IRS out of the conversation Jack. You know that just the mention of the word gives me the creeps," Dave said joking.

He sat down by Toni's side, and patted her on the knee.

"How's your drink Toni? It doesn't look so good."

"Maybe it needs a refill," she said smiling.

"My God it's empty," he said rattling the ice cubes on the empty glass. "How could you let this happen Jack?"

"Waiting for the host, I guess." Jack said.

"C'mon Jack, you know you're home. Take care of the ladies drink. I'm going to get some snacks. You guys must be starving," he said.

He got up and walked toward the kitchen.

Jack smiled and poured some Scotch for Toni and himself on their glasses. They could hear Dave in the kitchen, opening and closing doors and drawers.

"I hope that whatever he is offering us will be edible," Jack said.

"Is he that bad?" Toni asked, a worried look on her face.

"He's definitely no gourmet Toni," Jack said smiling, "but this is actually just a snack. I guess we'll survive it."

Dave was his old ebullient self when he came out of the kitchen.

"Here we are," Dave said holding a plastic tray, which he put on the table in front of them. There was a bag of cocktail crackers, a wedge of cheese with a small knife stuck on its top and a couple of cans of smoked oysters.

"Camille will kill you if she catches you serving your guests in this manner," Jack said slicing a piece of cheese. He hadn't realized he was so hungry.

"I know," Dave said, "but we're here among friends, right? Any oxymoron can open a can. Am I right Toni?"

Toni just nodded. She had already opened one can of smoked oysters, and was digging them out with crackers and stuffing them in her mouth.

"Let's hear what's in that cassette," Dave said inserting the micro cassette in the recorder and pushing the play button.

For a moment there was just the hissing sound of the tape rewinding, and the three of them stared at the little electronic gadget sitting on the table. After a few seconds they heard the voice of a man clearing his throat.

'My name is Carlos Hidalgo Arzon' a hoarse voice said, 'and I am part of a drug smuggling and money laundering organization run by my nephew Andres Hidalgo Santor. Andres recruited me to be his eyes in Miami regarding the money matters. His friend Jairo Dario Guzman, an established and well-respected Colombian businessman, handles the drug smuggling part. On the United States side of the operation there are several other people involved. Jimmy Hirshfield, owner and president of Arcadia development, the land and housing developer. Pedro Luis Agramonte, president of Intraterra Bank. Wilson

H. Margate, chief executive officer of Lincoln Savings and Loans. Joseph Eldridge, City commissioner. Harry Simpson, assistant to the chief of the Port Of Miami Authority and other lesser individuals on the government and law enforcing agencies. I also know, although I cannot prove it, that the helicopter crash that killed former resident chief DEA agent Bill Doherty in the mountains of Colombia, was no accident but sabotage ordered by my nephew Andres. I also was present in a meeting two years ago on Grand Cayman Island, where Mr. Margate asked Jairo Dario to help him get rid of his wife. This was accomplished a few months later by a faked boat accident on Biscayne Bay. I have evidence, which I am willing to supply in exchange for complete immunity by your courts and the benefits of your Witness Protection program. I am sending you a copy of this tape and will contact you in a few days. If you are not willing or able to come to an agreement, I'll send a copy to another agency.'

They watched as the tape came to its end and clicked the recorder off automatically.

"Impressive," Dave said.

"You know the people he mentions?" Jack asked.

"Some of them," Dave said.

"Me too," Toni said.

Dave got up from the sofa, and walked to the French doors. He stood there for a while, hands thrust into his pockets, his back to them. He finally turned around and looked at Jack.

"I'm afraid we need to have another private chat. If Toni doesn't mind," he said.

"Oh, for chrissake Dave, spill it out. Toni and me have been together in this from the beginning."

"It's kind of personal, Jack."

"How personal?"

"About your ex-wife."

"Alison?"

"Uhum."

"What about her?"

Dave took a deep breath, walked back and sat on the sofa.

"Remember I mentioned running into Alison when you first got here tonight?"

Jack nodded.

"Well." Dave sliced a piece of cheese, and poured some more Scotch on his glass. "I was in Palm Beach yesterday. Not on a case, just for some real state business I'm looking into. Myself and an associate went to have lunch at this private club an acquaintance of mine belongs to." He bit a piece of cheese and took a sip of his drink. "It's a very reserved place, and the dinning room it's not that big. Fifteen tables max, and it was almost empty. I looked the place over out of curiosity, and noticed the couple sitting on a corner table. They were having wine, deep in conversation and holding hands. The woman was Alison. The man was Wilson Margate."

Jack was at a lost for a moment, then the name clicked in his head. He was stunned, and sat back deep into the soft leather, holding his drink with both his hands. He felt dizzy all of a sudden, like if all the Scotch he had drunk had decided to rush to his brain at one moment notice.

"No wonder Jack considers you the best, Dave," Toni said, "you sure can deliver a speech."

"I'm sorry if it came out a little bit melodramatic, but under the circumstances . . ."

"Do you know this man, Margate?" Toni asked.

"I have never met him personally, but I know who he is," Dave told her.

"Could Alison be involved in any of this shit?" Jack said to nobody in particular.

Toni looked at Dave, but Dave was staring at the ceiling.

"Probably not Jack," Toni said lying her hand on his arm, "just one of those freaky things that happen."

"I hate to be blunt Jack, but I disagree," Dave said. He fished a cigarette out of the crumpled pack on the table, and lighted it. "This man planned the murder of his wife. Six months after the fact, Alison files for divorce without any reasonable cause. If I don't happen to go to this very particular place, on this particular day, there wouldn't be a reason in the world to link them together. As it happened, there's some connection here."

"There goes the attorney again," Toni muttered.

"What do you want me to do Ms. Suarez?" Dave said not to gently, "ignore the facts?"

"I need to take a shower," Jack said standing up. Toni and Dave followed, and stood up.

"You guys stay here tonight," Dave said. "Toni, down the hall there are two guests rooms. I'll put everything here in my safe, and we'll talk again tomorrow. Let us take a rest, okay?" He picked up the tape and the bundle of money.

"Feel free, if you want to get anything from the kitchen or whatever." He walked toward his studio. Jack and Toni walked toward the other end of the house.

The guestroom he picked was bigger than the master bedroom in his condo. He was familiar with it, because him and Alison had stayed on it a couple of times after some party had ended too late to drive home. Some time back, when life was normal. The other one was even bigger, he knew, because it faced the canal on one side. Both of them had French doors that opened into the huge terrace around the swimming pool.

He dropped his carry all on a chair, and opened his brief bag on top of the dresser and pulled all the contents out. The damn thing was really almost waterproof. All the stuff was damp but not soaked. He spread it on top of the dresser so the air conditioning would take the moisture out. He pulled the magazine out of the automatic, and worked the slide a couple of times. He would ask Dave for some gun oil and cleaning tools in the morning, and give it a good cleansing. He laid the automatic on the dresser, and looked at his reflection on the four feet wide mirror. He was a sorry sight all right.

His short hair was plastered down in some places, and stood up like wire in others. His eyes were bloodshot with dark rings under them, and he needed a shave. His blue polo shirt was streaked with white, salt-water marks, and he smelled like an abandoned fish bait bucket.

He walked into the bathroom and dumped his soiled clothes inside a hamper. He hoped Camille's maid would find them and take care of them, before they stank the house. He adjusted the shower spray to high and hot, and stepped under it. He tried not to, but couldn't help wondering what Alison was doing right at that moment. Sleeping peacefully on her bed, or having a nice mother to daughter chat with Jackie, who was supposed to have arrived in the evening? Or wriggling her ass under the body of Mr. Margate? Either way, none of his business, he thought. They were divorced, and she was free to do whatever she wanted with her life or her body.

He squeezed more hair shampoo on his head, and worked a fabulous lather. He would have to meet this asshole Margate somehow, see what he looked like. He wondered how Alison had met the man in the first place. Probably because of some legal procedure in the firm, Alison's specialty was corporate law, because socially they surely didn't rub elbows with the upper strata.

He turned the shower level to cold, and shivered under the shock of the ice-cold water. What could have turned Alison around, he wondered. The sudden apparition of a white knight riding his fucking horse? He was realistic, or maybe cynical enough to realize that that kind of apparition only occurred on the minds of young, naïve, single women. It had to be something else. Unmeasured wealth? Power? Palm Beach private clubs, and a peek at how the Jet Set lived? Whatever her dark reasons were, was she aware of the means to get to that end? Or was she just a spectator taken on for the ride? He shut the water off, and started toweling himself. Not his problem, he told himself.

He walked out of the bathroom, pulled a tan Bermuda short out of his bag, and slipped it on. Dave's crazy scam, about cleaning the sons of bitches offshore bank accounts, appealed to him more than ever. After that, they could turn the evidence over to the District Attorney. That would nail the lid on the coffin.

He picked up the phone on the dresser and dialed his answering machine. The first message was Dave asking his whereabouts, the second one was from Jackie.

"Hi daddy-o," the voice said, "I'm sorry but I'm not coming down after all. I'm going to Vermont with Sacha and some friends. I'll be talking to you." The other two messages were from Dave also. He dropped the handset on its cradle. He wondered who Sacha was. A boy, a girl, a dog? He didn't care. Vermont looked a lot healthier than Miami anyway. He was craving for a cigarette. After quitting for a few months, now he was back on square one. He opened the French door and stepped out on the terrace. There was a crescent moon that bathed everything with an eerie white light. The swimming pool lights were on, and the water sparkled with a translucent blue color. He smelled cigarette smoke and looked around. Toni was standing just ten feet away smoking a cigarette, the red tip glowing brighter every time she inhaled. "Hi Jack," she said.

He walked over to her. "You have any more of those?" he asked. She pulled a pack and a lighter from the breast pocket of her man-like pajama top, which reached down only to the top of her thighs. She wasn't wearing the bottom part. He lighted the cigarette, and returned the pack.

"Beautiful night," he said.

"That it is."

"You look more comfortable tonight, than you did last night," he said smiling. She flipped her cigarette off toward some shrubbery, and turned around.

"I can get into something even more comfortable," she said. She put her arms around his neck and pressed her body against his.

"I don't need any sympathy Toni," he said.

"It's not sympathy, you dumb man. It's just plain, old lust," she said smiling.

He followed her into the room, and closed the French door behind him.

TWENTY-SEVEN

"GOOD MORNING, GOOD morning," Dave said when Jack and Toni emerged from the hallway leading into the Florida room. He was sitting on a high chair on one side of the center-island of the kitchen. Camille was on another high chair, on the other side of the island, both of them holding mugs of delicious smelling coffee.

"I thought you guys would never wake up," he said getting off the stool, "coffee's coming up. Cream and sugar Toni?"

"Please Dave, thank you."

"Jack darling," Camille said sliding off her chair, "you look awful, if I may say so." She put her cheek against his, and blew a kiss into space. As always, Jack thought, she was immaculate, no matter what time of day it was. Her lush, dirty blonde hair, held in a ponytail seemed to float around her head, and smelled of some kind of flower. She was wearing a white pantsuit outfit with a heavy white cord around her slim waist. The flimsy material clung to her well-shaped hips and thighs in a very sensual way.

"Camille, this is Ms. Toni Suarez," he said.

"Toni," Camille said stretching out her hand, "glad to have you with us."

"Here you are," Dave said pushing mugs of steaming coffee into their hands.

"We missed you last night, Camille," Jack said.

"I'm sorry my dear, but you know how these affairs are. They tend to get complicated sometimes. A whole lot of friends insisted that we should go to this artist's apartment. Can't even remember his name, some young Portuguese painter. It was two in the morning before I could excuse me out of there anyhow," she said in her mellow voice.

"Jack and I are going to have coffee in the terrace while you girls fix breakfast. C'mon Jack," Dave said grabbing Jack by the elbow and steering him out to the terrace.

They sat on the table farthest from the kitchen area. Dave lighted a cigarette, and pushed the pack toward Jack. He leaned over the table, to get closer to Jack.

"Can you believe that woman?" he said. "'Can't even remember his name'", he mimicked. "She spent half of the night fucking the brains out of that sorry excuse of a painter, and now tries to pull that bullshit. Does she think I'm stupid?"

"I don't know Dave," Jack sipped some coffee. "She says she can't even remember his name," he said smiling.

Dave leaned over the table and looked at him for a couple of seconds.

"Fuck you too Jack," he said sitting back on his chair, and sipping his coffee. "That's not a big deal anyway."

That had been a cheap shot, Jack thought. Was he trying to get back at Dave because of what he had disclosed about Alison? He didn't want to think so. That would show a mean streak that he was sure he didn't posses.

"Sorry about that remark Dave," he said.

"I said forget it. It's not important anymore." He replied.

They sat silently for a while, sipping coffee and smoking their cigarettes. From their position, they could look down the length of the canal leading to Biscayne Bay. The part of the bay they could see in the distance, reflected the light of the raising sun and looked like a big silver tray, but the canal itself was a deep, cool green. Two sport fishermen motored by slowly, trying to keep their wakes to a minimum. Their occupants waved to them, and they waved back. Dave's open fisherman, moored to the wood deck, bobbed on the swells.

"Anyway," Jack said, "I touched bases with Toni last night about what you have in mind. She's kind of reluctant about the whole idea. She gave me all kind of reasons why we shouldn't go ahead with it. Which makes a lot of sense of course."

"Of course," Dave said pulling on his cigarette, "but was she very upset about the whole thing, or was she . . . well, kind of open minded?"

Jack thought about that for a moment.

"She wasn't shocked out of her mind, if that's what you mean. She's not that kind of person, she's got both feet very well planted on the ground. It was more a kind of analytical thing mixed with some moral concerns," he said.

"That's good Jack," Dave said squashing his cigarette on the ashtray, and lighting another one. "People with analytical minds usually see the light at the end of the tunnel." He turned around on his chair and looked at him. "We can't pull this thing off if she doesn't goes along with us, you know that."

Jack nodded in agreement. "Do you think we can do it?" he asked.

"There's just one way to find out, Jack."

"I think I know what you have in mind."

"Try me."

"Just a guess," he said.

"I'm all ears, Jack."

"We take the 350 grand and we go to the Bahamas. We open two or three secured accounts. We come back and try a transfer from the secured accounts in Grand Cayman to our accounts in the Bahamas. If the codes and everything else works, bingo. If it doesn't we still have some money, tax free."

Dave looked at him and his face broke into a broad smile, his little green eyes sparkling with pleasure. He put out his right hand, palm up. Jack smiled and slapped it, like two teenagers enjoying a good joke.

"With a little twist," Dave said, "we're not flying commercial. We can go in your airplane. The least paper trail we leave behind, the better."

Jack put out his cigarette on the ashtray.

"Not my ship Dave," he said, "I don't like to fly over that chunk of open water on a single engine airplane, but I can rent a twin engine. We can charge it as business travel expenses," he said smiling.

"And we have a big expense account," Dave said.

It was Jack's time to put his hand out. "We can leave tomorrow," he said, "it will be our little holiday."

Dave slapped his hand. "You got it."

"It looks like you boys are having a great time," Camille said approaching the table with a full tray. Toni was just behind her with another tray. "Mind telling us what's so funny?"

"Just old college jokes Camille," Dave said smiling, "just old college jokes."

The four of them sat at the table and started consuming the huge breakfast, making small talk. Without any previous consensus they didn't comment about their trek in front of Camille.

After cigarettes and an extra cup of coffee, Camille stood up and told them that she had to get ready to go to work. Dave mentioned that he should be moving along too.

"I would like to take the boat out Dave," Jack said, "maybe I can catch some fish for dinner."

"You guys just go ahead," Dave said standing up. "It's fueled and ready to go. The keys are on the ignition, and there are even some rigged ballyhoos on the cooler."

"We'll see you tonight then," Jack said, "don't work too hard."

Dave waved to them, and walked into the house.

Jack led Toni to the dock and helped her into the boat. He disconnected the power cord that fed the batteries and the coolers, fired up the motors and threw the stern line on the dock.

"Let go of the bow line and give it a little push," he told Toni.

The boat drifted away from the dock, its engines rumbling in neutral. He pushed the levers forward and started making headway down the channel.

He kept his right hand on the throttles and waited until he was far away from the moored boats on the canal, looking back to make sure his wake wouldn't reach them. The channel markers twisted slightly to his right.

"Hold on," he said to Toni. She grabbed the T-top supporting rails with both hands, and he pushed the throttles to their stop. The twin Mercury outboards roared and the stern of the 26 feet Mako dropped down, pulled by the bit of the propellers. After a few seconds the boat went into plane and shot forward, leaving behind it a rooster tail four feet high.

"Where the hell are we going?" she yelled over the roar of the motors.

"Out to the edge of the Gulf Stream," he yelled back. "About twenty or so miles, maybe we'll catch some nice fish out there."

He veered a little to his left, looking for deeper water, but keeping the same speed.

"I wish I could own one of those," she said motioning with her head toward Stilt City, a conglomerate of wooden houses built on stilts, on the shallows of Biscayne Bay many years before. It was impossible to build anything like that now days, but the ones existing were allowed to stay until they rotted away.

"You just might Toni, if there's one for sale," he told her smiling.

Fowey Rock lighthouse slipped by his left, and the water turned to a deep blue. He pulled back on the throttles until the boat was hardly moving, and steered to a northeasterly heading.

"What a beautiful day Jack," Toni said. "Are you sure we're going to catch some fish here? It looks so deep."

"We're not going to bottom fish Toni," he said. "We're going to troll. Try for a real big fish." He smiled while he made some small correction to the heading.

"Here," he motioned to her, "take the wheel and keep this heading, while I fix some rods."

She stepped to the console and he went back to rig a couple of rods and put the lines in the water.

He left the fishing rods on the gunwale holders and opened the cooler. He pulled two beer cans out and stepped up to the center console.

"How would you like to take a little trip to the Bahamas tomorrow," he said giving Toni one of the beers. He tapped the throttles with the palm of his hand a couple of times to get some more speed, but let her stay on the wheel.

"The Bahamas? What kind of a trip? You and me?" She slid into one of the bucket seats in front of the center console.

"Well, not quite. Dave is coming along too. It will be like a little holiday combined with some business dealings. We don't have to worry about Dave. He'll be in the Casinos most of the time," he said.

She looked at him and then looked toward the bow of the boat. "I don't know Jack," she said, "this is not what we set out to do. You came to me for some help to try to solve some kind of riddle, and the riddle turned out to be a big fucking mess. I'm in the middle of some shit I never thought I would ever be, and now you're proposing to go into some goddamn, even deeper shit. I don't think I can handle it. I swear, I don't think I can handle it."

He sat on the other seat and took the steering wheel from her. He changed the course a little to the East, and swiveled his chair around to look at the lines in the water.

"It's okay," he said, "you're right. I shouldn't have even mentioned it, it's just that I thought I should share it with you."

"Shit."

"I know."

"You're going to try to pull it anyway, aren't you?"

"I think so. Why not?"

"Because you want to get back at your wife somehow?"

"Of course not. She just came into the picture at the last minute. Just paying back the assholes that kicked the shit out of me. Or their bosses, really."

"It's not legal."

"It depends on how you look at it."

"I don't care how you look at it Jack. You know it's not legal."

"Remember Robin Hood? Steal from the rich to give to the poor," he said smiling.

"C'mon Jack, be serious. This is not a game." She gulped the rest of the beer and tossed the empty can on a bucket by the stern.

"You're right," he said steering the boat toward a patch of weeds. "Forget I ever mentioned it."

She walked around the seat one time and sat back on it again, not looking at him.

"We don't have to share the room with Dave, do we?" she asked.

"That I can guarantee," he said.

"At what time are we leaving?"

He smiled, and started turning the boat around. At that moment one of the fishing rods dipped its tip down and the reel started screaming.

"I think we have a fish," he said.

TWENTY-EIGHT

T HIRTY-FIVE MILES AWAY to the north, in Miami Lakes, Timothy Ambrose struggled with both his body and his conscience. He took a deep breath, held his stomach in and snapped the brass button of his designer jeans, on the corresponding hole. He looked at himself on the wall mirror of the walk-in closet. He looked like a fucking Coca-Cola bottle, and he hadn't put his polo shirt on yet.

He took off the six months old jeans in disgust, tossed them to the floor, and pulled on a pair of tan slacks, of a more recent vintage and two full sizes bigger on the waistline. He definitely had to start going back to the gym. For some reason, his overweight condition didn't look so obvious when he was in uniform.

He decided against the tight polo shirt and choose a white, short sleeved, cotton shirt instead. He stepped into brown Topsiders, and walked out of the closet. He had the house all to himself. Henrietta had gone to pick up her mother to go shopping, and his kids were nowhere to be found. He walked to the kitchen and looked around, trying to find something to occupy him that would stall for a little longer what he inevitably would have to do.

He finally grabbed a beer from the refrigerator, walked to his study and sat behind his desk. He didn't have Toni Suarez personal extension number at the paper, so he dialed the Miami Herald front desk and asked for her.

She was not in at the time, he was told but he could leave a message. He identified himself and told the operator to make sure to tell Ms. Suarez to get in touch with him as soon as possible, that the matter was of the utmost urgency. He hung up, and swallowed some of the beer.

He still didn't know how he was going to do it. Probably the best bet would be the warehouse they kept in South Dade. It was on an isolated complex, in one of the not yet too populated areas of Dade County. He would have to think of something to make her go out there, and make sure she brought along her new friend. Kill two birds with one stone, as the saying went. He hated the idea of having her tortured to find out the whereabouts of the man. Scott could pick them up there, and then it would be out of his hands. He had never killed anybody, not even on the line of duty, and he wasn't about to start now.

He finished the beer and tossed the empty bottle into the trash bin with such force, that it shattered in a hundred pieces.

He wouldn't be pulling the trigger anyway, he told himself, Scott would take care of the dirty part. Pull the trigger, or whatever else he would decide. For sure he wasn't going to ask him how he was planning to do it. A steel wire around the neck or a plastic bag over the head, were his specialties. The bastard had a sadistic streak a yard wide.

He pushed his head back on his leather chair and looked up at the ceiling, like if expecting that some answer from heaven would suddenly appear and tell him that he was right, or give him another option. Not a chance in hell about that, he knew. The situation was getting out of hand by the minute. It was self-preservation, he thought, it was almost self-defense. He had to produce. If he failed to produce, he would have to face the wrath of his associates. He shuddered at the thought. He had witnessed one disposal at the Miami River one time, and had heard of others. These people, if given the time and opportunity, didn't go for the fast and quick solution. They enjoyed the slow and painful one.

He looked at his watch. Time to leave for Elridge's BBQ party, if he was going to make it on time. They didn't appreciate the hired help showing up late. And he knew he was considered hired help.

TWENTY-NINE

"**I**'LL BET IT fought like a son of a bitch," Dave said turning over the huge Dolphin fillets on the BBQ hot plate. He brushed some more of the concoction he had made with olive oil, garlic, parsley and some other herbs Toni had never seen before. The result smelled delicious, though.

"That it did," she said, "I've never seen a fish jump so many times out of the water."

It was late in the afternoon, but the bright sun, without a cloud to contend with, gave the impression that it was midday. Under such circumstances, the three of them had agreed that the drink of the moment should be Vodka and tonic. Jack and Toni had washed the boat, while Dave filleted the fish on the dock's table. After a dip on the pool to cool it off, they had taken showers and changed into fresh clothes.

"Where the hell's Jack?" Dave said.

"Here I am," Jack said walking out into the terrace. "I was talking to Milton at Tamiami airport. We have a plane for tomorrow." He pulled a chair, and sat at the table.

"Nice plane?" Dave asked.

"A Cessna 310. It's an old model, but it's very well maintained. I have used it before. Don't worry Dave, it's a twin engine, we'll make it to Nassau."

Dave turned the fish fillets again, brushed them with more of his sauce and pushed a lever to raise the plate off the burning charcoals. He sat at the table and refreshed his drink.

"While you guys were out there on the ocean having a good time, I was doing some home work," he said. He pulled a pack of cigarettes out of his shirt pocket, and offered them around. All three of them lighted one. Dave pushed himself back on his chair, and looked at them with the kind of half smile Jack recognized he used when he had an advantage over someone.

"I called a friend, and he verified for me some questions I had, but wasn't one hundred percent sure of," Dave said. "I think it's the answer to the little problem we have in our hands."

Jack smiled. In Dave's lexicon, that meant that he had find out something that he didn't know shit about before it had been explained to him. But then, that was Dave's way to call attention to himself. He would gloat now and play the part of the guru in international banking and finances. Jack didn't care about the bullshit as long as it looked sound to him. If one thing he was sure about Dave, it was his thoroughness.

"What we need it's something called a Limited Partnership," Dave said, "I won't bore you guys with all the legal details. What it really comes down to is just a company incorporated in the Bahamas. The limited partners don't need to be residents of the Bahamas. My friend's friend will take care of that end over there, for a reasonable fee of course. The assets of that partnership are tax exempt, even transfers of cash to that partnership are not subject to excise taxes."

He took a long gulp from his glass, and looked at them both. "How that sounds to you guys?" He asked.

Jack dropped a few ice cubes on his glass, and grabbed the bottle of Absolute. He looked at Toni, and she nodded. He poured some vodka in her glass first, and then in his. He filled both with tonic water.

"You're comfortable with that, Dave?" Jack said.

"I sure am," he said getting up to look at the fish on the hot plate. He brushed some more sauce on it, and sat again at the table.

"Suppose that everything works out alright now, the way you have planned it," Toni said, biting off the end of a small Italian sausage. "What happens when the shit hits the fan and the whole thing cracks open? Money disappearing from accounts we're going to turn over to the DA. We will be investigated, Dave."

"So what? It could very well be assumed that if these people smelled some kind of problem, they would move their assets some place else. As far as we know they already might have, and we're wasting our time. It's worth the try anyway, we're not loosing anything," he said.

Jack lighted a cigarette. He knew what Toni meant, and her misgivings about the whole operation were well founded. He also had known Dave for a number of years and knew that he didn't reach conclusions, if all the options had not been exhausted. He decided to pave the road for him, instead of having to deal with explanations for Toni later on.

"I think that what Toni is trying to say is that if we can pull this shit through, would some agency, or somebody, be able to trace it back to us?"

Dave shook his head while sipping his drink. "No way," he said spitting a piece of ice back into his glass. "No way anybody could find any records. A limited partnership doesn't have to show publicly any records. Not the name of the partners, or a financial statement. We're pretty well covered on that part."

"What if some government agency tries to find out?" Jack asked.

Dave shook his head. "Not even them. The Bahamian Bank Secrecy Law won't allow it."

"You know that for a fact?" Toni asked.

"Yes, I do," Dave said smiling. Toni looked at Jack, and shrugged her shoulders.

"It looks like we're in business," Jack said.

THIRTY

"WE'RE IN BUSINESS now," Joe Elridge said pumping the hand of Timothy Ambrose. "You're a little bit late my boy, but you're here," the commissioner said resting his hand on Ambrose's back, and pushing him down the long corridor away from the front door. Ambrose couldn't help himself when he cringed unconsciously under the pressure of the older man's hand on his back. His mind also cringed at the mention of the word 'boy'. He was far from a boy, and he knew that the older man used the word not in a fatherly sense, but as some disguised racial slur.

When they reached the Florida room, the pressure of the hand on his back pushed him to the right, instead of straight ahead to the terrace around the swimming pool. They were going to Eldrige's studio, not the terrace. It meant that the BBQ party, if there was ever going to be one, was not going to be the happy good-old-boys category. It was actually what he had dreaded, a fucking meeting, with him as the central star. They reached the double doors of the immense studio, and the hand on his back felt more like if it was pushing him in than inviting him in.

"Our boy is finally here," Eldridge said to the group of men assembled inside the big room. The word stung Ambrose again, and he felt an urge to reach for the .45 Glock stuck on the back of his waistband. He smiled instead. Eldrige's studio was four times as big as his, with a huge desk in front of a wide bay window, which at the moment had its wooden venetian blinds closed shut. A floor to ceiling bookcase lined one wall, the other one was full of photographs and mementos from the thirty-odd years of its owner dedication to public service. All the walls were paneled in dark wood, and the carpet was a deep green. The two leather sofas and comfortable easy chairs were of different shades of brown. A couple of table lamps, plus the desk lamp, with its green shade, was all the illumination inside the room. The strong smell of good cigars permeated the room, and a little cloud of its smoke hung close to the ceiling. A very he-man room, Timothy thought, where a woman was admitted maybe once in a while to dust the books and vacuum the carpet.

"Hardly any introductions are needed, I think," the old politician said, walking to a portable bar in one corner of the room. "What will be your desire, my boy?"

Here we go again, Timothy thought. He felt like a beer, he was mostly a beer man, but he didn't see anybody drinking one, and was afraid that maybe there were no beers inside the small refrigerator. "Scotch and water will be fine Joe," he said.

"Hi'ya Timothy," Andy Ruiz said from one corner of the room, "heard that you guys fucked up again."

The remark took Ambrose by surprise, and he turned toward the man. He hadn't even told Joe about the debacle on the Keys yet, and the obnoxious prick knew about it already. To make it worse he said it like if it was some kind of joke, with a broad smile showing a lot of perfect white teeth, under his mother-fucking, gigolo mustache. If he ever pulled his gun in anger, Ambrose thought, Andy Ruiz was at the head of the pack to be the first notch on his gun butt.

"Sit down Tim, sit down," Joe Eldridge said handing him a tumbler of Scotch over ice, and motioning him toward one of the easy chairs. He went around his desk, and sat himself on his high-backed swivel chair. From where he sat, because of the green-shaded desk lamp, Timothy could only see half of Eldridge's face.

"Going through one of those bad luck streaks, uh Tim?" Harry Simpson said. Harry was the assistant to the chief of the City of Miami Port Authority, a sleazy, back-stabbing, unreliable piece of shit if he had ever seen one, Ambrose thought. He had never liked him, and had told Joe so, but the old politician had always dismissed it as some kind of grudge on the part of Ambrose. He couldn't underestimate the old politico, though. Harry was the key figure on the Port, for all the shit they were bringing in. Maybe when he was no longer needed, he would end up crushed under one of the containers he helped to smuggle in. Ambrose really hoped so.

"If you need some help Captain, just ask," the Colombian said with his suave voice.

"Thanks Jairo," Ambrose said, "but I can manage. Just one of those unforeseen situations." He smiled. "I'll keep you in mind anyway," he told the short, impeccably dressed, serious looking young man.

Jairo Dario he could understand, Ambrose told himself. The man was what he was, and never tried to be something else. A shrewd but fair business man, helpful and friendly; gentle as a dove when everything was going his way, ruthless and deadly as a rattlesnake, when they weren't. Not the kind of man you wanted to cross. With him, you knew where you stood.

"I can't see where you're managing anything Tim," Andy Ruiz said. "From what Scott said . . ."

"Shut the fuck up Andy," Eldridge said.

Ambrose stood up, spilling some of his drink on the green carpet.

"What the hell's this asshole talking about, Joe? Are you talking to Scott before you talk to me?"

"No, no, no Tim," Eldridge said, "simmer down, sit down, don't pay any attention to Andy. We just happened to run into Scott at the City Hall . . ."

"What the fuck was Scott doing at City Hall?" Ambrose asked.

"I don't know Tim," Elridge said in his conciliatory voice, "maybe running an errand for you. Who knows. Anyway, that's how we found out about the problem in the Keys."

"I was going to tell you all about it today," Ambrose said. Andy snorted, and Ambrose almost pulled out the Glock.

"Sit down Tim," Elridge said, the conciliatory tone gone. "We don't need to fight each other. We need solutions, maybe that what's Andy is worried about."

Like hell he is, Ambrose thought. He's trying to give me the shaft, and right now I'm not looking very good. I can't loose my cool now in front of all these assholes. By God, I am a *police* captain. I am the fucking *authority* here. Act like it, goddammit.

"I said I can manage the situation," he almost yelled, "so what the fuck's the problem?"

"Calm down Timothy, calm down," Elrigde said again, "nobody's saying you can't manage the situation. We're just trying to sort things out. Let me apologize first. I don't think I ever introduced you two. Mr. Margate is a . . . an associate of ours. I don't think you had met him before Tim, have you?"

Ambrose looked at the man sitting across the room from him. He realized that he had never seen him before. He seemed to be in his early fifties, Ambrose would say, with a full head of very well maintained, wavy brown hair. He had a square jaw, like some movie actors, but his small eyes looked like those of a rat. He was wearing a black, long sleeved silk shirt open at the front to the third button and white slacks, and black moccasins with no socks. He didn't even bother to give a nod of acknowledgement to the introduction. Ambrose caught the cold reception just in time, when he was about to get off his chair to shook hands or something, instead he wriggled his ass around, like if he was trying to find a more comfortable position, and remained seated, saving himself of a whale of an embarrassment. The man held his glass with the tip of the fingers of his left hand, which hung from the easy chair armrest at a precarious angle. The liquid was just a half-inch short of starting spilling on the carpet. From his shirt pocket he pulled a folded piece of paper with his right hand, which he opened with two fingers. He looked at the paper for a couple of seconds, and then looked at Ambrose with his rat eyes.

"Captain . . . are you sure that the man in question here is Jack Timberlake?" he said.

"Yes, I'm sure of that," Timothy said.

"Electronics engineer, working for some aviation company?" His raised eyebrows interrogated Ambrose.

"Yes. That's the one," he said.

Margate folded the piece of paper again in two with his fingers, keeping it between his index and middle fingers, and rested his elbow on the armrest, fingers pointed to the ceiling. Harry Simpson, in his usual ass-kissing role, jumped off his chair, grabbed the piece of paper from the extended fingers, and handed it to Ambrose.

"This man has a close friend," Margate said, "the name is on that piece of paper. He's a criminal lawyer with an office downtown. He lives somewhere in Gables States. I'm sure it won't be a *big* problem for you to find *him*. If I were you I would look into that. If this guy Timberlake has disappeared, he might be holed up in there."

Timothy Ambrose looked at the name on the piece of paper, and put it in his shirt pocket.

"Nice tip Tim, wouldn't you say so?" Eldridge said.

"Yes, sure. I'll look into this as soon as possible," he said.

"Not as soon as possible, Captain," Margate said, "you better start looking into it right away."

"What'd you say," Ambrose yelled jumping to his feet, "who the fuck you're thinking you're talking to, you . . ."

"Hold it, hold it!" Eldridge jumped from behind his desk and put his arms around Ambrose. "I need to have a couple of words with Tim here, you'll excuse us for a minute."

He pushed Ambrose toward the double doors, and both of them walked out into the hallway. Eldridge slammed the door shut behind them.

"Tim, listen to me," he said. His bulbous nose looked like a ripe tomato, and his elephant-like ears were sticking out to the sides more than ever, Ambrose thought. "There are a lot of nervous people around here, and with very good reasons to be so. We've been depending on you to take care of this little matter, and I hate to say it, but you keep fucking up. We need results Tim. Just find those fucking people, and get them off our hair." He gripped Timothy by the shoulders. "It can't be that difficult, I know that you can do it, but do it fast my boy." He pushed Ambrose toward the front door of the house. "We're counting on you. *I'm counting on you.* I can't emphasize enough how important this is Timothy. Don't let me down." He pushed Timothy out, and closed the front door behind him.

Ambrose stood on the front steps of the entrance to the huge house. He had never felt so miserable. He looked at the closed door behind him, and then walked to his car.

He got behind the wheel of his Cadillac, and slammed it with the palm of his hand. He was in trouble. Everybody in that room had wanted his balls, especially the man called Margate, if that was his real name. Apparently the asshole carried some weight, and if he – Ambrose – didn't make the chips fall in the right place, nobody would lift a finger for him. Ironically, the only person that seemed to care for him was old man Eldridge. He wondered now if when he called him 'boy', it was with a racial connotation, or if it meant something else. Nobody else seemed to have too much sympathy for him.

It didn't really matter, the whole majority was expecting him to give them some peace of mind and if he didn't, he was a very expendable partner. He had to find that woman reporter and her friend, because his one-way ticket for a trip to the bottom of the Miami River, was being discussed at this very moment. He started the car, and pulled out of the driveway, punching at the same time Scott's beeper number on his cellular phone.

"Get on this right away," he said when Scott called him. "David Hartman, criminal lawyer, downtown office, lives in Gables States. Might be harboring our friends. Find out and put a tail on him. He's expendable if it needs to be."

"It's Saturday chief."

"I don't give a fuck what day it is, or what your kinky plans are Scott, you just get on with it." He pressed the end button, and dropped the cellular on the passenger seat. He immediately regretted the mention of any kinky plans, you never knew how some people would react to certain comments. He took a deep breath.

What the fuck, he thought. He was wading in enough shit, a little bit more wouldn't make a hell of a lot of difference.

THIRTY-ONE

O N SUNDAY MORNING they arrived at Nassau Jet Centre, at around eleven-fifteen. He had decided on the Jet Centre, because it was not as busy as Nassau International and had all the facilities he needed anyway. After they cleared customs, and he had made arrangements to have the airplane refueled and parked, they took a taxi to Paradise Island, a small strip of land just across Nassau Harbour, attached to the main island by a causeway.

Dave had made reservations for them at the Radisson Grand Hotel. Very tactfully, he had reserved three separate rooms, although all three of them were on the same floor, and next door to each other. He had called his friend's friend as soon as they were accommodated, and they had met the man on the swimming pool deck at around three in the afternoon. The conversation had been mostly between the man and Dave, because tax shelters, limited partnerships, overseas incorporations, and other legal mumbo-jumbo were kind of foreign to him. The erotic massage Toni was giving to his leg with her bare feet under the table, didn't help his concentration either. She wore a black swimsuit that she had bought at the hotel boutique, which made the hairs on the back of his head stand on end, let along the rest of his anatomy.

On Monday morning they had gone to the lawyer's office and filled forms, and signed papers. Dave and the lawyer had taken off on their errands, and he and Toni had gone on a snorkeling trip. At night they had celebrated their new partnership, worth 300,000 US dollars, with a gargantuan seafood dinner, and three bottles of a very good white wine.

On Tuesday morning he was looking down from 2800 feet, at the incredible, translucent waters of the Bahamas banks, and fighting a mild headache. White wine somehow always gave him a headache. He felt like pushing the autopilot button and let the airplane flight its own way to Miami, so he could relax a little, but at this low altitude he didn't feel comfortable flying around if he wasn't constantly looking out for traffic. Toni was sitting on the right hand seat, and kept asking him to let her handle the plane. He gave her some instructions on how to keep the wings level and the plane straight on course, and sat back to enjoy the view.

"Don't go to sleep Jack," Dave said from the seat behind them, "I don't want to go scuba diving in the middle of the Gulf Stream."

"Don't worry Dave," he said leaning his head against the Plexiglas window. "Keep your eyes moving around," he said to Toni, "any speck out there could be a plane coming right at us."

She looked at him with surprise. "What if it comes from behind?"

"Well, there's nothing you can do about that, so don't worry."

She stared at him for a couple of seconds to make sure he was not kidding her, and then started scanning all the empty space around them. "Don't forget the gauges either," he said.

"What do you mean?"

"The gauges," he said motioning with his index finger at the array of instruments on the cockpit panel. "They tell you if everything is working all right. Look outside for traffic, look at the gauges for performance. Look outside, look inside." His jaws cracked open with a big yawn. "That's the trick."

"Shit Jack, this could be boring," she said.

"I never said it wouldn't be," he said.

"Don't I ever get to turn this thing around, and dive and soar like an eagle?" she said smiling.

"You will sometime, but not just yet."

He rested his head against the window again. He could use a couple of aspirins, he thought. He could also use a bigger dose of common sense, for that matter. He was still astonished at the strange turns his life had taken in just a few days, but was more amazed at the way he had reacted to the unforeseen changes. Instead of going to the proper authority, and drop on their lap a problem that was beyond his means to resolve, like any half-witted, middle-aged man would do, he had embarked in some kind of crazy quest that was none of his business, and dragged along the way two other people into a situation that could very well turn out to be very hazardous to their health.

The readiness with which he had agreed with Dave to rip off the accounts on Cayman Island, was something else to contend with. The moral and legal aspects of the scam had not even crossed his mind at that moment. It was a possibility, so why don't take it. Dave had seen the opportunity right away, while he was still looking some place else. Was Dave a crook at heart, or was it something else? For sure he wasn't pressured for money, it was probably more the excitement of the gamble; because it was actually a gamble. He himself had never been obsessed by the possession of extreme wealth. He had been happy being a professional, making a decent living in middle class America. Had that kind of wealth, the kind that doesn't know the meaning of 'I can't', what had lured Alison away from him? Had she an inner, never confessed to him, desire to reach the upper echelons of the money community? Did she really want to rub elbows with the rich and famous? He guessed he wouldn't know for sure, unless he put the question up to her, and that wasn't going to happen.

On the other hand, even if he had never before envisioned himself as a wealthy man, the idea of being a part time consultant, living in any part of the world he choose, with no particular deadlines or strings attached to hold him down, was very appealing. It would be a big disappointment if those accounts were dry, or proved to be inaccessible. That would be quite a joke.

"Are you awake Jack?" Dave screamed from the back, and brought him down to 2800 feet again.

"Yes Dave, don't get all excited now," he said. One way or the other, he still had to contend with the people that considered him a hazard to their future. Until he proved to them that he was not a menace, his life was as worthless as a closed bank account.

He decided he would call the Homicide detective, Rick something-or-other, and tell him the whole thing. Well, maybe not a hundred percent of the whole thing, but enough. He had more than enough information, and a good description of a couple of men that apparently were in the Miami Police force. That should get a detective salivating. And speaking of Miami, he thought, that's the Miami skyline right there on the horizon.

He had known he would have a ten to fifteen knots tail wind when he checked the weather in Nassau, and should have changed course a little more to the South some time before. He grabbed the seat release and pushed himself forward. "I've got the airplane Toni," he said in his no-nonsense, pilot-in-command voice. She let go of the yoke and sat back. He banked the airplane to the left almost forty degrees, diving at the same time to twenty-three hundred feet. He leveled off, and kept a southwesterly heading.

"Goddammit Jack," Toni screamed, "that's what I wanted to do! Why didn't you let me?"

He kept loosing altitude above Biscayne Bay, and south of Key Biscayne he banked sharply to the right. He tuned one of the radios to the Tamiami airport ATIS, and crossed the shoreline at fifteen hundred feet and almost two hundred miles per hour.

"Hoowee!" Toni said exhilarated, "this' the way I like to fly."

"I hate this hot dog shit, Jack," Dave said grabbing the armrest of his seat.

Jack smiled. He knew he was showing off, and bending a couple of good sense flying rules at the same time, but what the hell. Everything he was doing lately was bending rules with complete disregard for good sense. He pulled back on the throttles some, and gave them a smooth ride, if somehow low, toward West Dade County.

"It's incredible," Toni said, her face glued to the Plexiglas window. "Dave, have you noticed how many homes have a swimming pool in the backyard, and a fishing boat in the driveway? The whole city is full of them."

"I don't like looking down at the ground this close to it," Dave said.

"That's the point," Toni said, "you can't appreciate this when you're flying commercial."

"The point is, that if this asshole keeps horsing around, we might end up in one of those fucking swimming pools."

Toni turned around smiling to look at Dave, but he had his head against the back seat, looking at the ceiling of the cabin. Ten minutes later the control tower at Tamiami cleared them to land, number two behind a white and blue Piper Cherokee.

Jack parked the Cessna in its designated space on Arrow Aviation's parking ramp, and shut down the engines. He told Toni and Dave to take their baggage to Dave's car, while he secured the plane and went to Milton's office to close the flight plan, and wrap up the paper work.

They zigzagged eastward on North Kendall Drive, half of the time at ten to fifteen miles over the speed limit. The other half was a series of down shifting and hard braking maneuvers to avoid a rear end collision. Dave never stayed on the same lane for more than a few seconds. As usual, with him behind the wheel, Jack had his right foot buried into the passenger's side floorboard with such force, that the pressure was felt on his hipbone. His right hand was glued to the grip on top of the doorframe. He had given up hope long time ago to try to change Dave's murderous driving habits. Instead he tried to drive himself most of the times, or go in separate cars. He was sure one day Dave would miscalculate one of his split-second, razor-edge, high-speed lane changes, and bore a new asshole in some innocent, normal driver.

"Would somebody let me use a cell phone, mine is dead," Toni said from the back seat, "I have to call my office and let them know that I'm still alive." Jack handed her his phone with his left hand, his right one never loosened on the grip.

They reached Gables States and Dave's house, in what Jack considered a good shot at the world's speed record for alienated people, if such thing existed. They pulled their stuff out of the car, and walked to the main doors. They were so exhilarated about having arrived in one piece, that neither paid attention to the white car that drove by, while Dave was fumbling with his keys.

Jack came out of his bedroom where he had gone to freshen up, but mainly to place a call to Detective Rick Lopez, and joined Toni and Dave at the bar.

"Do you guys want to hear what one of my messages was?" Toni said when they were standing around the bar in the Florida Room, fixing drinks.

"Not yet my dear," Dave said opening a can of mixed peanuts, "let me go to my study, and listen to my messages first."

"I have to make a phone call myself," Jack said.

"Use any telephone you want," Dave said, "I have a separate line in my office." He grabbed a handful of peanuts and his tall glass of vodka and tonic. "I'll see you boys and girls in no time," he said, and disappeared toward his study. Jack picked up his drink and the half empty can of peanuts, and motioned Toni toward the big sofa. He slumped down in the middle of it, and rested his right leg on top of the Italian marble center table. That would give Camille a fit if she was around, but his leg was really sore after trying to push an imaginary brake pedal for so long, and it was Dave's fault anyway. He put the peanuts can on the couch between them. He used a cordless phone to call his own answering machine, but there were no new messages. He dropped the phone on the table, and picked up his drink.

"I called this guy, the Homicide detective, and told him almost everything," he told Toni, "and he really took some interest in our blonde friend."

"How do you mean?" Toni asked.

"Well, when I gave him the description of these two characters, he asked if I was sure how tall he was, exactly how blonde he was, how he dressed. You know, I get the impression that he knows who the guy is. He didn't ask so many questions about the other one."

Toni pulled a handful of peanuts from the can, and dropped some on her mouth. "That sounds good, Jack. Maybe we'll get a break," she said almost choking on the peanuts, "because you know who else wants to talk to me as soon as possible? Tim Ambrose," she answered herself, before he had time to ask. She finally washed down the peanuts with a gulp of vodka and tonic. "Probably Tim has found out something, he has been trying to get in touch with me for the last couple of days, they told me at the office. I have to give him a call."

Jack dropped his head back against the soft leather of the sofa. Maybe the whole thing was over, he thought. Maybe not over, but at least off their hands. He was sure detective Lopez knew who the blond guy was. Maybe he didn't know the man personally, but had probably had seen him around sometime or somewhere, in another department. His almost albino features could hardly be called unnoticeable. And Toni's friend, the captain, had apparently found out something that he wanted to discuss with her. That was great. If the Police Department started cleaning up their act, they would be out of the picture and left alone. No more running, and trying to hide. He sat back straight again.

"Call this Captain Ambrose, Toni," he said. "Find out what he wants."

THIRTY-TWO

"THEY JUST GOT in," Scott said on the phone, "it looks like they have been in some kind of trip. They were carrying some luggage."

"Okay. Good. Can they loose you? I know there's only one way in and out of that place."

"Not unless they go out by boat. Can't miss them if they drive out."

"Good. Let me make a phone call. I'll keep in touch," Ambrose said and hung up.

"It was fucking time, Tim," Eldridge said, "and now you're telling me they're still on the loose, and apparently back from some kind of trip? What kind of shit is that?"

"I told Scott to put this guy Hartman under surveillance since Saturday, Joe. He was nowhere to be found. He just turned up at his home a few minutes ago, with the engineer, and the woman reporter. All three of them got in together, and pulled some luggage from the car. That's why we assume they've been in some kind of trip," Ambrose said. "I left several messages at the Herald for the woman to contact me, so I imagine she will call anytime soon, and I'll take it from there."

There was silence on the other end of the line for a few seconds. Ambrose's hand was sweaty holding the cellular phone.

"I don't like this a bit Tim," Eldridge said, "not one fucking bit. I want to check something and I'll get back to you. Make sure that phone of yours it's ready and waiting, you understand me, boy?"

Ambrose swallowed hard. "I understand, Joe," he said.

"I can't believe it Joe," Wilson Margate said. He was in his office on the twenty-sixth floor of the Lincoln Savings and Loans building, on Brickell Avenue. "Are you telling me that that nigger policeman of yours hasn't done shit in four days? And now tells you that it looks like they were in some kind of trip? What the fuck he think he is, a travel agent?" He swiveled around and looked at Biscayne Bay, which was simmering in the afternoon sun. "Listen to me Joe," he said swiveling back to his desk, "this little unforeseen situation has developed into a real pain in the ass. We have planned against big contingencies, but we have to be prepared to handle small ones, like this particular one, that might pop up along the way. As far as I can tell, everybody is sitting on their comfortable asses, doing nothing and waiting for some solution to fall down from the sky. That won't happen Joe. Small nuisances that nobody really wants to take care of, can create a crack in our organization that will in the end affect all of us."

"Yeah, I know what you're saying Wilson," Joe said.

"Excuse me Joe," Margate said, his voice dropping to below zero degrees, "I really don't think that you know what I'm saying. What I'm saying is that you better get off that fat ass of yours, and take care of your part of our association. You have been wallowing in the gravy for too long, and you have lost your perspective. Shit happens, like they say, and now it's the time for you to scoop it up. The party is over, now it's time to rock and roll. If I go down you can bet your sorry political ass that you're coming down with me. You, and your whole fucking tribe. Are you fucking reading me, Joe?"

"I'm here."

"Did your people check if that trip they made was national or international? Did they check the airlines? Especially the ones going to the Caribbean?"

Eldridge had a fit of cough, which lasted almost a minute.

"Actually Wilson," he finally said, "I never thought of that. Checking the airlines, I mean."

"If I have to do all the thinking and all the planning myself Joe, I really don't see why I should be paying you all. Fucking wasted overhead, if you ask me. I might as well talk to Jairo. He's pretty good about cutting down on unnecessary overhead, as you know."

"I'll take care of it Wilson, don't worry. You have my word," Eldrigde said.

Margate slammed down the phone, and got off his chair. He walked over to the floor to ceiling bookcase lining one side of his office, pulled out a fake shelf holding some Caribbean Indians artifacts, and turned the knob of the safe hidden in the wall. He pulled out a small folder and sat back at his desk. He picked up the phone and opened the folder. There were several sheets of paper on it. There were no names, just numbers. He looked at the number in the left-hand corner of the top sheet, even if he knew it by memory, and picked up the phone.

THIRTY-THREE

THEY SAT ACROSS from Dave's desk, and waited for him to accommodate all the papers just the way he wanted them in front of him. When he was ready, he just looked at them and picked up the handset of the telephone. Nobody said a word. He punched some numbers and listened for several seconds. Then he started punching more numbers on the telephone keyboard, his eyes darting from the papers in front of him, to the keyboard. Jack realized that he was holding his breath while he looked at Dave's motions, and let out a long, silent sigh. He stole a side-glance at Toni, but she was sitting forward on her seat, holding her drink with both hands and staring intently at Dave, oblivious of everything else.

The keypunching, broken by stretches of deep silence, went on for what Jack thought was an interminable time, but which were actually just a few minutes. He took a sip of his drink, and fumbled in his pockets for a pack of cigarettes he couldn't find.

Finally, Dave sat the phone handset on its cradle and looked at them, astonishment written all over his face. He looked first at Jack and then at Toni in awe, and shook his head. His puzzled face started breaking into a smile, and he raised his hands from the desk.

"I can't believe it," he said, shaking his head.

Jack looked at him, but didn't utter a word.

"I just can't believe it," he said again, and started laughing.

"What happened?" Jack asked standing up. Dave looked at him.

"I just transferred twenty-two million dollars to our corporation in the Bahamas," he said.

Wilson Margate was about to start dialing a number, when his intercom buzzed. He punched the button with more force that was necessary. "Yes Lillian?" he asked.

"There's an attorney here Mr. Margate. A Ms. Alison Custer, she doesn't have an appointment, but she insists that I should let you know," Lillian said.

What the fuck was Alison doing here at this time, he thought. He had made clear to her that he didn't want her dropping by at his office during working hours. He was still mourning the tragic death of his wife, as far as all the people in his organization were concerned, and he didn't need any gossiping spreading around.

"Oh, yes," he said instead, "I completely forgot about it, Lillian. Send her in, please."

Alison closed the door behind her, and walked toward the impressive desk, twenty feet away across lush carpet.

"I didn't want to interrupt dear," she said, "but I was worried." She sat on one of the wing chairs across his desk, and rested her leather portfolio against the side.

"You have not called since Saturday, and what you told me about Jack getting to be a nuisance for you got me thinking. He's not bothering you because of us, is he?"

He really didn't need this crap at this time, he thought, but he hardly could tell her that. The odds that the ex-husband of the woman he was humping had chanced into some information that was damaging to his business must be one in a million or better, but it had happened. It was a reality he couldn't confide in her, though. He had drunk too much Saturday night and had talked too much. The only reward had been the name of the lawyer friend she had given him.

"No, of course not. As far as I know he doesn't know I exist," he said.

"I'm sure Jack won't create any problems," she said, "it's not his style."

"I'm sure he won't," he said.

"Are we going to that reception tonight?" she asked.

"I don't see why not," he said, "let me make a couple of phone calls, and we'll talk about it."

He dialed the numbers on the top, left-hand side of the paper he had in front of him. After a few seconds, he punched some more numbers. Alison looked at Biscayne Bay, and all the sailboats at anchor. To the left, in the distance, the huge cranes in Dodge Island looked like immense spiders about to grab some unsuspecting prey.

Wilson Margate slammed down the phone handset, but it missed its cradle and it bounced off the top of his desk. The annoying sound of a phone off the hook filled the office.

"What's wrong darling?" Alison said, moving to the edge of her chair. He didn't know it, but the color of his face had turned to a sand gray.

"I'll tell you what's . . ." he started to say, but couldn't finish, because a numbness on the left side of his jaw mumbled his speech. The numbness turned into a sharp pain that shot down his left arm all the way to his fingertips, and all of a sudden he felt like if an elephant had squatted on his chest. Such pain he had never experienced before. His whole torso felt like if it was caving in.

"I've been . . . ," he started saying, but then his eyes rolled back on their sockets, and he never finished what he had tried to say.

THIRTY-FOUR

J ACK DROVE SOUTH on the turnpike toward the address captain Ambrose had given Toni. It was way out in the southwest end of Dade County, and although he wasn't really familiar with the area, he knew it was on a part of the county still kind of underdeveloped. Toni had bitched because he had insisted in carrying the big automatic. She argued that if a police captain noticed that he was carrying a weapon, he might get the wrong idea. He didn't care what she thought, he had reached a point where he didn't trust even the police, whether the policeman was a friend of hers or not. The big gun felt physically uncomfortable stuck on the small of his back, but it gave him a lot of confidence. If the captain was not a moron, he couldn't get offended, he had argued back, not after what they had been through.

She was not convinced, and had gone into the silent mode, her head turned to the window, watching the landscape slid by. He shrugged the argument off, and looked at his watch. By this time Dave was probably sitting with Lillian Devore, the DA, and turning all the evidence over to her. He had called her office from his home and ran head-on into the defensive line all politicians erected around themselves, to keep unsolicited and bothersome callers at bay. He immediately went into his top-lawyer-in-the-court scheme. He dropped some names, mentioned graft at the higher official places and national security. Ten minutes later Ms. Devore was on the line, she agreed to meet with him in forty-five minutes.

They had left the house at the same time. Dave going downtown, to the DA's office, Jack going south to an uncertain meeting in some warehouse out in the boondocks.

He got off the turnpike in the exit he figured was closer to the address he had. He drove west along a wide four-lane avenue with lots of empty spaces on both sides. Most of the businesses were gas stations on the corners, and small shopping centers along the way, most of the stores empty. It was the typical businesses spearhead approach; getting in place before the housing developments started and the prices went sky high. He kept track of the street numbers as he drove at the minimum speed, and was ready one block before he came to the one where he had to turn.

There was a convenience store with gas pumps right on the corner. Behind that building was an empty lot, maybe three hundred yards long, and behind the lot, a row of warehouses extended for about two blocks along a lonely street down to a dead end. On the left side of the narrow street was undeveloped land. Just pine trees and scrub bush. He drove slowly down the street looking at the numbers on the front doors. The front of the long building was a repetition of itself. A small barred window beside a front door followed by a roll-up metal door, just one after the other. There was a dilapidated Mazda in front of the second warehouse, but not other car in sight. The number he was looking for was the last warehouse at the end of the building. A green metal dumpster sat at the dead end of the deserted street. Beyond it there were just more pines and sagebrush. There wasn't any car parked in front of the place he was looking for. As a matter of fact there were no cars in sight, but the dilapidated Mazda, period.

"This is it," he said to Toni. She looked around. It was not night yet, but the sun had set and the place looked forlorn indeed. "It looks like there's nobody here," she said.

"Let's find out," he said getting out of the car. Toni followed him, and they walked to the small front door. Jack knocked three times on it, and it was opened immediately by a huge black man, dressed on the blues of the Miami Police Department.

"Well, hello Toni. Please come on in," he said stepping back and pulling the door open wider. The overhead fluorescent fixture shone on his badge, and the twin golden tracks on his shirt's collar. He closed the door and shook Toni's hand.

"Glad to see you again girl," he said.

"I'm so glad to see you Timothy," Toni said. She really looked happy about meeting the man. "I want you to meet my friend Jack Timberlake."

"Jack," the man said smiling and putting out his hand. He was a couple of inches taller than Jack and had huge hands. His handshake was firm, but not the crushing experience Jack thought he was going to get. "But sit down please, sit down," he said in his deep voice, motioning them to a couple of metal chairs in front of a cheap metal desk that was pushed against one wall of the small office. Jack figured it was no bigger than about twelve feet wide by fifteen or eighteen feet long. Another door on the other end he assumed opened into the warehouse itself. Besides the metal desk and the two chairs, there was no other furniture. Toni sat on the chair closest to the front door, and he took the other one. He noticed that the small window had been covered with paper from the inside, probably to keep nosy people to peek inside, he thought.

"You said you found out something about the story I'm working on," Toni said.

"Yes, my girl, I did," he said, and leaned against the wall across from them. "I found out that you picked up something in a certain place on the Keys, that rightfully doesn't belong to you. I'm here, as a friend, to tell you to hand over whatever you picked up there. I'm sure it's of no use to you and it can only cause you some unnecessary aggravations."

Jack noticed Toni's jaw drop down and the astonished look in her eyes. He fidgeted on his seat and the captain's right hand dropped to the butt of the big automatic on his belt. He froze in place.

"I don't know what you're talking about Timothy," Toni said in a small voice.

"Ahh, c'mon Toni," Ambrose said shaking his head, "don't make this thing more difficult than it already is."

"I can't believe that you're mixed in something like this Timothy," Toni said.

Jack's head kept swinging from one party to the other. He had been right, he thought. A sixth sense had told him that this meeting was trouble. Nothing that he could really put his finger on, just a nagging doubt on the back of his mind. He hadn't wanted to question Toni about her friend, the police captain, he knew she would have exploded at the insinuation. He had hardly expected this confrontation though, he had worried about something going wrong, but nothing this bad. The pressure of the Desert Eagle against the small of his back had suddenly lost all its appeal. He sure wasn't going to try to beat the captain to the draw.

"Be sensible, girl. Just hand me over whatever you found down there, and we'll forget about the whole mess. I'll handle it from here on. I'm the only one that can help you." He smiled at both of them, but looked straight at Jack. "This gentleman is not even a journalist. I'll bet all he wants is to go home and relax, and forget about the whole thing. Ain't I right, Jack?"

Jack forced a smile, because he didn't know what else to do. He realized then and there, that they weren't going any place. He wasn't going home to relax and forget. Toni wasn't either. They were not coming out of there alive, period. He had to make a decision, and make it fast.

"I'm just going to forget that this conversation ever took place Captain," Toni said, and stood up. "I just hope that you will . . ."

"Not so fast girl," the captain said pushing her hard back into the chair, "just stay the fuck put. I'm trying to make it easier for you, can't you understand that?"

"The hell you are, you crooked bastard."

The captain hit the partition wall two times with the palm of his hand. In the small closed quarters, it sounded like two shots to Jack. The inside door opened and the blond man stepped into the office, followed by another one. He was smiling, and in his right hand, casually held by his side was the black gun with the long silencer.

He raised his hand slowly, and pointed the end of the silencer at a point between Jack's eyes, not more than four inches away.

"Get up asshole," he said, "and put both hands on top of your head." Jack slowly got off the chair, and crossed his hands on top of his head.

"Frisk him, Mike," the blonde man said, "our friend had taken lately to carry a small cannon. Too much gun for him, I would say."

The man called Mike holstered his automatic under his jacket, and patted Jack.

"Well, well, lookit here," he said pulling the Desert Eagle from his back. He looked at it, and dropped it to the floor. "Nice piece, partner," he said smiling. He continued patting Jack all the way down to his ankles. "That's it," he said.

"You can sit down now asshole," the blonde man said, bringing up his left fist in a swift arch. It hit Jack just under his breastbone. It knocked his wind out, and he collapsed down on the chair gasping for air. He felt like if a hot poker had been driven through his chest. He fought for small gulps of air to feed his burning lungs.

"I'm sure you all have met Scott," Ambrose said. "He's not the nicest guy in town. I was trying to spare you this part Toni. Please, think again girl."

She wasn't paying any attention to Ambrose, she was trying to hold Jack's head up so he could grasp some air. Scott switched his gun to his left hand, and hit Toni on the right side of her head with the back of his right hand with such force, that it knocked her off her chair. The man called Mike picked her off the floor, sat her again on the chair, and stood by the front door.

"C'mon cunt," Scott said, "talk to me."

His hand swung again, this time from the other direction, hitting Toni on the left side of her jaw, and propelling her against Jack. Blood flew from her mouth and nostrils, and her eyes lost their focus. Jack tried to hold her, but Scott grabbed a hand full of her hair, and yanked her back into her chair.

"Wait," Jack screamed fighting for some breath, "wait," he raised his right arm, "what you want," he said, and had to stop to get some wind, "what you want, was turned this afternoon to the district attorney. It's out of our hands." He started laughing and coughing at the same time. "Talking about assholes," he kept on laughing, and motioned to his watch with his right hand, "at this precise time the DA it's looking at your names and those of the ones above you. You're finished. No matter what you do to us, you're history you dumb prick," he said looking at Scott.

Scott switched the automatic to his right hand, and pressed the silencer against Toni's forehead. "For you," he said looking at Jack, "it won't be so easy."

"Enough Scott," Ambrose's voice sounded hoarser than ever. He had his Glock in his right hand, and it was pointed at Scott's midsection. The blonde man looked at the Glock, and then at his chief's face. The ugly silencer moved from Toni's head toward some point on Ambrose's midsection.

"What do we do now, chief?" he asked.

"We let them go," Ambrose said.

"Like hell we do," Scott said.

"You do like I tell you, you sadist piece of shit, or are you forgetting who's the boss here?"

"Joe was right," Scott said, "he told me that you would probably chicken out at the last minute. You ain't got the guts, captain, sir." He squeezed the trigger and the gun just made a small popping sound. The 9 mm. round struck Ambrose on his chest cavity, one inch under his heart. He recoiled back under the impact at such close distance, and his back hit the wall of the small office. His muscles contracted and the finger of his dropping hand squeezed the trigger. His .45 caliber Glock fired, the slug buried itself on the rug, but the deafening sound surprised everyone. Toni braced her hands against the sides of the metal chair, and kicked up her right foot with all her might. It hit Scott on his crotch, and the man yelled and jumped back. Jack sprung from his chair, grabbed the Glock from the hand of the falling captain, and hit the wall across from him with his shoulder, landing on the floor. He aimed the gun up at the two men, hoped he wouldn't hit Toni, and pulled the trigger three times.

The roar of three shots one after the other was ear shattering. The first round hit Scott on the neck, almost severing his head off his torso, the other two hit the man called Mike on the chest, slamming him twice against the front door. He slid to the floor with a surprised look on his face, leaving a red smear on the door.

Jack looked at Toni, still grabbing the sides of her chair. She looked awful, with blood all over her face. Ambrose, lying on the floor to his left groaned, and he turned over on his stomach and crawled the few inches to where the big man was bleeding to death.

"I couldn't girl," Ambrose said, "I, . . ."

Toni got off her chair and joined Jack on the floor. The way the man was bleeding, it was impossible to get some help before he would die.

"It's my name on those papers? My family . . ."

"No Tim," Toni said, "your name is not on the papers. Rest assured."

"Thanks girl." The big head rolled off Jack's hand.

Jack looked at Toni and started laughing again. He couldn't help it, maybe it was the nervous system taking over. They were alive.

"You look like shit," he said, and she started laughing.

He picked up the Glock, wiped it with his handkerchief, and put it in the hand of Timothy Ambrose. He pressed the hand around the butt, and pushed the index finger through the trigger guard. He rose to his feet, picking up the Desert Storm off the floor, and pulled Toni up. He pushed Mike's body with the door, so they could get out. It was completely dark now, but the surroundings were as peaceful as when they had arrived. He pushed Toni toward the car, opened the passenger door and helped her in. He got behind the wheel, and backed out of the parking space.

Four blocks away, he drove into a gas station and stopped in front of a bank of public phones. He dialed 911, gave the address of the warehouse, and told the operator that he had heard several gunshots fired inside the office. He hung up, ignoring the operator's insistence in trying to keep him on the line and get more information out of him.

THIRTY-FIVE

JACK DROVE OUT of the gas station parking lot and headed North on the deserted street. He was sure that somewhere along this same road on their way in, he had seen one of those signs that point in the general direction of the closest hospital, but he couldn't remember exactly where. It was just one of those things you catch while you're driving and get stored on the back of your mind, without real recollection. All he could remember was that it was close to a cemetery. He floored the Taurus, passing the sparse traffic he found, sometimes driving on the wrong side of the road. Toni was leaning back against the seat holding a scarf or some piece of cloth against her bloodied face. She wasn't talking or moving and he wondered if she had gone into some kind of shock. He shook her shoulder with his right hand and she stirred a little, but didn't say anything.

"I know there's a hospital around here somewhere," he told her, "I'll find it in a minute." He was disoriented after the several turns he had made around the darkened residential streets, realized he was loosing precious time, and fought down the wave of panic he felt creeping on him.

"I don't want to go to any hospital," she mumbled from behind the piece of cloth she was holding to her face.

Listening to her voice gave him some confidence and he accelerated toward the end of the long dark street. He looked both ways when he reached the stop sign, and spotted the hospital fluorescent logo a couple of blocks away on his left.

He drove past the front of the hospital and made a left turn on the corner, following the lighted sign that pointed to the emergency entrance. It didn't look like the biggest hospital in town, but it was a hospital.

"Please Jack, take me home," she said, "I don't want to go in there." She pleaded with her eyes.

"You need a doctor to look at you Toni," he said, "you might have a broken jaw or something."

"I don't have any broken jaw, just a loose tooth. Let's get out of here please," she begged.

A burly security guard knocked on the driver's side window and Jack lowered it.

"You need any help?" He asked.

Jack looked at Toni's eyes, and then at the security guard.

"No. Not really, thank you," Jack told him. "We changed our mind."

"The lady looks hurt, sir," the man said.

"It's OK. Good night," Jack said and put the car in reverse, so the security man couldn't look at his license plate, and backed into the side street. He knew exactly where he was now, and turned toward US 1 just a few blocks away. He picked up his cellular phone when he was on the main thoroughfare, and dialed Dave's number.

"I'm on my way to Toni's house," he said when Dave answered, and gave him the address. "Meet us there in about an hour and we'll talk. It's such a fucking mess that you won't believe it." He hung up and turned to Toni. "Don't you dare die on me or go into some kind of shock lady," he said.

"I won't Jack," she said trying to smile. "Just take me home."

He nursed a scotch and water from the bottle he had bought on their way to Toni's house, and roamed around the house while she was on her bedroom showering and taking care of her injuries. She had told him that the damage was not as bad as all the blood all over her made it look like, because a lot of it didn't belong to her.

He had insisted on washing her face as soon as they had arrived at her house, and after wiping some of the blood off her face it didn't really looked that bad. She had swollen lips, some cuts on the side of her face and a loose tooth she kept pushing into position with her tongue. It looked awful but not really life threatening, so he let her go into her bedroom to take care of herself. He asked her to leave the door open just in case she didn't feel too well all of a sudden, but she wouldn't hear about it. She said she wouldn't lock it, but he could stay outside, have a drink and just wait for her.

He figured that the chances of her going into some kind of shock at this time were kind of minimal. The lady apparently was tougher than he had ever thought. He smiled to himself and started walking around the small house, looking at the little details, something he really hadn't done on his last visit.

He had read some place that you could learn a lot about a person's personality if you could see how the person lived and kept it's home. He looked at everything. The furniture was casual and comfortable, but sparse. No extra baggage, just enough to accommodate a small amount of people, if it needed to. There were lots of real plants that he imagined needed some personal care, and a few oil and watercolor paints hung on the right places, as far as his limited knowledge of art matters could tell.

His cellular phone rang, and he pulled it out of his back pocket. "I can't find the fucking place," Dave said.

"Where are you now?"

"On Main Highway and Poinciana Avenue."

He gave Dave instructions on how to get to the house. He peered trough an open door into what looked like Toni's den or small office. It was also sparsely furnished. A small tile topped breakfast table served as a desk, with a comfortable leather chair behind it. Against the back wall a computer sat on a stand, just a convenient half turn on the armchair away from the table. Three mismatched bookcases stood against the other walls. Framed pictures, photographs and some diplomas and mentions, in no particular order, covered the rest of the walls. He flipped the light switch off, and walked back into the living room.

Toni came out of her bedroom when he was standing in the middle of it. She was wearing a thick, white terrycloth bathrobe. Her lips were puffed, and the red welts on the side of her face were starting to turn purple. She hesitated for a moment at the end of the hallway and then ran to him. He embraced her and she buried her face on his chest. "I'm so sorry I got you into this mess Jack," she said between sobs, "we almost got killed, my God."

"You don't have to be sorry about anything Toni," he said. "We were together in this from the beginning, remember?"

"Yeah, but you warned me that it could be a trap," she said raising her head and looking at him, "you were right and I was wrong."

"Forget it Toni," he said, "it was a risk we had to take." He smiled down at her. "All things considered we didn't come out so bad. I don't have a scratch and your swollen lips look kind of sexy to me."

A loud knock on the front door made them jump apart, and Jack's hand went automatically to the butt of the automatic on the back of his waistband. He then remembered about Dave's call. He walked to the door and grabbed the doorknob with his left hand, his right one still on the butt of the automatic.

"It's that you Dave?" He asked.

"Who do you think, asshole."

Jack yanked the door open, and Dave stepped inside, one bag in each hand. He looked at Toni.

"Goddamn. You look like shit woman," he said. She rolled her eyes up, and dropped on the sofa.

"If you guys keep telling me, I'm going to believe it," she said.

Dave dropped the bags right where he was, walked over to Jack and smelled his drink. "We don't have any vodka around here?"

"Sorry pal," Jack said, "it's either scotch, or plain grape juice. Take your pick."

"Scotch will be fine then. Go easy on the water, Jack."

He dropped on the sofa beside Toni, and patted her on the knee. "It's okay dear. You'll be your normal beautiful self in a couple of days. It's just that your kisser reminded me of the Camel cigarette add." He cracked up laughing.

"Fuck you Dave," she said.

Jack came out of the kitchen with a fresh drink, and one for Dave. He sat on one of the easy chairs across the center table, and handed Dave his glass.

"She didn't want to go to the hospital," he said.

Dave looked at Toni again. "It doesn't look that bad," he said, "one time I ran into an open door and it did more damage. I have two implants to prove it."

"You must have been blind drunk," Jack said. They both laughed. Toni wasn't so happy.

"Do you guys realize that the only one that had been slapped around is me?", she slurred through her swollen lips.

"I've been shot at," Jack said defensively.

"Yeah, but you never got hit."

"I need another drink," Dave said, "this one was kind of weak."

"I guess I'll have another too," he said. He felt the tension he had been under for the last few hours slipping away, and was starting to feel kind of comfortable with himself. "Are you sure you don't want one Toni? It won't heal your lips but it will sure help your ego."

She thought about it for a moment. "Yeah, what the hell, get me one too," she said, "but Jack, put a lot of ice on it and don't make it too strong."

Dave moved to the edge of the sofa, and pulled a pack of cigarettes from his pant pocket. "You don't mind, do you?" he asked her, because there was no cigarette ashtray on the table. Toni shook her head. "Jack," she said as loud as she could, "there's a plastic ashtray somewhere there in the kitchen, please."

He stopped pouring whiskey for a moment, when he heard her. It sounded too familiar he thought. Jack this and Jack that. It raised conflicting emotions on him that he wasn't sure he liked. Not yet anyway.

He pulled a couple of drawers and found a cheap black plastic ashtray on the second one. He grouped all three glasses together, put the ashtray on top of them, grabbed the whole thing with both his hands, and walked back into the living room.

Dave sipped from his drink and became somber all of a sudden. "Do you guys want to talk about what happened at that place?" he asked.

"No, I don't," Toni said immediately, "I want to forget about it." She raised the glass to her swollen lips, started sobbing at the same time, and spilled whiskey all over the front of her robe. Dave wrapped his arm across her shoulders and hugged her to him. "It's alright girl, go ahead cry. It's over. Everything's going to be all right," he said soothingly.

"I'm so sorry I insisted on going to that place," she said between sobs, "Jack told me it could be a trap." She wiped her face with the sleeve of her robe. "My God, Timothy was part of it, I couldn't believe it." She put her glass on the table, writhed away from Dave's embrace, and curled on the end of the sofa. She looked at some point across the room, but her eyes were glassy and unfocused. She covered her face with her hands, and started crying again. "I'll never forget the face of that man," she said between sobs, "blood from his neck fell all over me." She curled tighter into a fetal position at the end of the sofa, and shook with sobbing spasms. Dave patted her back with his hand.

"Shouldn't we take her to a hospital?" Jack asked Dave. He shook his head.

"This is a normal reaction. The adrenaline has slowed down, and reality has caught up with her. It's actually healthy to break down like this. If you keep everything bottled up inside you it's going to be worse." He stood up, "C'mon Jack, give me a hand and let's take her to bed."

They walked her to her bedroom and tucked her into bed.

"I'll be on the living room if you need anything Toni," Jack said. She just nodded, and Dave pushed Jack out of the room, closing the door behind him.

THIRTY-SIX

THEY TURNED TOWARD the living room. Jack cracked open the door to Toni's room, in case she needed anything. He followed Dave into the living room and they sat back on the sofa. They sipped their drinks in silence for a while.

"What about you Jack?" Dave asked.

"What about me?" He said.

"Do you want to talk about it, or are you going to keep it inside until you burst."

Jack thought about it. He sure didn't feel like crying. He wasn't too sure about what he felt. He felt some kind of disappointment, not overwhelming guilt or regret. He didn't know if he would snap later on down the road, but at the moment he was not the guilt-ridden patient in need of a shrink. He had just reacted when confronted with a life and death situation. He had had not time to think. He didn't doubt for a minute that if he had done something different, Toni and him wouldn't be alive now. He hadn't looked at the face of the man, like Toni had done. Both of them had just been a deadly threat to be contended with. Never before, in all his years, had the idea of taking the life of another human being crossed his mind. It was just not on the scheme of things he lived for. All of a sudden, in just a few days, all he had been doing was trying to keep somebody else from taking *his* life. It sure had changed his perspective about live and let live. He didn't feel any regrets or any huge feel of guilt, and that scared him to some point, but not to the point that he felt he should discuss it with Dave.

"It was a mess Dave," he just said.

"That I can figure by myself," he said drinking the last dregs of his glass. "Do you think you're going to need any help to cope with it?"

"I don't think so," Jack said, "not at the moment, anyway."

They both looked at their empty glasses. "We might as well get drunk then," Dave said. Jack went to the kitchen and brought the bottle and a bowl full of ice to the table.

They refilled their glasses, and sat silent for a while, each lost on their own private thoughts. Jack ran through his mind again the events of the last few hours, trying to find at which point he could have done something different that could have changed the outcome. He was sure there wasn't one, he had been a pawn in a game not of his choice. It all had begun as a game for them, but the chips had been in place way before they had dreamed it.

"How was your meeting with the DA?" he finally said.

Dave turned to him, but the look on his face was one of somebody that had been mentally miles away from the present time and place.

"I'm going to tell Camille tonight that I want a divorce," Dave said.

"I asked how was your meeting with the DA," Jack said again.

"When I tell her that I will leave her the house and some securities I know she won't argue," he said.

"She keeps fucking around?" Jack asked.

Dave looked at him like if he hadn't seen him in a long time.

"The meeting with the DA went beautiful," he said, "she really loved it. She went into high gear right away. I bet those assistants are going to be working overtime tonight."

"Where does that leave us?" Jack asked.

"Just where we are," he said. "When she listened to the tape and went through the papers, she didn't object to complete confidentiality as from where I had gotten the evidence. You and Toni don't have anything to worry about."

"And the money?"

"Safe in our little corporation," he said smiling, "I checked again today to make sure I was not dreaming."

Jack refilled their glasses, and lighted a cigarette. He kicked his boat shoes off, and planted his feet on top of the center table.

"So. What do we do now?" he said.

Dave put out his cigarette on the cheap plastic ashtray and smiled at him.

"Whatever we want, pal. We sure have the capability."

"It's a big chunk of money."

"It sure is," Dave said sitting straight on the sofa. "I'm worried about her, though," he said nodding toward the bedroom, "she might crack open. She has gone through a lot, you know."

Jack exhaled a long stream of smoke, looked at the tip of his cigarette, and grounded it on the ashtray.

"I've been thinking along those lines myself," he said. "What happens if she decides not to go along with us, and instead wants to bring everything into the open?"

Dave fidgeted with the pack of cigarettes, but didn't light one. He picked a couple of ice cubes, dropped them into his glass, and poured some more scotch over them. He took a sip, added one more ice cube, and pushed himself back into the softness of the comfortable sofa.

"I really don't want to think about that," he said. "She's a journalist. If she decides to go public and tells what we have done, all kind of legal shit it's going to hit the fan big time. We will be charged with at least three criminal charges to start with." He lighted his cigarette and blew smoke toward the ceiling. "Probably a few more if you give me a couple of minutes to think about it."

"And the money?"

"The money is kind of invisible as we talk right now. It's protected by Bahamian banking laws, and unless somebody has the codes to access the account, it will stay there forever."

Jack put out his cigarette on the ashtray, ran his hands through his hair, and kept them on the back of his neck, looking at the ceiling. "The money really doesn't belong to us," he said. "The point is, that we have set a machinery in motion that is going to bring a lot of crooked people down, and we don't have to be on the midst of it."

"Yes, that is true," Dave said. "But you would like to keep that money, wouldn't you? We actually didn't steal it. We just separated it from a bunch of crooks."

"That's a very nice way to put it Dave," he said smiling. "It sure is very tempting." He leaned over and picked his glass from the table. "Let me tell you *dishonestly*, that I wouldn't mind keeping it," he emptied his glass and put it back on the table. "We have to discuss this matter with Toni, though. All three of us have to agree on what we're going to do."

Dave crossed his legs one time, and then crossed them again. He kept rubbing his chin with his right knuckles. He finished his drink in one big gulp, and immediately poured some more whiskey and dropped some ice cubes on his glass.

"I don't think that we actually have to discuss anything with Toni," Dave said looking into his glass. "She was there for the ride Jack, this is something between us. We have been friends for years, we don't need a third party involved in what we do." He picked up his drink, and sat back on the sofa. "She's really a liability and you know it. If she doesn't open her mouth, everything it's okay. If she decides to open her mouth, we're screwed. It's just as simple as that. We just have to make sure she doesn't open her mouth."

"How do you plan to do that?" he asked.

"Oh, I'm not sure Jack. Maybe suffocate her with a pillow, now that she's sleeping will be the best choice. It will look like these crooked cops she was after did it to her," he said.

"I don't believe what I heard, Dave. Start again and don't bullshit me," he said smiling. He picked up his drink, but the glass was empty.

"I'm not bullshitting you," Dave said. "It's the only way Jack. Think about it." He moved forward and sat on the edge of the sofa. He looked toward the hallway to make sure Toni hadn't come out of her room. "Tomorrow all hell is going to break loose on Dade County, Jack. There are going to be bodies all over the place, including a Police Captain. The DA it's going to have a field day. Toni's involvement in this mess could be disclosed, and her death would be considered one more casualty." He swallowed the rest of his drink, and lowered his voice some more. "Somewhere along the line you might be subpoenaed to testify, but I'll be there to help you out. Nothing can be traced back to us. You'll have tons of money to spend. We can go around the world and have the biggest time ever."

Jack looked at Dave in disbelieve, his eyes were glassy, but not because of the drinks.

"You must be out of your fucking mind Dave," he said. "Do you realize what you're saying?"

Dave moved closer to the edge of the sofa. "Listen to me Jack. We are talking about more than twenty million dollars, asshole. There's no cunt that's worth that much."

He looked at Dave straight in the eyes, trying to fathom if his friend was kidding him or if he really meant what he was saying. He didn't like what he saw in his eyes.

"You're mad Dave," he said. "That money really doesn't belong to us. You don't need it. I don't need it. Not to keep on living." He fiddled with his glass, and finally decided to drop a couple of ice cubes on it and pour some whiskey over them. He stirred the drink with a finger, and looked at Dave. "If we decide to keep it, we have to agree on how we're going to do it and split it between the three of us." He raised his glass, but barely took a sip of the drink. "I'm going to try to forget what you said."

Dave shook his head several times, and looked at Jack. "I don't trust the bitch," he said.

"She's not a bitch and I do trust her," he said.

Dave refilled his glass, and took a small sip. "It seems like you don't like my proposition Jack," he said. He got off the sofa and walked over to where he had dropped the bags he had brought in, right by the front door. He picked one up and sat back on the sofa, setting the duffel bag between his feet.

"Let me show you something Jack," he said pulling the zipper back on the duffel bag.

"What the hell's that," Jack said when he saw what Dave had pulled out of the bag.

"My friend, this is a beauty," Dave said hefting the small black automatic pistol with its bulbous silencer, on his right hand. "It's a .380 PPK. Nice little fucker, not as nasty as the big cannon I loaned you, but it gets the job done. It came my way some years ago as a present from a client." He smiled at Jack. "Illegal as hell and not registered to my name, of course. One of those things you keep around for a rainy day. I put it in your bag before coming here because I thought that maybe you wouldn't agree with my options." He pulled the hammer back and pointed the gun at Jack's chest. "One more body won't make a hell of a difference, don't you think so? I'm sorry Jack, but this is a chance in a lifetime."

Jack kicked the center table with both his feet and it hit Dave's legs just under the knees. There was hardly any noise, but he saw a flash a fraction of a second before he felt like if he had been hit on his left shoulder with a baseball bat. The impact of the soft-nosed bullet at such close range slammed him backward, and he crashed on the floor taking the chair with him. The initial numbing blow changed to a fiery burning pain as he tried to sit up. His vision blurred, and for a moment he thought he was going to pass out. He shook his head and looked at Dave. He was standing up and aiming the small automatic down at his face. He locked eyes with him a second before he saw the back of his head explode in a rainbow of red and gray matter. Blood spurted from a hole under his right eye, and the gun fell from his hand. He fell back into the sofa, eyes wide open with surprise. The white material of the sofa started turning pink, as it soaked what was coming out of what had been Dave's head. For a fraction of a second it all looked to Jack like a movie played in slow motion, until the roar of a shot filled his ears and reverberated against the walls of the small room. He rolled to his right, dragging his useless left arm around, and saw Toni standing on the hallway, a big black automatic held on both her hands and still aimed at where Dave had been.

"Where the hell did you get that gun," he yelled.

"I picked it off the floor when we left the warehouse," she said.

END